Timely Persuasion

Timely Persuasion

A Novel

By JL Civi

Note to my mother:
The word "fictitious" means that character names such as Mom, Dad, Me,
My Sister, or My Brother do not correspond to actual members of our family
or any other family, including the Farkles.

Note to Mrs. Conway:
Did I say John Conway? I meant Jon Mack.

ISBN: 978-1-7330421-0-9

For Alane

Prologue

"I CAN'T BELIEVE YOU WANT TO MARRY THIS GUY!"

That was the last thing I ever said to my sister. At least it was the last thing of any real importance. Our argument over her fiancé continued on from there, but it was clear she wasn't listening to reason. She was "in love," which meant that her usually impeccable judge of character had been compromised. Her view of the world was so distorted that she didn't see that a future with Nelson was not something she really wanted. She wouldn't see that not one of her friends or acquaintances understood the coupling. And she couldn't see that we all discussed this fact ad nauseam behind her back. She was "in love," and neither I nor anyone else could talk her out of it.

Of course, we still tried. "We" isn't really the right word. Others confided in me that this could only end badly, but nobody had the guts to bring it up on their own. Friends of my sister with whom I had never had more than a brief and awkward "Hello" with in my entire life would pull me aside to ask what I thought of Nelson. Upon hearing that I shared their collective sentiment they would tell me I had to fix it. That I was the *only* one who could fix it. Friends are supposed to show support, but family could use the blood is thicker than water excuse to stage a socially acceptable intervention with minimal repercussions. Thus the only party included in the "we" became "me." (Me, myself, and I actually, but what's the difference?)

So I was elected scapegoat, which brings us closer to my final line: "I can't believe you want to marry this guy!"

I prefer not to recall any more of that conversation now, but I suppose it's the best starting point. She could and should have done better. She was selling herself short. Nelson had already proven himself to be controlling and smothering during their courtship, leaving my sister a mere shadow of her former self. He had already been the death of her with his constant negativity, and he would continue to pull her further and further from her joyous true self if the relationship continued.

But it wasn't too late for her to save her own soul. Everyone makes mistakes, it's just a matter of recognizing these mistakes early enough to correct them. Since the relationship would in all certainty not last forever, the end result would be more easily achieved now before things would inevitably become complicated with wedding plans, shared finances, a home, and children. (Thank god their union never resulted in kids!) It would be so much better for everyone involved if she were to get out before it was too late. I wanted to believe that she could break away, but I knew she'd never leave him. Unfortunately, I turned out to be right.

She said I was being unreasonable. That settling down was just a part of growing up. "Settling down" is a strange saying. Conversationally it tends to mean staying put with a spouse and a home and a job and some kids, the good old-fashioned perfect American family. And once in a blue your dreams come true and that blissful state is achieved. But far too often people are pressured into initiating this chapter of life before they are ready for it. The concept of "settling down" becomes very literal: settle for less than your ideal, a lower mate that may not meet all of your standards just to have the charade of security. And it is a charade. Fall in love, settle down, be alone in a lonely town. Eventually people figure out that this isn't really the better life they had hoped for, leading to constant bickering, illicit affairs, trial separation and actual divorce.

I thought I had a valid argument with the statistics to back it up, but as I said when you are blinded by "love" you don't tend to listen to reason, especially if the "love" is of a more contrived and delusional variety.

What is love? What is life for that matter? One is an illusion and the other is a dream. But which is which? They say love is a stream that will find its own course. You just know it when you see it. When you feel it. But humans are often forced into a false feeling of love once the realities of life strip their idealism away.

I used to argue that love itself doesn't actually exist at all, at least not in a concrete sense. As I said, it's always contrived and delusional to some degree. You need to form your own definition and build on it over the course of a lifetime until you are left with the only answer. That answer won't come immediately, and you know it don't come easy. There will be many pitfalls, red herrings and false hopes along the way. And in those very cases you need a good friend to set you straight; to show you the big picture and pull you out before you hurt yourself and everyone who cares about you.

That's all I was really trying to do here. Not that I should have expected to be listened to. I'm not trying to sound blameless. The blood is thicker than water concept was certainly good in theory, and had previously proven itself true in practice as well.

I had always been rather protective of my sister. This protectiveness most often manifested itself when it came to her selected boyfriends. Nobody was ever quite good enough, and my opinion was always voiced. Too mean, too smart, too arrogant, too nice, too mundane, too reclusive, too fake, too erratic of a speech pattern, too promiscuous, etc. The list of faults went on and on.

There were even a few occasions when I attempted to set my sister up with my most trusted friends, but those pairings would also end with my own objections when I came to realize that the qualities I sought in a friendship were not suitable traits in a mate for my sibling. Some might say I should have held my tongue and let her learn her own lessons, but there was a part of my conscience that just wouldn't let me. The voice inside my head that couldn't let me live with the guilt of knowing that my implied consent could possibly lead to a future disaster. So my mind was always spoken, and that may have had a lot to do with the sick irony of what actually played out.

My sister did marry Nelson, and I blamed myself for the entire thing. Had I not allowed her into my inner circle she likely wouldn't have been at the card game where they met. And had I not become known as the boy who cried wolf in my previous boyfriend objections, perhaps I would have been listened to when this most crucial case came along.

Everyone tells me it was just a series of coincidences that I had no real part in, but I know better. Maybe they think I take solace in assigning the blame to myself rather than putting it back on her. Or perhaps I need to occupy my guilty conscience with feeble attempts to reconstruct what might have been different since this wasn't supposed to happen.

You may come to the conclusion after reading this that it really was my fault, though that will depend on your feelings regarding which one of us is me. But hopefully you'll also see that it doesn't necessarily have to be that way.

If only…

One

I WAS IN A BIT OF A TESTY MOOD when I arrived at the bowling alley on league night for a variety of reasons, but mostly because the anniversary of my sister's death was approaching. Shortly after she passed I packed my life into my car and drove away from it all. A distant voice told me it was time to go, so I did. Made it clear across the country in four days.

That was almost a year ago. I hadn't been back home since, but I did have a plane ticket that my parents bought me so I could attend the upcoming memorial mass. At first I resisted. I don't fancy myself a religious sort and wanted to keep the memories cased away undisturbed. Eventually I conceded to having a ticket sent to me, though I had yet to decide if I would use it. For now I just wanted to drink, bowl, and forget about life for a while.

None of the regulars had arrived yet. I was here earlier than usual, a perk of my newly christened unemployed status. Laid off from a mindless call center job a week earlier, the lack of work was actually a welcome change. Severance pay and unemployment would keep me afloat while I plotted my next move. What could it be? Road trip? Back to school? Steal my daddy's cue and make a living out of playing pool? The options, they were infinite. It was essentially a paid vacation, albeit a semi-permanent one. Thinking about it almost lightened my mood for a moment, until I saw that my spot at the bar was taken.

An old man I had never seen before was sitting on my usual stool, tightly clutching his mug as he held it about an inch above the bar. I gave him a dirty look for no good reason other than that and took an adjacent seat, making sure I was still in view of the Hot Spot lottery screen. I knew that I was in no position to even consider playing the lottery since my disposable income had taken a hit, but I figured it was just funneling money right back into the system that was sponsoring me. Was there really a better use for unemployment funds?

The cute French bartender started pouring my drink without asking. I nodded a brief acknowledgement as I fished in my bowling bag for my lucky lottery form. A beer was already in front of me by the time I found the orange Scantron paper. I eagerly took a sip and watched the current drawing play out.

Twelve. Twenty-two. Twenty-four. Forty-seven. Sixty-nine. All five numbers shared the screen, making my mood just that much worse. I looked at the filled out but not yet handed in betting slip in my hand, then back up to the numbers on the screen, then back down to the ticket. They matched. Every last number matched, beating the 1 in 1,551 odds.

Every Tuesday for the last five months I played those same five numbers on five drawings at five dollars a game. Throwing away twenty-five bucks a week for a chance at greatness, but I never got them all. Often zero, occasionally three, rarely four, but never all five. Why these numbers? I've never really known for sure. They just popped into my head. This was the first time I had even seen all five of them on screen together. But there they were, grinning down and mocking me. And if this old fool hadn't distracted me by sitting in my seat, I might have had time to get my ticket in for this draw.

There was still time to kill before it was time to bowl, but the thrill was gone. Although I knew that any combination of numbers had the same odds of coming up in each and every drawing, I also knew that these five wouldn't come up again anytime soon. Some may call it the gambler's fallacy, but the gambler was a pretty smart guy. It was time to fold 'em, time to walk away, and almost time to run.

The way today was going the team would be better off taking my average minus ten, so I chugged down half of my beer in hopes of slipping away before my partner arrived. Tilting my head to drink drew my gaze back towards the lottery screen, hoping to see different numbers but knowing better. (Or knowing I wouldn't see them but hoping better?) Something in my head told me to look again, but something up there lied. I crumpled the ticket and dropped it onto the bar.

"Play 'em," a voice said.

Out of the corner of my eye I saw the old man on my stool take a long sip of his drink. I pretended not to hear him and did the same with my beer, keeping my gaze on the now inactive lottery screen while mimicking his action.

"Your loss," said the man.

"Excuse me?" I've never been one for small talk, especially from a stranger butting in on a matter that didn't concern him, even if the matter was something as trivial as a game of Hot Spot.

"Your numbers. This is your game."

"I think I'm done. They're not coming up twice." I paused before curtly adding "And how would you know what numbers I'd play?"

The man took another long sip and smiled, keeping his glass in his hand the entire time. "Twelve, twenty-two, twenty-four, forty-seven, sixty-nine. They all come up this time. When you're feeling greedy you think about adding two, four, and seven. Now would be a good time to follow through. This time you got it."

He was right. Those were my numbers. And when I felt greedy I did always think about adding the related permutations of the same, and I always chickened out in the end. But how could this man I'd never seen before know my lottery routine? Maybe he saw me play the same ticket every week, but he couldn't have guessed the extras. A bit spooked, I tried to blow him off with a wiseguy retort.

"If it's such a sure thing, why don't you play it?"

"That's not possible. And it's your lucky day, not mine. My lucky day has come and gone."

"What do you mean it's not possible?"

"Too late now. Here they come."

The man focused on the small screen. I took another sip of my beer and also watched, trying for a look that was more casual than intrigued. Not much suspense was needed, as the first five computer animated numbers to bounce onto the screen were mine. At first I was excited, then angry. I actually found myself rooting against my own numbers. This guy couldn't be right. He was just a kook getting his kicks with some Mountain Dew rock. But he had picked them all, even the final three extras. I uncrumpled my lottery form to check the back for the odds and nearly fell off of my stool when I saw the answer. 1 in 230,115.

The numbers faded and were replaced by the official game clock advertising the next draw. Noticing the time, I really had to get out of there before practice started and my teammate arrived. I drank down my last swallow and headed for the door. Three quarters of the way there I abruptly turned back as I realized what was going on.

"It's fixed, isn't it? You work for the lottery, and the game is fixed."

The man smiled as he suppressed a laugh. "No, it's not fixed."

"Then how?"

"Easy," he said, standing up and pausing to enjoy the last sip of his drink. "I'm from the future."

That said, he put his beer glass in his pocket and walked past me to the exit while I stared after him in disbelief. At first I told myself it was just a prank and following the man was what he wanted, so I decided to stay put. But the whole thing still didn't have a satisfactory explanation, so I had to follow.

The parking lot was brimming with cars but devoid of people. Reasoning that one of the cars must belong to the man, I checked the nearby handicapped spots first. (I realize now that just because he was old wouldn't necessarily mean he was handicapped, but that was the first thought that came to mind at the time. Ageism isn't a quality I'm proud of, but unfortunately it's there.) Peering into the first window, I was pushed and pinned against the side of the vehicle. I struggled, then winced as I felt a sharp pain in the back of my neck. My attacker released his grip, allowing me to whirl around in time to see the old man stash something in his pocket as he walked away.

"What the hell was that?" I yelled while rubbing the throbbing welt left by the ambush.

"It's something you'll thank me for later."

"Thank you? I'm calling the police!"

"Suit yourself, but they won't believe you. Nobody will. Just go in and bowl. We'll meet again someday soon."

"Again? You're insane! You watch out, I'll…"

Again I was grabbed from behind. I covered my neck, kicked back forcefully, and turned to see my bowling partner splayed out on the ground.

"Whoa man, what the hell?" he said as he pulled himself to his feet.

"Sorry, I thought you were with him."

"Him who?"

I turned and pointed out the old man still slowly walking away.

"Him!"

"Him who? There's nobody there."

I could still clearly see the man walking away as plain as day, so my friend's disbelief was really pissing me off. I didn't need this crap on top of everything else. Either he was playing a very unfunny game, or I had kicked him harder than I thought.

"That old man about to cross the street. He poked me with something."

"Did you get high without me? I know you think it makes you bowl better, but now you're seeing shit."

He had a point. A couple of quick hits before entering the bar to start the prebowl drink up did wonders for my nerves and had me raring to go once practice started. And it did make me bowl better, regardless of what anyone else thought.

"Yes, I'm stoned. But I really was just attacked."

"When I pulled into the parking lot I saw you trip and fall into the side of that car, then turn and start yelling. Nobody attacked you. Nobody else has even been in the parking lot."

"Then what is this?" I said, turning and pointing to the still sore bruise on the back of my neck.

"It's your fat neck. Nothing special. No cut, no bruise, no tattoo. Not even a bug bite."

I looked in the street once again, but this time the man really was gone. Or had he ever been there? Was this all just a stress and drug induced fantasy? I'd never hallucinated on pot before. I didn't even think you could. My fingers could still locate the tender lump on the back of my neck, but my bowling buddy sounded so serious when he said he saw nothing.

Across the way I spotted a tan van idling at the far side of the parking lot. It was reasonably close to where the man disappeared, so I started towards it. A hand on my shoulder stopped me.

"Quit fooling around. Let's go in there, have a beer and get you calmed down so you can bowl. We're going against the Blackouts tonight and need your arm for the victory."

After a dramatic pause, he lifted his bowling bag above his head and added "I, Bowlingus the God of Thunder, can't always do it alone." That crazy nickname came up from time to time, mainly just to get me fired up. He didn't need to try too hard tonight.

"Let me check something out first. I think he's in that van."

"Too late now."

The van peeled out of the parking lot. Not concrete proof of anything, but something strange was going on.

"First round is on me," said my partner. "Grab Glitzy and let's go."

Protesting would do no good. I agreed, checking one last time for the man in the tan van before following Bowlingus into his Olympus.

Two Of Us

GLITZY WAS MY BOWLING BALL, named for her flashy shine and the letters GLTZ at the start of the engraved serial number. By the time I rolled my fifth warm-up ball I had more or less calmed down. Although still concerned by what had happened in the parking lot, for the moment I was content to let my subconscious ponder it while the rest of my brain worked on strikes and spares. I was in the thunder zone, landing my shots in the pocket and either obliterating the pins or leaving easy singles for marks. My confusion and aggression seemed to be channeling well. Bowlingus thought it was the beers that soothed me. I figured it was the remnants of my high that allowed me to compartmentalize so well.

When it came to bowling, we weren't that good but we weren't that bad. We owned that middle ground where non-bowlers thought we were savants and league bowlers thought we were—pardon the pun—out of our league. Our averages didn't inspire fear in anyone (I was at 158, he at 161), but when we got hot we could do some damage. Case in point: the God of Thunder had rolled a 270 in the third week that somehow still stood up as league best for the season. He was pretty excited that we were scheduled tonight on the very same lanes on which he had completed that historic accomplishment.

Unfortunately I hadn't been there to witness it, as I had to work late. (And considering my lack of employment, a lot of good that did me.) He was still a little bitter that we lost the match despite his gem. Normally it would have been strong enough, but his other games were only about average and we were playing the top team. All three games were close, and even a slightly below average showing from me could have earned us both a sweep and bragging rights.

Our dynamic duo was known as the Bowling Stones. Team names in our league came in a variety of distinct styles. Some kept with the theme of the sport, including the Explosive Nines, Rollin' Blackouts, Splitters, and Gutter Balls. Others added a suggestively dirty spin to the bowling reference such as the Ballsacks, All Seven Digits (I don't even know what that means), or my personal favorite: "Bowler? I Hardly Know Her." Then there was Team 8, who just went by Team 8. I hoped this was because they didn't know how to work the electronic scoreboard, as it's not all that hard to come up with a team name. Rounding out the league was the only all female pair known as the Protestant Girls. Bowling league wasn't really a place to pick up women for most guys, except for Bowlingus, who had done some fucking with the Protestant Girls. I preferred to focus on the sport of it all, especially tonight.

Practice finished. We each gave the treasurer our six dollars for the weekly sidepot and wished the Rollin' Blackouts good luck, rhetorically confirming that our usual beer frames and losers buy drinks rules were in effect tonight.

The Blackouts were a fun team. A couple of reckless tattooed biker guys who heckled and drank heavily but could still roll with it. We were evenly matched on both bowling and drinking ability, and were separated in the standings by a mere two points. If we could take three of four tonight we'd crack the upper echelon and be tied for fifth place.

I led off, feeling confident that I still had the 'A' game I flashed during practice. Tightening my grip on Glitzy, I dropped my right arm back and started my approach. Three quick strides to the line, a hard foot plant … and I fell flat on my face. The ball swung wildly to the left, clipping two pins.

"Nice shot, Blondie!" yelled one of our competitors.

I hate it when they call me Blondie.

Trying not to make eye contact with anyone to spare further embarrassment, I picked myself up off the ground and limped back to the ball return. My next approach was more tentative, but I overcompensated and tossed this one wide to the right.

"Hey Goldilocks, you want the ones in the middle," was the dig I heard this time.

"At least someone else is finally the butt of a blonde joke," giggled the Protestant Girl Bowlingus knew best. I ran my fingers through my now popular pale hair and hoped the night would be over with quickly.

"God of Thunder" Bowlingus lived up to his name when he opened with a booming strike and marched back to the table trying to hold back a big grin. I just nodded, slapped his hand, and hoped I could do the same on my next turn. We rarely spoke to each other while bowling, especially when someone had a perfect game going. One strike does not a perfect game make, but you never talk to or about a guy throwing all strikes, just as you never talk to or about a baseball pitcher working on a no hitter. If you do and he blows it, the jinx is on you.

I picked up my ball and waited for the Blackout on the opposite lane to finish his shot, but backed off and put my ball down when he ended up with a split. Our other big bowling superstition is to never throw an opening shot when there is a split on an adjacent lane. Splits are contagious, and catching a bad case of them can ruin your night. My opponent playfully shook his fist at my ritual, then finished off his turn with a field goal. I didn't even have to look to know that someone behind me would have thrown their hands in the air like an NFL referee. I grinned a bit through closed lips, delivered my shot towards the pocket, and headed straight for the bar without looking. I thought I had nailed a strike, but was humbled when it ended up being a split despite my precautions.

Bowlingus rolled another strike on his second turn, but his toe crossed the foul line, negating the shot. The loud buzzer censored the majority of his tirade. I handed him a beer and shrugged, then marched up to shakily resume my game.

I continued to flounder and still had nothing through the ninth frame, ruining the beautiful pastiche of Xs and /s that Bowlingus had going on our side of the scoreboard. My line boasted six consecutive open frames including four splits, a couple of embarrassing turns converting half the pins or less, and an absurdly undeserved strike leading into the final frame.

My accomplice still refrained from talking to me, partly due to my rough showing and partly due to his game being ruined by a second foot foul in the seventh. If I could talk I'd tell him we somehow still had a chance of winning this game due to his performance thus far, but he probably knew that already. Eyeing the scores and the handicaps, my bowling math told me we needed thirty-five pins between us for the victory. Normally I can't add to save my life, but pincounts plus bonus balls are almost second nature. My next shot counted twice, so a strike from me now would all but put it away. Otherwise any mark would still leave us looking good pending Bowlingus' final turn. Normally I'd say we had it in the bag, but the way I was rolling tonight nothing was easy.

Pulling Glitzy from the ball return, I noticed that her thumbhole had been chipped. I showed the others and asked permission to tape it up before my final roll. They agreed and I was on my way, but not before reminding me that I needed all the help I could get. At the pro shop I borrowed a roll of tape for some impromptu surgery. While in the process of fixing the hole, I sat on a stool at the bar with the ball in my lap and tried to analyze what I was doing wrong tonight. It was ironic how our league bowling routinely went like this. Tonight I was having my worst performance of recent memory and we still had a shot in the tenth. But a few weeks ago Bowlingus hit a level we can usually only dream of and we still got beat. Why couldn't he do it again this time? A blowout like that would have been amazing, even with the potential for sandbagging accusations by the other team.

This thought was interrupted by a throbbing pain in the back of my neck, centered on the fresh bruise. Concentrating on the match had allowed me to forget the incident temporarily, but apparently my preoccupation was contributing to my lack of bowling ability. As I rubbed the bump with my cold beer mug it was all I could focus on. Who the hell did that guy think he was? And what did he do to me?

It was something sharp, definitely not his bare hands. I remembered him taking his mug with him when he left the bar. Broken glass used as a weapon? When was my last tetanus shot? Or was it something worse, like a new drug in a syringe? I did feel three feet thick. Hopefully not AIDS or some biological warfare agent. Maybe a steroid? No, steroids should make me bowl better, not worse. And anyways, they probably wouldn't have taken effect yet. Then again, I never actually saw a needle. For all I knew he just scratched me with a sharp fingernail. But for some reason I felt I knew this was definitely an injection. The whole attack didn't make much sense, but the memory was too vivid to have been made up.

There would be plenty of time to ponder after bowling was done. For now the pain had subsided, allowing me to make a mock bowling motion with the newly taped ball. Satisfied with the feel, I returned to the lane to take my shot.

Not wanting to waste more time or endure further heckles, I marched past the other leaguers and assumed the starting position without even so much as a glance at anyone. After a deep breath to get focused, I carefully started my approach and launched a beauty just right of the head pin. I thought about turning around for dramatic effect, but this shot felt so good coming off my hand it would be a crime to not witness the impact. The ball curved majestically towards the pocket, and went right through the pins.

But they were all still standing.

The ball had literally gone THROUGH the pins, as if they weren't even there. I turned to my partner with a look of disbelief, but he didn't seem to notice. Instead he got up to take his final shot.

"What the hell? Did you see that?" I asked.

He ignored me and took his spot at the starting line.

"It's still my turn, man. Do I get to take it over? How did that happen?"

He continued to ignore me and started his windup, drawing his arm back and stepping forward even though I was still standing on the lane between his body and the pins.

"Hold it! What's going on?"

Undeterred, he walked right through me without making contact, just as my ball had passed through the pins.

Dumbfounded, I whirled in time to see the last pin topple off the back of the rack as Bowlingus pumped his right arm in victory. A small gathering of other league members surrounded him, each offering high fives. I tried to join in, but my hand passed right through his. I tried to touch my left arm with my right and had no problem. I pinched myself, yanking out an arm hair in the process and feeling the pain I expected.

Looking up, the electronic scoreboard flashed 270. Congratulations were announced over the intercom system. A sea of outstretched arms waved in a show of solidarity. I overheard someone mention it was too bad I wasn't here to see it.

"Not here? I'm right here! But he didn't just roll a 270, that was a month ago."

More people walked through me as I just stood there stupidly. My heart raced in disbelief. I noticed the Rollin' Blackouts a few lanes down playing with the Protestant Girls. Our lane was shared with the league leading Explosive Nines. I grabbed my head and tried to think, gathering my hair into a mini-ponytail and absentmindedly grazing my neck bruise in the process.

Suddenly I was falling, and found myself sprawled out on the floor of the bar. Dazed, I staggered to my feet and ran back down to the lanes. Spotting my cohort, I grabbed him roughly by the shirt, brimming with great relief upon feeling his collar between my fingers.

"Can you see me?"

He gave me a very strange look that indicated he could, but didn't actually respond.

"You can't see me!"

"Yes I can see you. Quit spazzing," he said through clenched teeth as he pushed my hands away, trying for discretion but failing. "Take your turn and finish them off. I shouldn't even be talking to you."

"I did go, but nobody saw. Nobody could see me!"

He gave me another incredulous look, similar to the one he had given me when we first met up in the parking lot. "C'mon man, I just need a spare from you. Where's your ball?"

Good question. Where was my ball? I didn't remember having it with me when I ran over here. Suddenly I felt a lot less crazy, as my missing ball was proof that something had happened.

"I already threw it. It went through the pins, but they didn't fall and it never came back."

"You're starting to scare me. Call the desk and ask for a ball return."

"You don't understand. I'm serious. I already went, threw it real nice, but it missed. It couldn't have, but it missed."

I had awoken the fury of Bowlingus. He was pissed.

"Stop talking crazy and throw the fucking ball," he replied in a quiet growl.

"But I don't have it!"

"Use mine!"

He shoved his overweight weapon into my gut. I walked up to the line with the unfamiliar ball and promptly sent it into the gutter.

My teammate put his hand on his head in disgust. "I don't think you've ever thrown a gutter ball on an opening shot."

My head spun with all kinds of thoughts.

The 270.

The ball going through the pins.

The man and the attack.

The lottery numbers.

The needle and the damage done.

The Future.

I couldn't take it.

"I'm sorry, I don't feel well. We have to forfeit the match. I'm going home."

Amidst a variety of astonished looks and protests, I left.

Gimme Three Steps

"I'M FROM THE FUTURE."

The words echoed in my head as I drove, repeating over and over and over again. I tried to fight it and think things through, but any thought sunk before I could get my mind in enough order to theorize what it all meant. I was having trouble keeping my eyes on the road, and in all honesty hardly remember the drive at all. I was on autopilot, thinking about nothing and everything all at once. I can't even recall what album I listened to that night, and that's rare for me. Next thing I remember I was lost in an unfamiliar neighborhood. My sense of direction has always been rather poor, but this was a drive I'd made countless times before. My attention continued to drift, but I fought through the haze and eventually found my way.

Finally in the safety of my home, I paced around the apartment in a frenzied thinker's walk. I felt like I was tripping, and very likely I was. The old man had probably drugged me, leading to hallucinations and other various acts of dementia from my subconscious. I'd never experimented with LSD before, sticking to the relative safety of marijuana and alcohol. How bad could anything from the earth really be?

"I'm from the future."

Having decided that I was most certainly on something, my thoughts went back to exploring the time travel option for the fun of it. In my altered state I was actually starting to believe it again. It couldn't be, but it almost explained what had happened.

Or did it? Suppose I did go back in time to the night of the 270 game. Why didn't anyone know I was there? I clearly knew that the old man who claimed to be from the future was there when we had our conversation.

And not only did they not know I was there, but they could all pass right through me. I was a ghost. But that didn't make sense. The time traveling man had pinned me down and scratched me with something, and I had the battle scar to prove it. Or at least I thought I did.

I fell onto my bed to focus better. If it was a drug that allowed me to travel in time, maybe it hadn't been completely absorbed by my system yet. That would make me ghost-like, whereas the old man was fully acclimated to the time travel serum and thus really there and able to interact. I was getting somewhere in theory, although I had no real scientific knowledge to back it up.

Then there was the issue of my bowling ball, which was with me during the hallucination but gone when I returned to reality and never touched by the old man. Maybe my thumb was bleeding? No, no scab. Or sweating? Maybe my sweat gave the ball the same physical properties (or lack thereof) that I had. Furthering that line of reasoning, the same question and answer applied to my clothing. I wasn't a naked time traveler like the Terminator.

Following the same thought, I took inventory of my wardrobe to make sure it was all intact. Pants, socks, belt, shirt, shoes, watch. And speaking of my watch, I noticed it was about seven minutes fast. Odd, as it typically kept good time. And seven minutes seemed about right for the amount of time I was in that ghostly state, though that was hardly conclusive proof of time traveling.

If any of this was even remotely true, why me? Maybe it hadn't happened and I was just completely insane. Or tripping. Yes. Tripping. I kept forgetting that I was tripping.

The best way to figure out anything is to try it again. How? I was just thinking about that 270 game, and then I was there. Where to now? My mind was a blank slate, waiting for the thoughts to come.

Birthday!
Fourth of July!
Christmas!
Leap year!
Nothing.
Figuring I wasn't thinking hard enough, I got up and dug through my desk. Eventually I found a word of the day calendar that hadn't been changed since late January and randomly flipped to a page. March eleventh. The word was blink, as in "I'll be back in a blink." Sounded good to me. Let's blink!

Aside from making me go cross-eyed, staring at the page didn't do a damn thing. I threw the calendar across the room in disgust. Wiping my face, I realized that I had broken into a cold sweat and started talking to myself.

You're just tripping on ecstasy or LSD or something similar.
The drugs don't work.
Time to stop acting crazy.
Let it run its course, everything's gonna be all right.
There is no time travel.
You lost your bowling ball, but you'll get it back.
This is not real, this, this is not really happening.
You bet your life it is. Turn up the radio, close your eyes, and just go with the flow.

The pep talk with my inner self seemed to work. I traipsed through volumes two and three of my CD collection in search of suitable inspiration, but none of the old favorites were doing it for me. I eventually dug out an old mixtape and a cassette player I hadn't used in years and retired to the couch to ride out the rest of this long, strange trip. Midway through the second song (from an acoustic set my roommate had done on my college radio show), I managed to pass out hard.

I had an awesome dream, but couldn't for the life of me remember what it was. Probably nothing important. Before I knew it I was jerking awake with a start when I felt the couch move.

It wasn't just the couch. Everything was shaking.

A glass rattled on my kitchen counter. Books toppled like dominoes on a shelf, knocking a golf ball onto the floor. A picture fell off the wall.

"Earthquake!" I thought aloud as I scrambled towards the doorjamb out of habit and instinct. The effects of the injection had seemingly run their course. I was a bit groggy from my nap but scared sober from the adrenaline rush of the quake. People say I'm crazy, but I actually enjoy the thrill of a good California earthquake as long as nothing breaks and no one gets hurt.

When the tremors subsided I tentatively started to put my apartment back together. Walking over to retrieve the golf ball, I stopped when I saw the signature on it. Huey Lewis. I've had this ball since 1986, the year of my first concert. After a year of constantly playing the *Back to the Future* soundtrack, my uncle took me and my sister to see Huey Lewis and the News. On the way to the concert we randomly bumped into Huey on the street. Having nothing autographable with me, my uncle gave me a golf ball that was still in his pocket from his round that morning. This was fitting, as the tour was in support of their *Fore!* album. At least Huey seemed amused by the whole thing, though I'm sure it wasn't the only golf ball he'd ever autographed.

The bruise on my neck started to burn. I rubbed it, and suddenly I wasn't in my apartment anymore. I guess technically it was still my apartment, just minus the "my" part. Definitely the same shape as the apartment I called home, with the same carpeting and floor plan. But the furniture and decor had instantaneously changed around me.

The walls were mostly bare, my feeble attempts at decorating completely eliminated by a light shade of green paint. The furniture actually matched and was part of a full set rather than the assortment of hand-me-downs, discontinued sale items, and yard sale trophies that made up my place. My do it yourself fifteen-dollar bookcase was now an ornately hand-crafted antique piece. The wall that was once blocked by my beat up futon was now bare, with a grandma-style couch in the center of the room facing a small TV with rabbit ears on a wheeled cart. And on that grandma-style couch was a grandma-style old woman.

I crept up to her slowly, trying not to be seen. Her eyes were closed. She must have dozed off watching the late night newscast. Still holding the golf ball, I tentatively lobbed it towards the opposite end of the couch as an experiment. It passed right through as if the couch wasn't even there, continuing through the wall on the other side.

Still moving slowly, I reached down to touch the couch. My hand passed through it. I tried to gently touch the woman on the arm, but my fingers went right through her as well. Now more comfortable that I wouldn't be seen, I waved my arm back and forth through the sleeping woman's head several times. She didn't even flinch.

Was I really in 1986? Had the ball brought me here? Tripping was one thing, but this was just surreal. I ran to the TV and tried to change the channel to find something 1986ish, but like everything else my hand passed through the knob. I had to get out of here.

I found the Huey Lewis ball on other side of the wall and picked it up. As with the bowling ball, I could throw the golf ball at anything and it would just keep traveling through solid objects until it lost all of its momentum. Likewise, I could still walk through any object as needed in order to retrieve it.

I decided to work my way up and down the street, peeking into houses until I found some verification of my time travel theory. After two vacancies and a set of amorous neighbors, I finally found something that met my criteria.

A family sat in front of another rabbit ear adorned television set engaged in their nightly viewing ritual. On the screen was a movie trailer for *Peggy Sue Got Married*. 1986 sounded about right for that. The commercial ended and an episode of *Cheers* resumed. The little boy in the group turned to his father and asked:

"Will Sam pitch for the Red Sox in the playoffs?"

That was the clincher.

The father laughed and started explaining that Sam Malone was a fictional character, but I didn't need to hear the rest. I reached back to finger my neck bruise, and was instantly home in front of my own bookcase again. My watch and my house clock were about ninety minutes out of sync. It was as if I'd never left, with the time discrepancy being the only evidence of what may have happened.

Is this real? It certainly seemed to be. I wasn't quite sure what to make of everything yet, but had a pretty good idea of what I wanted to try next.

Four Hours In Washington

KEEPING ONE EYE ON THE ROAD AS MY CAR SPED NORTH, I glanced at the printed Internet driving directions on the passenger seat. Approximately 1144.3 miles (give or take) to my ultimate destination: 171 Lake Washington Boulevard in Seattle. I could have found "exact" mileage had I bothered to enter my own home address, but my big brother paranoia always left me wary about giving out my real details on the Internet, even to a mapping engine. Where do you think junk mail comes from? If my conscience told me that they were watching, who was I to doubt it? Just because you're paranoid don't mean they're not after you. Besides, on a trip this long I only needed to know the highways. I can get to the freeway from my house without any help from Mr. Mapquest, thank you very much.

I eyed the speedometer and the clock to do some quick math as to my pace. (Driving math and bowling math are closely related.) Good, but not great. Even though I was a man on a mission, I reluctantly accepted it was best to split the sixteen-hour drive into two parts. Today's goal was to break the halfway point. I should have hit the road as soon as inspiration struck, but I foolishly decided to get some rest first. So instead of setting forth in an adrenaline fueled blaze of glory I let insomnia kill my buzz, dozed off somewhere in the wee hours and finally sputtered out the door with a coffee and radio aided kick-start just after sunrise.

I could see no reason to rush the drive since my intent and ability made a traditional schedule unnecessary. It was more my eagerness calling for the urgency than anything else. Mulling my options after the accidental time trips, I decided that whatever had happened to me both at the bowling alley and at home was definitely more than just a chemically induced fantasy. And if it was real, I wanted to explore it to its fullest potential before it went away forever. I'd also been itching for a road trip ever since I found myself without a job, which is why I set forth on an observational journey to unravel a great mystery of history: the death of Kurt Cobain.

I call it a death rather than the generally accepted suicide ruling since I subscribe to the conspiracy theory that something just didn't fit. There's a private investigator who thinks Courtney Love had her husband offed when he threatened to divorce her. Evidence includes the level of heroin in Kurt's blood being far too concentrated for him to handle (let alone fire) a shotgun, the allegation that the suicide note was actually a retirement note, two different handwriting samples on said note, sloppy police work based on assumptions rather than facts, and various other anecdotal inconsistencies. I had written an article for my college newspaper about the case that got picked up and syndicated nationally among other college papers. That article turned out to be the big break that got me into music reporting.

I realize I haven't mentioned my old career yet. Once upon a time I was a freelance music critic. Most of my writings critiqued newer artists by comparing and contrasting them with the classic sensibilities of other songwriters—both domestic and foreign, contemporary and historic. Growing up on my parents' collection of "The" bands (The Beatles, The Rolling Stones, The Eagles, The Clash, and The Ramones) along with a sprinkling of Billy Joel, Paul Simon, Van Morrison, and Harry Chapin kept me musically grounded yet still diversified enough to appreciate the importance of the singer songwriters among the rock and roll forefathers.

I briefly migrated towards grunge and metal as I came of musical age, but my roots ensured that my tastes were more eclectic than my peers. As a young writer, my heyday was covering the new British invasion of the mid to late nineties when Alternative paved the way for Britpop to enter America. I started a little late, but wrote many primer articles that allowed me to catch both myself and my readers up on the scene. None of the bands to come out of this era were ever as big as The Beatles, but quite a few shared some similarities. Blur, Carter USM, Cast, Supergrass, Black Grape, Oasis, James, Kula Shaker, and The Wonder Stuff were all on my radar. Great hooks, poppy melodies, and a holier than thou, bigger than Jesus English swagger combined with topical, punny lyrics that really meant something.

I also wrote an odd review here and there on an American band, but mostly stuck to the Brits. The exception was Nirvana, for whom I always had a soft spot without really knowing why. Maybe it was because the cacophony of controlled chaos embodied in the music spoke to me more so than anything ever had before. Or that they were the first band I could really call my own. Or the Beatlesque mania that surrounded the release of *Nevermind*. Or maybe it was because the article on the murder conspiracy theory got me noticed. Or maybe it was just because they were so damn good.

Back to that conspiracy theory, I'd never been certain either way, but I always felt that the evidence didn't rule out murder. Not that my opinion mattered, for if all went well I'd be days away from joining the select few who knew the real truth. I didn't know what I'd do with the information once I had it, but that wasn't very important to me at this point. Maybe deep deep down I thought it could revive my sagging writing career, a worthy cause that was something to believe in. Of course, all of this presumed I actually had traveled in time, and if so I was suddenly a master of time travel after two short accidental lessons. For this I had a plan.

Caught up in my thoughts and the stereo, I made it thirteen hours on the first leg before stopping at a motel in Eugene at around 7 PM. I asked the woman at the front desk if I could get a discounted room rate due to the short duration of my stay and my lack of employment. Although I was trying my best to dole out the charm, she wasn't having any of it and declined my advances while citing company policy.

At times like these I wished I could be more like my father. He had this uncanny ability to interact with secretaries, waitresses, telemarketers and other female service professionals to get whatever he needed with a wink and a smile, regardless of the quote unquote rules. Unfortunately that's not a characteristic I inherited from him. How his sexism became my ageism is beyond me.

Settling into my full priced room, I perused the free newspaper left on the dresser for some entertainment. The movie listings weren't all that exciting, and the television had fifty-seven channels but nothing on. Eugene didn't have a major league baseball team, and the minor league team was out of town. Flipping past the entertainment section, I saw an advertisement for an upcoming Bob Dylan concert on October 5 at McArthur Court on the University of Oregon campus. That date was almost a month away, but would that really stop me?

I drove to the University and wandered around a bit until I located McArthur Court. Surprisingly enough it actually was a "court," as in the basketball court the college team plays on. Although I was annoyed at myself for not figuring that one out, I had more important things to think about.

With basketball season not starting until November, the venue was closed on this September evening. The gates were locked, but that would be even less of an obstacle than the time barrier. Opening the newspaper again, I stared into the face of old Mr. Zimmerman, massaged my neck, and focused hard on that soon to be day in October. Future, here I come!

Apparently this was easier said than done.

Time travel lore and theory are pretty split as far as access to the future is concerned. The Grandfather Paradox is often cited as the logical reason why travel to the past is impossible, but travel to the future could scientifically work without having this problem to deal with. They say it would require travel at the speed of light and possibly a zero gravity black hole, but the rest of the science involved is over my head.

Both myself and the old man had allegedly visited the past, so that disproved half of the theory. And I was pretty sure my travel occurred while standing still, nixing the speed of light aspect. I used to be of the mindset that travel to the future would be impossible since it hasn't happened yet, and thus there isn't any future to go to. But if the old man had come here from the future, he obviously had to return there. Just because I'm not aware of the future relative to me doesn't mean it isn't out there.

But how could I get there? Remembering the two previous trips, blinking backwards seemed to follow a pattern. I needed to focus on an event I had specific knowledge of, be it via an actual memory (meeting Huey on the street in 1986) or a good secondhand account (Bowlingus and his 270 game).

Thinking of a birthday could have been too vague, and staring at a black and white advertisement for a Dylan concert that hadn't yet occurred was neither a memory nor a secondhand account. Hmmm. Why not try to retrace the other trips?

Autograph!

Fore!

"Is this the '50s, or 1999?"

Golf ball!

Bowling ball!

Either I was missing something, or one of my baseless theories was completely wrong. But those last images may have been a subconscious reminder. I was holding a bowling ball before my first trip and a golf ball for my second. The answer was obvious. You need to have balls to travel in time.

—⁂—

Back at the motel, I sat on the floor at the foot of the bed bouncing a tennis ball against the wall. I had to break down how this time travel thing worked. Assuming another injection was unnecessary, I decided to stop at a store to at least test the far-fetched ball theory. But more reasonably, maybe I was using the newspaper in the wrong way. If the future was off limits, using news from the past should do the trick. Scanning the still open entertainment section, I found a more detailed article on the upcoming Dylan show that I hadn't read in my earlier haste. It was a standard concert pitch type article that I could have written in my sleep, but one section stood out:

> If this visit to Eugene is anything like the last one, we're in for a treat. True fans are still talking about the rousing set played on June 14, 1999 at the 1,000 seat EMU Ballroom. A last minute solo show added to his summer tour with Paul Simon, Dylan treated the intimate crowd to an acoustic six song set at the start of his performance. Over the course of the evening he dusted off eight tunes that hadn't been played on the current tour, including the live debut of "Down Along The Cove" from his 1967 *John Wesley Harding* album.

That would have been a heck of a show to be at. I lobbed the ball at the wall as I turned the page, but it never bounced back. Before I had a chance to look for it, I was distracted by a screaming baby beside me.

The motel room was still the same, but a young couple and their child now accompanied me. Surprised, I jumped up and tried to press my back against the wall, ending up splayed out on the carpet of the adjoining room. Standing up, I raced over to the newspaper sitting on the dresser. June 14, 1999. I was miles away from the show, but I was back.

Noticing the noise had subsided, I poked my head back through the wall into my original room to investigate. The baby had calmed down but the family was still there. Clearing my throat didn't draw any attention to me, nor did a clearly stated greeting. Back in the adjacent empty room, I walked over to the bed and was able to put my apparitional hand right through it. (Not surprisingly, as I had just walked through yet another wall.) Between the bed and the nightstand sat my missing tennis ball.

Was it really the ball? Everything seemed to be the same as before. I still couldn't be seen by anyone, which seemed to rule out the theory that whatever was causing this needed to be absorbed into my system. Maybe interaction was learned over time, or maybe I'd need a separate, stronger dose to gain that power. I had hoped to have acquired the ability to inter-act by now so my current mission would be more than just observational. What if I could save Kurt Cobain? What would the next Nirvana record sound like? Would the mystery song from the Fitchburg show be on it? Would the new music cause Wyld Stallyn-esque world peace? Would the world be spared the boy bands and dance pop that would poison the ears of youth for years to come? Rock could still reign supreme, copycat sui-cides would be stopped, and I might even have a career again.

Like most others, I had always thought time travel would be achieved by a machine of some sort if at all. Since my experiences were clearly not linked to any machine, it seemed to argue that time travel is mostly mental. Was I tapping into the unused portion of my brain? If so, how could my brain have such vivid memories of events I'd read so little about, let alone seen first hand? And how the hell did the balls play into this?

This was reminiscent of the *Quantum Leap* argument on whether it was the body or mind of Sam Beckett that did the leaping. Internet newsgroups often debated the benefits of both, and individual episodes would tend to contradict themselves. Sam gave birth as a woman once, giving a point to the mind theory. But as a man with no legs, he was able to walk across a room, while others saw his host seemingly levitate. That was definitely a vote for the body traveling. Maybe it changed as needed by the situation God or Fate or Time put him in? Or the situation the episode writer needed to solve a problem?

My new train of thought must have broken the spell, as I found myself sitting on the floor in front of the newspaper having touched neither bruise nor ball. How long had I been here for? I retrieved a second tennis ball from the canister, gave it a squeeze, then smiled a wide grin as my new plan fell into place.

—⚬—

God bless the library. I always thought that the Internet would be the death of the public library system. It still may be in the far future, but as the Internet becomes more and more pay per view and the library stays free, you just can't go wrong. Not wanting to become a paid member of various newspaper websites or pay three bucks per article, I signed up for a free library card that earned me unlimited access to their extensive archives. Moments later I was at a computer, sipping my morning coffee and viewing the full text of articles circa April of 1994 while awaiting the actual paper copies from the librarian. The power of the newspaper from the night before had given me an idea. I just needed to find an event that would be memorable enough to get the focus right.

Cobain's body was found the morning of April 8. That should be the easiest, as the event itself was etched into my soul from the moment I heard the news that my idol was gone. I didn't believe it at first, thinking that my source was still confusing the Rome coma with this new incident. That was pretty illogical since the occurrences were a month apart, but the irrational mind isn't too keen on logic in times of emotional upheaval.

The coroner placed the approximate date of death on April 5, so I focused my data quest on the fifth through the seventh. It didn't take long to dig up the full newspapers from the days in question. My only idiotic snag was not remembering until after I had the papers in front of me that the newspaper of April 7 is telling the events of April 6. Blame the Internet for spoiling me with instant gratification.

April 7: Shannon Doherty files for divorce from Ashley Hamilton. I had a bit of a celebrity crush on her at the time and seem to recall smiling at this turn of events, but I don't think it had a profound enough effect to get me to where I needed to go.

April 6: A plane carrying African presidents from Burundi and Rwanda is shot down. We probably discussed it in my only college history class, but I seldom paid attention.

B-1B Lancers break 11 world speed records. I remembered this one, as it was in part the impetus for a term paper. We had to take a pair of existing technologies from today and combine them to form a somewhat reasonable practical application for tomorrow. My lab partner and I paired the English Channel "Chunnel" tunnel with supersonic travel to predict a tunnel from New York City to London. Our professor called it ridiculous and lectured us over not taking the project seriously, but we finished third in a national science contest. He had to publicly apologize and change our F grade to an A+. That one just might work.

April 5: Talk about a slow news day. From what I can determine, nothing important happened. Scientists report that the Milky Way is in the process of eating a lesser galaxy it had collided with. The governor of Maine signs a bill repealing a state ban on juice boxes. (Juice boxes? What's wrong with juice boxes?) American Airlines employees are given a four percent stake in the company. A judge blocks the purchase of McGraw Cellular by AT&T. Crayons are recalled for lead content. Aerosmith wins big at the Boston Music Awards. Pink Floyd releases *The Division Bell*. Right here and now, unbeknownst to the world, the most important musician of the current generation possibly lies dead while Aerosmith and Pink Floyd continue to milk out glory that has long since passed. Isn't it ironic?

What could I do for a backup plan? April 1, 1994 was a red-letter date in my personal history: The WBRU April Fools Day Low Dough Show at Lupo's Heartbreak Hotel featuring Carter USM, Possum Dixon and more for the low low price of one dollar. That night was my introduction to both bands, and they instantly ranked among my favorites. Especially Carter. They just blew everyone else off the stage. Between my best friend and myself we bought all of their albums the next day. Funny that less than ten years later neither band was still together. Pearl Jam was the closest thing my generation had to an Aerosmith or a Pink Floyd. (Including the similar shades of mediocrity post *Vs.* ...)

If all else failed, I supposed I could go back to April 1 and stay there for a week. It was just a shame I wouldn't get to relive the show since I was three thousand miles away.

Could I stay back in time for a week? I hadn't yet tried, but I didn't see why not. I could hang out, show myself around. There was no reason why I couldn't sleep while back in time aside from my usual insomnia. I'd have my choice of places to stay since nobody could see me. Food and water may be a problem, but I should be able to bring supplies with me since I had already inadvertently carried the bowling, golf, and tennis balls back with me. I might not even need food or sleep, since as far as my real body was concerned I wasn't actually gone at all.

Better still, if I hung around all day on the first and into the second, I'd now have memories of the second. Considering what I had already learned, that could be enough to allow me a free pass back there whenever I wanted. Unless my memories of the second were filed with my memories of the day I left in the present, which would lead me back to the bring some food plan.

Tired of speculation, I decided I wouldn't need any of these plans if I could find some more memorable news from the week in question. Needing two hands to dive back into the computer archive, I accidentally dropped my coffee while placing it on the desk next to the monitor. Looking around to make sure I wouldn't be caught making a mess in violation of the "no food or drink" policy, I noticed something was wrong. Not wrong, but different. The flat panel Dell I had been standing at was gone, replaced by an older green-screened terminal with the library logo in ASCII characters. I tried to type on the keyboard but my fingers went right through it.

I spotted a calendar on the librarian's desk. April 1, 1994. My reminiscence of the concert was so strong that I had blinked back without even realizing it. I had also done so without the aid of a ball, ruling out that ridiculous theory. This would bode well, as I had confirmed that I had the power to reach the first of April. I fingered my neck bruise and was immediately in front of the properly modern computer. I was sans coffee, but ready to track down more articles and verify my ability to reach other dates in the vicinity.

Five Seconds
To Hold You

FURTHER RESEARCH ON THE WEEK PROVED FRUITLESS. I stole a few newspapers worth of record reviews, bought a map of the state, and printed a Bob Dylan concert chronology to keep me amused while waiting around (and to fuel my internal Mr. Fusion), but that was about it. I did accidentally discover the name of a city 76.7 miles east of Seattle on Interstate 90 via the map, but aside from stoking my unforgettable fire it wasn't all that relevant to our story.

Most importantly, my abilities to blink back with an appropriate event in mind went off without a hitch. In addition to April Fools Day, I was also able to reach the sixth based on the term paper memory and the fourth based on the birthday of an ex-girlfriend.

Time of day was still a curious missing link. Though I had figured out jumping back to a specific day, I always returned to the exact same clock time I left from and never changed locations. As much as I concentrated on being there for the start of the concert and the birthday party, I still couldn't break the time barrier. (Well, obviously I could, but you know what I'm trying to say.)

My plan of attack (finalized on the second leg of the drive, from Eugene to Seattle) was to blink back to late at night on the sixth, allowing me to sneak into the seventh first thing by crossing midnight as the days changed. If I needed to go back further, I could then jump to the early morning of the sixth. If I hadn't solved the mystery by this point, I still had the fourth to fall back on. And if all else failed I'd jump all the way to the first and camp out until I had my answer.

In the back seat I had a small cooler with a loaf of bread, some cold cuts, and two gallons of water. Nothing fancy, just enough to sustain me if needed. I also had a red rubber ball I bought from a machine outside the grocery store, just in case.

It was nearly midnight when I pulled onto Lake Washington Boulevard. I parked the car outside of Viretta Park, ignoring the sign saying it was closed from 11:30 PM to 4 AM. After placing the cooler on my lap and synchronizing my watch to the clock in the car I felt ready to blink, but remembering Glitzy decided to get out of the car first. Ideally I'd want to take the car with me, but I didn't want to risk leaving it back in time. Or even worse having something weird happen where I only take the steering column with me, leaving my getaway car inoperable. I pocketed the newspaper clippings and made my way down the steep stone staircase into the park proper. At the bottom of the stairs I stopped and focused on the genesis of the old Chunnel project.

Nothing.

I tried again, remembering how the professor had been a dirty old man who hit on all of the girls in the class.

Still nothing. (I should have figured, since that could have been any day.)

What was wrong? I had no problem blinking back from the library, and I was using the same memory. Making matters worse, I was in danger of missing my easy window into April 7 if the clock slipped past midnight, which was now less than a minute away.

Trying not to panic, I retrieved my newspaper headlines for a different approach.

Justice Blackmun resigns!

Earthquake in LA!

Beer kegs in Maryland!

Biosphere! African Presidents!

Not even a tingle. Maybe I really did need a ball.

Now desperate, I squeezed the superball and turned to the page of music reviews for new and upcoming albums.

Smash by The Offspring!

Rusty by Rodan!

This was no good. I didn't care about either of those bands. Scanning down further I found something that struck a nerve but was worth a try: *Live Through This* by Courtney's band Hole.

Nope. The other reviews in my stack didn't seem to be worth the effort, as *Mellow Gold* came out way too early and *Parklife* was born too late.

Dejected, I plopped down on a graffiti covered bench and read the entire paper from April 7 cover to cover, never feeling close to blinking back at any point. Worse still, it was now 1:15 AM, which meant that my plan to backdoor the seventh was out unless I wanted to wait an entire day. I couldn't even get back to the April Fools Day concert, and that was one of the most vivid memories of my life. In some twisted way it felt like my historic bad concert karma was haunting me once again.

Bad concert karma is Murphy's Law applied to rock and roll. Tickets sell out early, a secret show occurs without your knowledge, a set time gets changed, an opening act doesn't show up, or someone breaks an arm in the mosh pit forcing a trip to the hospital mid-set. You name it, it's happened to me. The Reverend Horton Heat/Butthole Surfers show sells out inexplicably, leaving me to listen to the opening song from the sidewalk through the door of the club. All of the toilets overflow an hour before the Mighty Mighty Bosstones are set to take the stage and everyone is sent home. A bouncer throws a stagediver towards an exit at a 311 show, knocking over a friend's chair and breaking her knee. Black Grape can't get into the country to play the Enit Festival. I can't figure out how to travel back in time to one of the greatest shows of Bob Dylan's later career until I'm back in my motel room.

One of the fringe benefits of being a music critic was my guest list access and insider connections, which I had thought would eliminate the bad karma and give me a one up on the competition. I was wrong. Carter USM canceled the one date on their American tour that I had a press pass for, and two weeks later they call it quits. I hear on the radio that Nirvana won't be headlining Lollapalooza as they were originally scheduled to, and I'm so mad I punch a wall and break my hand, which is a bit harsh considering that Kurt turned up dead the next day...

The next day! I punched the wall on April 7th! The cancellation had been announced earlier than this, but in the days before Internet ubiquity it was the first I had heard of it.

A hard rain had begun to fall. The graffiti had washed away from the bench, but the paint wasn't running. The bench wasn't even wet. Even though the rain was steady, I wasn't getting wet either. The graffiti wasn't gone, it just wasn't there yet. I'd already blinked back to the scene of the crime.

It was 2:20 AM. Approaching the house, I began to experience a chilly sense of déjà vu. Although I'd never been here before, I had seen video and photos on the news and in magazines, and often envisioned it in various daydream/nightmares after the infamous tomorrow that from my perspective hadn't happened yet.

A garage/greenhouse hybrid loomed diagonally to the left of me just past some thick shrubs and a wooden fence separating the park from the property. I walked through the fence, intending to make the greenhouse my first stop as it seemed the most logical choice. If the body was there, it would mean I was too late and needed to keep pushing further back. If not, I'd just wait it out and all would be revealed. Good in theory, but in execution I faltered.

Part of me didn't want to visit the scene of this "murder" for fear that it would bring back memories of the other death that hit much closer to home. I'd never visited the scene of my sister's death while it was actually considered "the scene." I just couldn't bear to. Irrational guilt that I had set the events into motion, fear of confirming this, and a variety of other factors played into the decision.

I also didn't want to confront Nelson, as I'd likely kill him on the spot. Although I don't really see myself as being capable of committing murder, I wouldn't be above a heat of the moment attack on a highly deserving party. So I laid low, held back, attended the funeral, and skipped town. My guilty conscience was more or less a ridiculous way of taking control of the situation (or more accurately not taking control), and it certainly did its job.

The slamming of a car door reached my right ear, breaking my concentration. Two men were approaching the Cobain house. I had already ducked into the shadows to hide when I remembered I probably didn't need to. I crouched down to confirm my invisibility by sinking my hand into the ground, but something stopped me. I couldn't even reach the ground—my palm struck an immovable force about an inch before it should have. Partial blades of longer grass penetrated my hand, but that was as far as I could go.

Confused, I walked back to the fence and tentatively extended my arm. As expected, it passed through without resistance, just as my full body had moments before. Squatting once more, this time I couldn't even get within three inches of the ground. This was not only true of my hand, but my feet as well. I hadn't noticed before in my excitement, but they weren't quite touching the ground either. Through my thoughts I heard a voice call Kurt's name, reminding me why I was here.

The men had circled the perimeter and were climbing in through a ground level window. Was I actually here right on time? Unbelievable. I ran through and into the house to catch up. The window led to the kitchen. Both men were now inside, still yelling Kurt's name. I inspected each room of the surprisingly clean house trying to find him, hoping that I'd be able to do something, that my mere observational presence on the scene could persuade a change. (If a tree falls…) Moving through walls, I was able to get around the house much faster than the two intruders. It was pretty vacant, with the only sign of occupancy being the sounds of a television drifting down from somewhere upstairs.

Actually getting upstairs was my undoing. I just couldn't go there. Physically. It wasn't an invisible barrier as it was when I tried to touch the ground outside, but instead the lack of something solid to climb on. When I reached the stairs, I went right through them.

"You've got to be kidding me!" I yelled for no one to hear.

Looking down, I noticed my feet were now about a half inch below the bottom level of the house, wading in a puddle of floorboards. Since the house (and the world, for that matter) is rarely ever on a plane or completely level, I supposed this made some sense. By extension, I shouldn't be able get to the basement either. Or the… shit!

Not wanting to accept my realization, I ran back outside to the greenhouse where the body would eventually be if it wasn't already. I had no way of knowing, since the body was found upstairs, above the garage. It just wasn't fair. Pacing around the garage looking for a way up would be a foolish waste of time. I hurled the ball at the ground in frustration, watching it prematurely ricochet in the space above the dirt and launch into the night sky.

Eventually the two men left the house. They didn't even look in the direction of the other structure, let alone search it. Either they knew what was there and had no reason to look, or they didn't know and were in too much of a rush to find out. Some resolution.

So close and yet so far. My ability was more of a curse than a gift, with limited powers of observation and no power to interact. There had to be more to this. I needed an explanation. Trial and error just wasn't enough.

My only chance at understanding was to find a teacher.

6ix

"**A**RE YOU DOING ALRIGHT? It's not even your night to bowl. Don't you have a job?"

"I'm on sabbatical."

I nodded, smiled politely, and held out my beer in a toast-like salute to hammer home the point to the bartender that I'd essentially become a regular at the bowling alley bar.

"Regular" probably wasn't the right word, as I was far exceeding even the Cliff and Norm definition of the term. Since returning from Seattle early Saturday afternoon, I had been here waiting for the man anytime the bar was open. I was drinking like it was my job, and in a way it was. The actual "job" was a stakeout, with the drinking just something to do rather than a true desire to drown my sorrow. My alcohol tolerance was so high I was practically immune to the effects of light beer, but I couldn't very well sit at the bar all day and not drink. Besides, I needed to be there in case the man showed up. A definite long shot, but what other option did I have?

"Can I expect you at your usual time tomorrow?"

"Probably not. I'm waiting on a friend, and with any luck tomorrow I'll be leaving on a jet plane." I fished out my lottery form. "Can I play five more?"

I was gambling a lot, unreasonably figuring that retracing my actions from our first meeting would be the best way to get the man to reappear. Considering I only intended to gamble but didn't actually place a bet on the day of our first meeting indicated that this plan was also far fetched, but it was a logical companion to the gambler's fallacy. At least it was something to do besides sip beers all day. Though my numbers never came up all at once, I had more or less broken even by landing a few pairs. Yet even the dull repetitiveness of my new routine wasn't much of a comfort. I needed answers, or at least a sense of direction and purpose. I was singled out for a reason. But why?

A group of bowlers entered to start their pre-match drinking, but I didn't recognize any of them. This was Monday, my league was on Tuesday and didn't have any dual-leaguers like these guys. They were giving an older fellow a hard time, saying he had his chance at immortality on the previous Thursday and it would never come again.

He had tossed a pair of perfect games and was well on his way to joining the ultra exclusive 900 club, but he choked on the last ball, closing with a 291 game and 891 series. A stupendous feat, but it's known to all league bowlers that the only way to score 291 is by picking up nothing more than a single pin on the thirty-sixth and final throw. I wasn't about to participate in the ribbing, as I'd be thrilled with a single perfect game and wouldn't care if I finished off the series with a pair of rare double-digit scores.

In need of a break (and wanting to verify I still had the power), I used the recent library memory to blink back to the Thursday in question. In my world he'd at least have his chance at greatness again, though he'd inevitably be doomed to repeat his failure. I had an hour to kill before the league started, so I walked the lanes for some fun. Took a look at the pins up close, tried in vain to will balls that were gutter-bound into being strikes and balls that were strikes into being gutter balls. It was fascinating to note that the bowling lanes were well kept and well built, as my feet stayed perfectly in sync atop the level pine and maple boards of the playing surface.

After becoming bored with having no effect on the games in progress, I wandered through the pinsetter and into the back room behind the scenes. I had always been curious to see what goes on back there but too shy to actually ask an employee for a tour. Quite an amazing piece of machinery, with all sorts of gears and pulleys on the pinsetter and the ball accelerator.

There was some space for a mechanic to get in there and check things out if needed, but not a whole lot.

Done with my snooping, I was returning to the lanes in search of the near 900 show when a red bowling ball in the middle of the pathway behind the pinsetters caught my eye. Glitzy?

Reaching for her tentatively, I was able to nudge the ball into a slow roll. I picked it up, and my fingers fit perfectly into the custom drilled holes. There was fresh tape on the chipped thumbhole. I rocked my arm back and smiled. A glance at the serial number confirmed what I already knew. This was my girl.

I shouldn't have been so surprised. My ball was essentially right where I had left it after throwing it through the pins, the wall, and the pinsetter almost a week ago… or make that two days ago based on my current time. And the fact that I could touch it, hold it, feel it in my arms… what did that mean? I supposed since both myself and the ball were displaced in time we were real to each other. Or maybe it was because I was the one who had displaced it to begin with.

Excited to have a new project, I carried the ball out to the front of the lanes. Carefully placing it on the bottom shelf of a ball rack didn't work, so I left it on the floor and partly inside the ghostly rack before blinking myself back to the present.

I was back at the bar where I had started, with the older bowlers still razzing their buddy over his big choke. I ran out to the rack where I had left my ball moments (days) ago, but it wasn't there. A beat up yellow rental ball sat in its place.

As I considered the physics involved in this, a little YABA girl walked up to the rack and struggled to pick up the yellow ball. She awkwardly succeeded and ran back towards her baby-sitter at a bumper lane. Sitting in place of the yellow ball was Glitzy, as if she had been nestled inside.

I picked her up without any problem, making me think that maybe I wasn't here. I took the ball to the bar with me, resting it in my lap as I ordered another drink. The bartender happily complied, so obviously I was visible. I was also sitting on a stool and resting my arms on the bar. I tried to set the ball on the counter, but without the support of my lap it fell straight through to the floor and rolled away.

This was getting curiouser and curiouser. I had retrieved my lost bowling ball, but it wasn't really of any use to me since only I could interact with it. Maybe I could steal some pins to bring back in time with me as well. Or maybe not. If the pins and ball were from different times they may not be able to interact either. Clearly the ball traveled in time with me initially, but could it travel back? What purpose would it serve to have an invisible object in the present?

Presuming I wasn't the only time traveler out there (a known fact counting the old man), I wondered how many other pieces of time traveler debris there might be. This whole room could be littered with secret items only accessible and visible to the unique person that left the item behind. Maybe the old man had a whole collection of knickknacks in here that nobody knew about.

Just then it hit me how stupid I had been. All I had to do to find the man was blink back to our first meeting and confront him there. It certainly shouldn't be hard, as it was far and away my most vivid memory of the recent past. Smiling, I slid my hand back towards my neck bruise. As I was about to make contact, someone grabbed my arm and twisted it away from my neck.

"Don't, or you'll ruin everything!!"

I turned around and was eye to eye with the old man.

"Ruin what?" I asked, trying not to wince from the improper bend in my elbow.

"Don't do anything. We can't talk here. Meet me outside."

He slowly released my arm from his grip, then walked past the bar and through the wall to the parking lot where it all began. I started to follow, but was interrupted by the bartender.

"Are you sure you're okay?"

"Um, yeah. It's just something about my neck. I need to get some air. Keep my tab open."

Outside, the man was pacing as he waited for me. I wanted to start the questioning, but he beat me to it.

"Who injected you?"

"So it was an injection!"

He grabbed me, shaking my body for emphasis.

"I saw the bruise. You were going to use it, so you obviously know about it. But you don't know much about it, or you'd know that you don't really need to use it. It's not a switch. I need to know who, where, and when!"

"Are you crazy? You gave it to me! Why can't anyone else see it?"

He ignored my question while pondering my answer. A smile seemed to come to him slowly. "Yes, I would have. I must have. But when?"

"About a week ago."

"About a week ago, or a week ago? I need to know exactly."

"Last week. Bowling night. Right after you told me to play…"

He interrupted before I could finish. "Hot Spot! That's when I would, so that's when I will."

The man was suddenly in much better spirits, far calmer than he had been in our previous encounter. I took advantage of this mood swing to take control of the conversation.

"Can I ask some questions now?"

"Certainly. I'm sorry." He sat next to me on the sidewalk, his butt sinking below the raised asphalt. "I warn you that I may not have answers for everything, but ask away."

I took a deep breath, considering the order in which I wanted to state my case. I decided it best to talk about what I thought I knew first, then let him correct me as needed.

"The injection. What was it?"

The old man reached into his pocket and pulled out a small syringe filled with a clear, bubbling liquid. He held it up for me to inspect, but pulled it away when I reached for it.

"Look and ask, but don't touch."

"Fine. Obviously it allows me to travel in time, and I'm grateful."

The man smiled and nodded while returning the syringe to his pocket, so I continued.

"You've already told me you're from the future. So we both have this power. But I don't think I'm doing it right. I could use some lessons."

Nothing really changed in the man's face, he still just grinned an awkward grin and nodded slowly.

"You don't need lessons. And I think you know why I need you. Where was the first place you went?"

"To the scene of the crime. To save…"

He stopped me with a raised hand and a slight lean forward.

"Scene of which crime?"

How did he know there could be more than one? This threw me, though I suppose I should have expected it as it was what I wanted to hear.

Flustered, I held back my emotions and clung to my game plan.

"Kurt."

The man laughed. "Ahhh. Kurt. Noble, of course. But I think you'd rather save your sister."

I'd had it with the mystery shit. "Of course I'd LIKE to save her, but how can I save anything if I can't interact with anyone! And how the hell do you even know about her? What good is it to time travel just to observe? You can obviously have an effect on things, and obviously know more than me. A little help would be appreciated. So why me? And how come you can wrestle and inject me, but I pass right through things? Did you invent this? Is it some sick time traveler's joke to go around passing out limited abilities?"

Another flippin' nod and smile. "As I said, I'll answer what I can. It won't be everything, but it should be enough for now. You have the same abilities I have, though you may not have learned to fully control them yet. And, alas, I also have very limited powers of interaction, identical to yours. Time travelers are only able to interact with themselves."

"I figured that much. We can interact because we're both time travelers. But your powers are stronger. Why can you hold that syringe? Or sit on a stool? Or drink a beer?"

The man laughed. "You're quite observant. I can hold the syringe since I brought it with me from my time. As for the stool and the beer, you must have left them behind. I suppose I owe you a thank you. It's great how the beer stays cold when temporally displaced."

I remembered landing on the floor of the bar after my first blink and was embarrassed for not figuring out that much on my own. It was just like my bowling ball experiment. The stool and the beer must have gone back with me.

"So I can be on the receiving end of your syringe because we're both time travelers? That can't be right. I wasn't a time traveler before you injected me."

Laughing again, the man replied. "You're not listening. We can't interact with other time travelers. We can only interact with ourselves."

"Ourselves? But that doesn't make any sense." It suddenly hit me. "Unless…"

With another smile and nod, my sentence was completed for me.

"Exactly. I'm you."

Stunned by this turn of events, I studied the old man's face for the first time. In a bizarre way it was like looking into a living mirror—a living funhouse mirror that made you look older. He wasn't just an old man, he was an old me. But that couldn't be right, since they always said…

I realized that this was a situation where I couldn't speak to myself in internal monologue, so I actually vocalized my thoughts.

"They always say that meeting up with your past or future self could have drastic consequences and really muck up all of space and time."

"They say it, but that doesn't make it a fact. All that is *said* about time travel is based on theory. Sometimes theories are right, sometimes wrong. It wouldn't be any fun if everyone was always right."

"I guess not."

Smile, nod. "And we've just proven that theory to be false, just as we have before and as we will again."

"This has happened before?"

The man lifted a hand to stop me, giving another nod and smile before resuming.

"Another unproven theory is that you shouldn't know too much about your own future. I do subscribe to that one to a certain degree. I'm not going to tell you much about how we turn out, especially since it isn't necessarily set in stone anymore. The one exception: You now know that you will go back in time and meet yourself."

Loving a good argument, I played devil's advocate. "I disagree. By having this conversation, I won't need to have it with myself again, since I'll already know what I said on both ends."

"Wrong. My first rule of time travel: If you interact with yourself, you must repeat all interactions to keep the flow going. The interaction doesn't have to be repeated exactly, but it has to occur. When you are on the other end of this conversation it may be very different, but you still have to have it unless you undo it on another trip, in which case you still have to make *that* trip."

I nodded dumbly even though I was lost. Older me continued.

"That's the reason I asked when you got injected, so I could know when I have to go there and do it."

"You're saying you never injected me?"

"I didn't. Another me did. But I will. I just did it in the wrong order, but you can do it in the right order when you play this end, tidying up the flow a bit." He stopped his soliloquy, noticing my vacant stare as I smiled and nodded back at him. "Does that make sense?"

"Not at all," I confessed.

He exhaled a silent sigh and tried again. "You now have the ability to travel in time because you went back in time and gave yourself that ability. Therefore, you must go back in time at some point later in life to give yourself that ability again, or else you never would have gotten the ability, and you're caught in the loop of paradox."

I was sure I was wrong, and was not afraid to tell myself. "I think you're already in a paradox. I mean, how did you get the ability to give it to yourself the first time? It had to start somewhere."

"Suppose we were involved in the discovery of time travel, using people as lab rats in a slew of experiments over a period of years before finally getting it right. Learning from our mistakes, we decide it would be better for everyone's sanity if this ugly episode never happened. So I go back in time to before the experiment and give you the ability to travel in time. From that point on you can do everything differently from what I did so long as you still go back to give yourself the power. The early experiments are pinched away as if they never happened, but we get to keep the time travel. Paradox is avoided, and everyone wins!"

I was still confused on the whole picture, but had to admit it was getting better. "I think I understand. You want me to try not to forget about what hasn't happened yet?"

"Theoretically."

"Then how did we invent time travel? Did the experiments never happen, or just never happen to us?"

"That example was hypothetical. Also, I said we were 'involved' in the discovery, not the actual inventor." He gave me the same knowing look I was fond of giving before continuing. "Any more questions?"

"What did you mean when you said I'd ruin everything before?"

"Where were you going?"

"To find you on the day we met."

"That would have ruined everything, since you can only go to the same time once."

"So I wouldn't be able to get there?"

"No you would, since you're younger. But I wouldn't, which would mean I didn't, which would mean you couldn't, which would be the big bad paradox."

"Why can't you visit the same day twice?

"I don't know. It just doesn't work."

"But that doesn't make any sense without a reason. You should be able to."

Old me was becoming impatient. "Of course you should be able to, and maybe one day we will be able to. Time travel is still in its infancy. Once upon a time we could transmit audio signals through the air but not video. Video was finally figured out, but for the first few years you couldn't do it in color. I'm sure everyone will be making repeat trips in time someday, but as of today we cannot."

His analogy was reasonable, but I wanted to continue debating. "But if that ability was developed in the future, couldn't you just go back and pass it on earlier?"

"I suppose that would be likely."

"So since that hasn't happened, that would mean it never will. Right?"

He sighed again, less silently than before. "I don't know, but I wouldn't necessarily want to find out. The inherent risk in disproving the theory is far too great."

I gave him a look of half confusion and half fear, still not fully understanding how this worked.

"Don't dwell on it too much. Bottom line is to just be careful."

Though not the answer I wanted, it was good enough for the time being.

"So, what's next? How do we save our sister?"

Tram #7 To Heaven

"**A**TTENTION PASSENGERS. THE CAPTAIN HAS turned off the fasten seat belt sign and it is now safe to move about the cabin. Approved electronical devices may be used at this time."

Electronical? Did I hear her correctly? Is that even a word? I considered opening my eyes and asking the passenger riding next to me for his take on "electronical," but decided I didn't want to encourage him.

I wasn't particularly tired, but had decided to feign sleep before takeoff once it became clear that my seatmate was going to be quite the talker. The thought of five uninterrupted hours of unintelligent conversation didn't sit very well with me. I really hoped he was stopping at the layover and would not be on board for the second leg of the flight. If he was on board, I'd be on bored. Had my assigned companion been a cute girl I may have changed my tactics, though I'd likely still end up singing in silence unless she started the conversation. Funny how it was always an annoying, older male bending my ear on a cross-country flight rather than some sweet young thing.

So I remained awkwardly wedged between the seatback and window with my eyes closed, listening to the hum of the 747 engine and occasional snippets of a tale regarding a five dollar tomato being told to an unsuspecting soul across the aisle as I plotted my rescue mission. I really wished I hadn't forgotten my headphones.

The plan I helped myself concoct was complicated, but understandably so under the circumstances. I needed to go back and convince my younger self to convince my sister not to wed, thus preventing her death by preventing the inciting incident. The first question that came to mind was obvious.

"Why can't you do it?"

Older me had done his smile and nod thing upon being asked this. I wondered at which point in my life I would pick up that habit.

"You know how we were in our youth. Extremely antisocial. You're still the same way. I can't get close enough to a version of us that can be helpful. He'll think I'm a crazy old man."

Based on my reaction to my neighbor on the plane, he was certainly right about that. But how had he convinced me to help him? He made me come to him. It was genius really. I was ready to banish him to Ignoreland until he intrigued me by knowing the Hot Spot numbers. That's probably what I would do if I were him. Or when I become him, as the case may be.

Thinking about it now, I might have been approached by my older self many times in the past and not even realized it. Part of my mind almost started to remember it, though it could very well be a false memory based on the power of persuasion.

Eyes still closed, the internal, unspoken debate with my real self drifted towards figuring out how to convince my younger self to cooperate in this venture, and then on to selecting the most appropriate dates and events to base our rescue from. You may think that you know yourself well enough to anticipate how you would react to any given situation, but this was turning out to be quite a stumper.

My mind continued to wander without much serious deliberation, and my fake sleep inevitably and unknowingly morphed into real sleep. I dreamt I was falling. Or not really falling, as there was no wind resistance, no chill. Just the helpless, dizzy with a sense of vertigo feeling where you know you're dreaming but it's still frightening. Usually you wake up with a sudden start, catch your breath, and that's that.

I forced my eyes awake and realized I really was falling. Clouds passed through me, and when I emerged I was floating in free fall waiting for an inevitable encounter with the ground below me.

But...

For some reason it didn't seem so inevitable. The ground wasn't coming any closer. My body was hovering in space, falling sideways if that makes any sense. Or actually not falling at all, as I could again feel that invisible barrier beneath me.

It reminded me of the old cartoons where a character is able to defy the laws of physics and walk on air until such a time that he realizes that this is happening, at which point he'll wave briefly at the camera as gravity takes over and his fall begins. But for some reason I wasn't really falling. I tentatively took a few steps, then sat down cross-legged in mid-air. Was it because I wasn't really here?

This started me thinking as to how the time travel effect really worked. Were the sky and clouds around me real and my body an illusion, or was it the other way around? Or were both person and place very real, but existing on differing planes of reality? With my hovering and such it would probably make more sense for me to be a disembodied observer. The most reasonable conclusion I could draw was that the inventor of time travel (maybe even me, I still wasn't certain on the history) decided to give the appearance of a body to minimize any potential disorientation that would be felt by an apparitional spirit in the sky. As usual, I grew tired of internally debating something I knew so little about and turned my attentions back to my surroundings in a practical rather than theoretical sense.

Looking up, another plane was upon me. Caught like the clichéd deer in headlights, I broke the trance in time to brace myself for an impact that never came. The aircraft flew right through me, so fast that I barely caught a glimpse of the inside.

Apparently I had blinked back while thinking about my sister. I wanted to rationalize that since I wasn't really here nothing could hurt me, but my mind wasn't up for being rational. I started to scream as another jet approached...

...and snapped upright in my seat.

"Are you okay?" asked my annoying fellow traveler.

"Me? Um, yeah. Bad dream. Thanks."

"I always have the strangest dreams on airplanes," he started in an attempt to comfort me. "Once I thought the entire plane was full of Lilliputians. You know, from the book? They had plans to hijack..."

I returned to my fake sleeping posture and blocked out the rest of his odd recollection. Every time I thought I was used to this time travel thing I'd have a reminder that it's not all fun and games. Perhaps I should have been encouraged that I was able to blink back with less and less effort on each subsequent trip (no effort at all in this case), but on the other hand I now had to worry about where I went with my newfound knowledge of the one visit policy. The circumstances and panic of that last blink back didn't allow me any time to note when I'd been. Hopefully it wasn't to a time of any importance to my mission.

I suddenly realized the significance of my library daydream back to April 1, 1994. I didn't know it at the time, but that trip had effectively eliminated my plan to wait out the week before Kurt Cobain died. That was also why I couldn't get back to any of the prearranged dates I had rehearsed for that trip, since I had already taken the memories for a test drive at the library. At least that took some of the fickleness out of my supernatural ability. There were real rules that needed to be adhered to. Now it was just a matter of learning them all.

In this most recent airplane blink I wasn't actually falling, more hovering when the plane flew through me. That may mean that my height (for lack of a better term) while in the past is linked to my altitude (the elusive better term) upon departing. Paired with the minor levitation I experienced back in 1994 this made some sense. If I was right it might prove useful later. And the tree house would be just the place for further experimentation.

—⁘—

"He said in love and war all is fair, he's got cards he ain't showing."

My father had picked me up at the airport and was singing along to the Jonathan Edwards oldie as we sped home on Route 24. Due to the intended purpose of this visit, Dad wasn't in very good spirits. He tried to fake it with some small talk and scattered impromptu song fragment sing-alongs, but I wasn't so easily fooled. Since I had a slightly different plan for coming back East, my own mood was better, almost hopeful. Dad more than likely thought I was faking it too, and that wasn't necessarily a bad thing.

"How's the job search coming?" he asked, abruptly lowering the radio volume without taking his eyes off the road.

"No offers, just a come on from the whores on seventh avenue."

"Don't mock one of the greats," Dad said without even a hint of a smile.

People seldom catch on when I speak in song lyrics. I get a lot of strange looks based on my frequent non-sequiturs, but little recognition. I can't even tell why I do it. They speak to me in riddles and they speak to me in rhyme. Oops, I did it again. Sometimes the fragments aren't even from songs I like. It's mostly just a word association game my brain plays that manifests itself via lyrical tourette's. So stand up and fight, stand up for your rights, and dance to the music that nobody likes.

Dad often understood the sources, though he never appreciated the concept. He considered it a sacrilege for me to pilfer words of wisdom like that, even though he never complained when my Mom spoke the same way. Maybe it was genetic.

"How is my quoting any different than the cover songs you play on the guitar?"

"My songs are a tribute. You speak as if the words are your own. That's the part that isn't right. Now seriously, do you have any job leads?"

In need of a better answer, I restated. "I'm almost happy to be on the dole and avoiding people for a while. Besides, only fools and horses work."

The "almost" was a lie. I was actually thrilled to be void of responsibility for the time being. And the way things turned out, it was perfect timing to have some freedom to do what I had to do here.

The music critic career I alluded to earlier had imploded shortly after the turn of the millennium. It wasn't so much that my talent was fading, but more so that I just didn't feel the passion for it anymore. An early musical midlife crisis is probably the best way of describing it. I had passed my musical peak and done quite well for myself being in the right place at the right time. But as popular tastes evolved, no new music really moved me anymore. Most of my few and far between freelance pieces covered the solo careers, new projects, or even deaths of my earlier heroes. Fluff pieces saying "This new album is great not because it's actually any good, but because it reminds me of the glory of my misspent youth." Artist loyalty and nostalgia tours may be good for the performers and the fans, but not so much for a journalist who is supposed to stay relatively objective at all times.

Solicitations for my articles and reviews kept coming, but I couldn't bring myself to fake it. After being essentially blacklisted from most of the major publications for refusing assignments and not having anything inspire me enough to submit a review to the online and offline 'zines, I turned to a string of personal assistant and call center jobs just to pay the bills. The most recent of these had ended in a massive layoff a few weeks back, and the downtime and unemployment pay were quite welcome.

Not that I really needed a great deal of time per se anymore. The ability to time travel essentially gave me unlimited vacation days if and when I returned to the working world. Vacations would have to be all sightseeing tours, but that wasn't too bad considering my antisocial nature.

"Just make sure you do something practical with your time off," Dad continued as he exited the highway. "I don't want you just laying around drinking beer all day."

"I won't just drink. I'll drink and complain."

Dad didn't think that response was as funny as I did, so I politely thanked him for the advice. He looked like he was about to say something else, but changed his mind and responded by turning the volume back up on the stereo and air guitaring out the last few bars of "Sunshine" as he held the steering wheel with his knees.

I tried to convince myself that he was actually jealous of the position I was in but didn't want to show it. It probably wasn't true, but I knew I'd certainly be jealous if things were reversed. Regardless, he seemed to be holding something back, but it wasn't really my concern at this one moment in time.

—⁂—

"It's so good to see you. Let's take a picture!" was the first thing my Mom said upon my arrival. It was always the first thing she said.

"No flash photography, please," was my reply, also the same as it ever was.

It wasn't so much photographs in general that I didn't like, as I agree that they are a great way to capture a memory. It's amazing how the image of one split second can set your mind whirling to remember an entire day, week, month, or even a year. But this was not true of the photos my Mom liked taking. She must have been a portrait photographer in a past life. Her compositions always had us sitting up straight with the living room fireplace as our backdrop. Mom on the right, me in the center, and Dad on the left when he eventually figured out the automatic timer on the camera. Then just me and Mom, and then me and Dad. Always the same poses, the same setting, and sometimes even the same clothing. (I admit I'd often try to wear the same outfit each time I visited just to prove my point about the lunacy of taking the same exact photo 8,000,000 times.)

We had so many of these photos, if handed a pile and asked to put them in chronological order I'd be willing to bet that not a single one of us could do so. How could we? The slightly younger looking ones would go on one end and the slightly older ones on another, but month to month and even year to year not much changes without context clues. Late spring or early fall? Birthday or holiday? Prom, wedding, or funeral? If Mom could pull off the ordering feat without assistance I'd never complain about her picture taking again.

Once upon a time my sister had her place in these photos as well. There was even a part of me deep deep down that thought the only consolation prize to come of my sister's death would be the end of my Mom's staged photos and a move towards happier candid shots. In a candid shot of a group the event takes center stage. You may not even notice that a particular individual wasn't present at any given time. But omissions become painfully obvious when everyone is assuming the assigned positions. I'm not saying that I want to forget, but why would you want a constant reminder?

After the photo session my Dad wandered off to noodle with his guitar while my Mom predictably started grilling me about my love life.

"Have you talked to…"

"Don't say her name."

"How did you know I'd ask about a girl?"

"It's always about a girl."

It was always about a girl, and I was always elusive, this particular time for three reasons.

First (and most obviously): It wasn't any of her damn business.

Second: Without fail, the moment I utter the name of a girlfriend in my mother's presence and she repeats it aloud, the relationship will immediately begin a downward spiral towards certain doom. It sounds crazy, but even my sister believed in this phenomenon and she was always the more levelheaded one. I'm not sure if it's psychological witchcraft or if she's some kind of hypnotist. Of course I don't really think Mom does it on purpose if it is something more mystical, but if I can accidentally travel in time, why couldn't my mother be a sort of accidental anti-cupid? (If this theory is true, I've got absolutely no one but myself to blame for not having her start chanting a mantra of "Nelson, Nelson, Nelson, Nelson, Nelson, Nelson, Nelson" a long, long time ago.)

Third: There really wasn't much to talk about as of late. Mom was referring to the one that got away just before the sister situation played out, but I'll get to her later. Since my sister's death I had considered myself jinxed and avoided most social behavior, including proper dating. I didn't want to feel the same guilt over causing a bad relationship for another of my friends or myself, so I kept away. Save a drunken one night stand here and there with minimal initial conversation, that was that. And that certainly wasn't something you brought up with your mother. I knew I'd get over it eventually, but the timing still wasn't right.

Mom continued. "Don't you want to get yourself a good job and find a nice girl to settle down with?"

"Don't get me started on settling down."

She read my tone before I had time to restart my famous rant.

"I know, I know. You just want to have fun, sow your wild oats and keep your freedom. And there's nothing wrong with that. You'll stop when you've found the right one just like your father did."

"Or like my sister didn't."

I realized my poor judgment in bringing this up as soon as the words were out of my mouth. Mom's eyes began to well up as the memory we were both avoiding rushed to the pinnacle of her consciousness. Needing to get the conversation resumed as distraction, I said the second thing that came to mind.

"What do you know about Dad and his wild oats? I thought you always said 'The past is still the past.'"

Mom laughed. "That is what I say, but it doesn't mean I don't know what goes on."

She smiled a knowing grin as she wiped the tears from her eyes. "Your father was quite the smooth operator back then. He could seduce any girl he wanted to. But I was the only one who ever played hard to get. That's why I won out. I was intriguing to him. He couldn't have me unless he decided to settle down. Right, dear?"

Dad had walked in with impeccable timing holding his acoustic guitar in one hand and two beers in the other. He just shrugged and handed me a bottle.

"Whatever you say, sunshine. I'm trying to remember how to play the rest of this song. I've almost got it."

He kissed my mom on the head and winked at me as he left the room. She half followed, goosing him as he walked out.

I didn't know if I should feel uncomfortable in this conversation or not, but since I had never heard this part of my parents' origin story I was oddly intrigued. Awkward discomfort was certainly better than tears. I looked towards Mom to resume our conversation, but the moment had passed. That faraway look again overcame her.

"I guess what I'm saying is that you'll just know when it's right. And if you don't, others might see it for you."

The tears came quickly this time. "I just wish that Nelson was able to see what was going on before it was too late. I mean, it's not his fault, but…"

More sobs abruptly ended the revelations. I gave my mother a hug because it was the right thing to do, although I was a little taken aback that she didn't blame Nelson for this as I had. From my perspective he was clearly the responsible party.

"It's going to be fine, Mom. I'll find a way to make it right."

"I know," she sniffled. "I'm just glad you're home."

With the embrace ended and the tears slowed, I thought it best to get away before my emotions caught up to me.

"I feel like taking a walk now that I'm back in my old neighborhood. Want to come with me?"

"No thanks. I have to be up early tomorrow. And you do too, so don't stay out late. Did you write something to read at the service?"

"Still working on it," I lied. "That's why I need a walk."

I had no intention of attending the service, but now didn't seem to be the right time to get into that with Mom. Besides, I wouldn't have to write anything if there wasn't a service to attend.

"Good luck. And put on a jacket!"

Mom kissed me goodbye and left the kitchen to join my father in the family room. I grabbed my jacket as instructed and exited through the back door. As I walked outside, I could briefly hear Dad playing something that resembled the chords to "Sunshine" when Mom opened the door and released the sound to the world.

"In this old world she's gonna turn around, brand new bells will be ringing."

Eight Days A Week

The neighborhood hadn't changed much in the year since I'd been gone. I couldn't outright pinpoint any major changes over the past several years either. Surely some things were different, but a slow evolution often goes by unnoticed, whereas a larger jump is more jarring.

The first thought to come to mind was how I missed the crispness of a New England autumn. Time just blurred on by in California with picture perfect weather every day. After making it less than a quarter of the way around the neighborhood, the second thing to come to mind was that I was freezing and didn't really miss crisp Septembers at all.

The lights were still on when I returned home, meaning Mom and/ or Dad were still up. Not yet ready to venture inside and talk more about the supposed reason for my trip home, I wandered into the backyard to further ponder my true plan. Aside from the tree house, I hadn't sorted out as much as I would have liked to on the plane. I've always been the sort who kept the real planning until the last minute. Internal debate is my prep work, used to keep my mind limber more than anything else. Need to give the synapses some work to keep them clear for times when serious thinking is required.

I decided that I should make all contact with my other selves in reverse chronology. That way if he happened to freak out I could avoid severe mental trauma by pinching off each episode by moving the first contact up earlier. The last thing I needed was to be known as the guy who was always talking to himself, or worse yet always trying to talk to himself even when there was no other self to talk to. Using days of the week as a simple analogy, if I went back to Friday and screwed up, I could still go back to Thursday and try again, essentially erasing the Friday trip from the flow as far as my younger self was concerned. On the other hand, failing on Thursday and Friday in proper order keeps both strikes "on the record" so to speak.

Although I didn't know all of the blinking mileposts on the path I would take, the most obvious would be to go back to just before she died and make sure I was there to stop it. I considered cutting to the chase of what older me really wanted to do by eliminating the problem at the most probable source: the wedding. We were both all but certain this was the beginning of the end, but Mom's comments had given me a slight case of doubt. Suppose there was even the smallest chance that I was wrong. Would it hurt to have some verification first?

After much consideration, I decided to do the right thing and play it straight by first trying to save her life directly. I could always stop the wedding later since it wasn't necessarily dependent on the success of this primary mission.

Breaking from my thoughts, I realized I had been walking around in circles within the fenced-in perimeter of my childhood backyard. This was a common walk for deep thought when I was younger, and I had picked up the trail where I left off. I remembered jumping the fence to retrieve wiffle balls hit into the woods during epic games of home run derby. Hitting homers over the four foot chain link fence used to be hard, but as I grew it became easier and easier until I finally had to rotate the field to aim at the twelve foot deck on the back of the house as a more challenging target.

Continuing counterclockwise, I finally reached the tree house. It overlooked the open area where the family dog used to frolic. He wasn't around anymore. Hit by a car during my freshman year of college. We never got another dog, but kept the area either as a tribute or out of laziness. I was never sure which.

At the vacant doghouse I kicked around in the dirt at the back left corner until I heard my heel knock on plywood. The hiding place was still there. During high school I'd bury my marijuana stash here in a tin box under a small square of wood. And here it was, undisturbed after all these years. I pried open the box and found a lighter, a book of matches, and a plastic bag with some ancient shake and two clumsily rolled skinny joints, now yellow with age. The matches didn't work, but the lighter was still in fine working condition.

I climbed up the creaky ladder, flipped open the trap door in the floor, and emerged in the creakier tree house. Leaning out the side window towards the temple of the dog, I lit the crumbly parchment. A bit harsh, but still refreshing. On many a summer night the neighbor girl and I would get stoned up here and fool around a bit. Or—no, wait. We got stoned once and I made a move, but she was less than receptive and stormed off into the night. We never hung out again.

Did we?

Yes.

No.

Maybe?

No.

Definitely not.

Why couldn't I remember? How could I forget? Which version was right? I guess I was choosing to remember the happier fantasy. Either that or I was already stoned. There was only one way to find out. Time to party like it's 1991.

The dog was barking uncontrollably as he often did when he had company. I stepped through the wall of the tree house and looked down at him from my hovering position. He immediately calmed down and sat quietly. Could he see me? I guess that made sense, since animals and small children could see Al the hologram on *Quantum Leap*. I ran a short spiral above my dead dog's head, wanting to check his eyes for yellow matter custard if I could get close enough. He remained still and didn't even look up at me. I yelled his name in an attempt to attract his attention, but still he held his ground. Guess he couldn't see me after all. Even though there isn't much science to my time travel theories, I decided I should probably try to keep them separate from movie and TV logic.

Blinking back from the tree house was a calculated move, as it would allow me access to the upstairs of the raised ranch house. (Too bad I hadn't thought of this in Seattle.) The floor of the tree house was almost exactly in line with the backyard porch. When I was younger I had ambitions of building a bridge between the two structures, but my Dad knew it would be an eyesore and rightfully disallowed it. Leaving the dog behind, I walked across the invisible bridge to the kitchen window.

Taking care to be discreet so my high school self wouldn't see me, I felt like a bit of a peeping tom as I voyeured inside. My sister and I were at the kitchen table playing cribbage. The game was played more or less on autopilot, while the primary focus was her grilling me on the events of the evening.

"So, who was that girl with you in the tree house?"

Younger me blushed as he tossed two cards into the crib. "I have no idea what you're talking about."

My sister had just turned fifteen and was trying to learn the ropes of teendom from me, not quite realizing that I wasn't the best teacher from an "are you experienced" standpoint.

"You just had a smoke by yourself? That's the sign of a true junkie."

I laughed at the lesser of two evils entrapment game she often played. Even at this young age she could casually manipulate without arising suspicion. It must have worked wonders in her teaching career, effortlessly convincing kids they were taking the high road in revealing one secret while protecting another. My high school incarnation foolishly thought he could play along.

"I don't know what you mean. I don't smoke."

"You don't smoke cigarettes," was her immediate reply. "But I've heard about some other things. You should let me join you. That is, if you really were alone up there…"

I watched myself redden as he tried to hide behind his cards. Though I wasn't recalling this exact conversation, I did remember the general scenario. Sis wanted me to be her doorman to the world of underage drinking and drugs. I wanted to set a good, know when to say when, functional alcoholism, recreational in small doses from time to time type of example that kept the stoner that I was under wraps. But she had friends among the high school gossip circles of other sibling pairs, and thus knew a lot more than she was letting on. She was playing this one perfectly, knowing that dragging me down one path would force me to retreat down the other when I changed the subject.

"Fine. I was with a friend out there, but her name is not of your concern. Lesson number one, which I'm sure you'll learn the hard way one day, is that a gentleman doesn't kiss and tell."

She laughed. "If you think you're a gentleman, your advice should be a gentleman doesn't kiss, unless he wants the girl to cuss at him and run away."

I pushed the cribbage board away, effectively ending the game as the argument escalated.

"You were spying on me!"

Mom walked in at that moment, looking younger than I could ever remember. "Kids! Do you know what time it is? What's going on?"

My sister and young me exchanged a brief glance, trying to telepathically get on the same page for a cover story. I couldn't very well tell our mother: "She was watching me try to seduce a girl with a joint," as I'd be in trouble for the drugs, in trouble for telling my sister that I did drugs, and on top of that get the third degree about the girl, eventually revealing her name and falling victim to Mom's jinx. Any way you look at it you lose.

Sis started. "He's pegging extra holes and trying to cheat."

Young me took her lead and responded perfectly, throwing down his cards. "Whatever. I'm not playing anymore."

Mom bought the ruse. "Remember: the name of the game is fun."

Outside the window, I smiled at another of Mom's catch phrases.

"The name of the game is fun."

"The past is still the past."

"Because I'm the mother."

Remembering all of these in succession kicked off a fit of laughter, at which point high school me looked towards the sounds and made eye contact with modern me.

"Hey!" he yelled, tripping over his chair as he ran for the back door.

Stunned, I left the porch and sprinted through the air towards the woods behind the house. Behind me I could hear the anarchy play out. My father had joined the group when he heard the commotion, and the dog resumed barking upon seeing the gathering outside.

Mom: "What is it? A robber?"

Me: "There was a man watching us. He jumped off the deck and ran that way."

Sis: "I didn't see anything."

Dad: "I see him, he's in the tree house. You better run, motherfucker!"

Mom: "Language!"

Catching my breath as I turned back, I saw my father descend the stairs and charge in my direction. He was holding his guitar as if it were a club and seemed fully prepared to utilize his weapon of choice. He looked angry. Very angry.

"Be careful!" I heard my mother yell as Dad gained ground.

Realizing that running wasn't the best option here, I did what I should have done from the start. I fingered the neck bruise and instantaneously returned to the modern day tree house.

Drivin' On 9

I WOKE UP IN THE MORNING AND FELT A PANG. Actually I didn't sleep well and woke up quite a bit during the night, but this was the first waking period that could be considered "morning" rather than "in the middle of the night." I absentmindedly stared at the row of identical clocks on the wall, one for each time zone in a bizarre attempt at postmodern decor. Trying to fall back asleep, I wondered if the constant ticking contributed to my inability to sleep solidly. Now the clocks seemed almost silent, but in the still of the night the second hands echoed in a series of sonic booms. Not the best environment for an insomniac with a headache.

The couch in the basement wasn't particularly comfortable, causing my sleep to come in short bursts rather than a single continuous block of rest. My body usually needs a few days to acclimate itself to a new bedtime resting place, after which I'll pass out and sleep with no problem. I can nap anywhere, but always have a problem with real nighttime slumber. The desire is there, but I reach a point where I'm so tired I can't sleep whenever a scenery change is involved. Of course, upon returning to my own bed I'll have to be reacclimated to it as well and the cycle starts anew.

I'm sure my overworked brain had something to do with the will to drive myself sleepless. During the restless hours I replayed my previous blink. It was nobody's fault but my own. I'd have to be more careful going forward. But what about Dad? Had he really been able to see me? Was I starting to fade in for real? At some point would everyone be able to see me as I originally theorized? Old me hadn't said anything about that, but then again I never asked.

Maybe Dad was just putting on a show so younger me wouldn't look foolish in claiming to see things. Defending the honor of his only son, that sort of thing. He did have a tendency to do that from time to time. Hell, maybe he knew I was stoned and was quietly giving me the business about not keeping my shit together.

There was another major question at hand: Did I (real, here and now me) remember seeing myself in the window? I didn't think I did, but of course I should since now I know I was there. You would think I'd remember the day a peeping tom spied on us and the whole family chased after him. That's not something you forget. Maybe my memory was clouded since I was now on both ends of the exchange, causing my recollections to fuse together as one memory to conserve brain space. If a brain worked like a computer hard drive, how many gigabytes could it hold? Just thinking about it gave me another headache.

A strategy adjustment was in order for the next time I met my younger self. I decided it might work to my advantage if I jumped right in his face and gave him the ghosts of Christmas style *"I'm from the future"* speech. Walk through some walls for extra effect, provide vague answers to direct questions, rattle my metaphorical chains and we'd be ready to save the day. There wouldn't be any need to tell him the real purpose of the mission, just to stick to our sister like glue for a couple of days and the bad bits would all be history.

My sister's life ended on September 11, 2001. Nine eleven. The biggest tragedy in American history, and I'll always remember it for one unrelated death a few hundred miles away from ground zero. It's ironic, as her passing had nothing to do with the infamous events of that day. It was just a coincidence of the calendar. She was probably gone before any of that happened.

People tend to remember quite readily where they were when certain landmark events occur, most often events of a tragic variety. Where were you when JFK was shot? When John Lennon was murdered? When Kurt Cobain died? When the space shuttle blew up? Etc, etc. Nothing like a generational sea change to anchor a memory and make it familiar to millions.

Then there are the not so universal "where were you when" memories; mostly happier recollections that are more personal in nature. Where were you when you first heard your favorite song? When you learned to drive a stick shift? When you met your best friend? When you had your first beer or your first joint or your first kiss? When you learned to travel in time? When your sister died? (Maybe they aren't all happy memories.)

Of all the defining moments above, nine eleven was the biggest of my generation. Probably of any generation for that matter. Strangely enough, my mind works in such a way that I can usually recall the day before and after such major events just as well as each D-day itself. The day before 9/11 I had been out late partying with some friends and really tied one on until the wee hours of the morning. My boss was on a business trip, so I figured it wouldn't be noticed if I waltzed in a few hours late. But you know how that story goes. I nearly got caught.

The telephone rang at what felt like an ungodly hour, although it was really after 10 AM. Dragging my hungover body out of bed to answer, I was surprised to hear the voice of my boss. He said he figured I had stayed home because of what was going on, which was odd since he normally made an overly big deal about attendance. He apologized for calling me at home and asked me if I could change his travel plans and get back to him. I had no idea what he was talking about and confused by being "asked" rather than "told" to do something, but played along with a somewhat believable happy jolly voice that was met by an awkward sense of bafflement. My best guess from the context clues was a freak storm of some sort, but as I faked my way through the conversation I turned on the TV just in time to see the second tower collapse while Dan Rather deadpanned that this was all in fact really happening.

Much of the next thirty-six hours were spent glued to CNN, save for another, more typical call from my boss ordering me to contact the airline and demand that he be put on a plane. I told him that all air traffic had been grounded, but he just didn't get it. He wanted me to tell them who he was so they'd HAVE to act. I told him I meant no offense but rather doubted he had that much clout. The next time the phone rang I was about ready to tell him to buy a pogo stick at a toy store so he'd fire me and we'd be done with it, but the call wasn't from him. Instead it was my father. I couldn't really understand him over his sobs, which was striking as I'd never heard him cry before.

No need to get sidetracked by this now. That part of the story is all in the past, which is exactly where I was headed to fix things before getting lost in this tangent.

I borrowed my mother's car under the pretext of running an errand before the mass for my sister (not technically a lie) and drove over to my former apartment on the fringe of the city. Parked outside, I stepped out of the car and habitually rubbed the neck bruise, which wasn't exactly a bruise anymore now that it had a few days of real time and even more cumulative time to heal. The blink back to September 10 was quite easy based on the barhopping memory. All that was left was to walk through the wall of my street level apartment and wait for myself to return from work.

It was funny how when I really lived in this place I had wished it was on an upper floor, figuring it was safer from potential crimes if a robber had to lug everything down a set of stairs, giving witnesses a better view of his activities. Had I succeeded in moving upstairs, today's trip would have been more difficult. Like the imaginary thieves I feared, I needed access to the lower level in order to be discreet about meeting myself.

My apartment was just as I remembered it: a total dump. Being the first real world residence of my own, it was essentially a dorm room projected into a medium sized studio in the corner of an inexpensive double-decker building. Several mismatched blankets covered a newly inherited (and perpetually unmade) bed in the corner, a card table served as a desk when poker wasn't being played on it, and a varied smattering of chairs rounded out the furnishings. I had sold my computer once I admitted to myself that I was no longer a writer, and the stereo would have been next if I could ever bear to part with it. To be honest, my current west coast residence was also a nice bit of frugal living, but at this place discarded dumpster discoveries made up the bulk of the furnishings. One man's trash is another man's couch, coffee table, TV stand, desk, and settee.

The office I worked in as a bitch (or more officially, "administrative assistant") was just around the corner, and I would be due home for lunch any moment as it was now nearing noon. Dining out wasn't much of an option on my salary (as I used to joke in those days, "Call me Edgar Allan, 'cause I'm so Po'") and I'd prefer to walk home to eat rather than pack something and eat it alone in my cubicle. I also preferred to answer the calls of nature in the privacy of my own home. Aside from a fancy hotel, nothing beats home field advantage in the bathroom.

I couldn't remember if I had come home to eat today or not, but the blue flashing light on my answering machine provided a clue that I would be stopping in at some point to find out where my friends were meeting. (This version of us wouldn't own a cellphone for another year or so.) I would typically play the messages at lunch, go back to work, and then proceed straight to the bar at quitting time. At least that was how it went when I lived it. If I could get my point across, I wouldn't be going to the bar this time around.

I tried to play the messages to confirm, but was quickly reminded that I couldn't when my hand passed through the machine. Feeling stupid, I sat on the floor and awaited my return.

—◊—

Waiting for myself was beginning to feel like waiting for Godot. Apparently I did not come home for lunch on this day, or if I had it wasn't at an hour that would be deemed lunchtime by a reasonable person. By 3:15 I was becoming impatient and once again found myself cursing the inability to select the times of my arrivals. It would be far more effective if I could just fast forward through the boring bits and get this party started. In the midst of making a mental note to prioritize this feature when I either met or became the man who invented time travel, I heard someone fumble their keys and throw the latch.

I dove into one of the walls and cautiously peered through. With only my cheekbone and left eye exposed, I witnessed the arrival of slightly younger me, circa 2001. He shut and locked the door, dropped the mail on the couch, put a Soul Coughing disc on the stereo, closed the blinds, double-checked that the door was locked, and walked into the kitchen.

He/I emerged seconds later with a leftover meatball sub in one hand and a bag of weed in the other. Apparently this wasn't just a lunch break, as I never went to work under the influence. (Well, almost never. And never on purpose. But those brownies are a completely different story for another time.) After a bite from the sandwich, he painstakingly packed the small blue bong our sister had given us for our birthday. He took a hit, smiled, and noticed the answering machine. He got up to retrieve the messages, checked the lock on the door a third time, and was already back on the couch for another hit from both sub and water pipe before the first message had started to play.

"Hey man. We're going to the bowling alley for happy hour. And it's guys night, so don't bring the girlfriend," was the typically short and to the point message left by one of my drinking buddies. The second message caught me off guard.

"It's me. Just saying hi. Thanks for the note earlier. I love it when you speak in lyrics like that. It's so poetic. Anyways, enjoy your night out with the boys. I'm sure you'll give me a drink and dial later."

It was her.

I hadn't heard her voice in a long time. I wondered if she'd changed at all. Even though she wasn't really my type, the cute little redheaded girl and I had a promising fling that had been going on for longer than most, but it all went for naught after my sister…

I snapped myself out of the memory. Plenty of time to go back and change that later, but right now I was busy making other plans. Younger me had left his vices on the floor and was hunkering down for a nap on the couch, lying on his side and embracing a throw pillow as if it were his absent bedmate.

A part of me almost missed that simple life. Easily amused with food, tunes, dope, and the mental image of a pretend girlfriend as he floated his way upstream through dreamy dream land. Why wouldn't you want to live in this world? I smiled as I remembered all of the naps I used to take on that couch, even after getting my first proper bed that now sat unused in the corner.

Watching myself drift off to sleep, I decided it was time to act. Crouching down on all fours, I crept over until I was literally beside myself. I was close enough to whisper in my own ear, but what would I say?

"I don't wanna go and party. Maybe I'll call my sister and play cards."

In my moment of hesitation I must have practiced my lines a little too loud.

"Hmmm…" grunted stoned sleeping me. "That's not a bad idea. But she'll say no. We haven't spoken in a while. And it's guys night." Upon completing his thought, he sighed and gently kissed the pillow he was snuggling with.

Subliminal persuasion was not my initial plan, but if it worked this could go far better than I had hoped. In my half asleep, half altered mind I didn't even seem to realize that I was talking aloud to myself. Did I always do that? Did I think I was talking to her?

I tried to brace myself on the couch to stand up from kneeling, but my hand dissolved in the armrest and I keeled over, head-butting my sleeping self in the chest. Stoned and startled, he immediately sat bolt upright. We stared at each other with the same shocked expression, my second encounter with the living mirror. Launching into Plan A, I jumped onto the couch, pinning myself down while awkwardly putting a hand over my younger mouth to silence myself.

"Don't panic."

The look in my eyes seemed to agree as young me tried to nod, so I eased up with my hand.

"Who are you? You look like me."

"I'm from the future. I have a message for you. Don't go to the bar tonight. Stick to your sister like glue for the next twenty-four hours. I can't tell you much more."

Young me smiled. "What the hell, I'm only dreaming. I'll play along. You came here in a time machine I invented, and need my help to get you back to the year 1985."

"No! This is the real deal. Just keep our sister company until this time tomorrow, okay?"

"Do I have to hang out with her boring loser husband too?"

I had raised a good point. "No. Take her away. Maybe go to the Cape house for the night."

"But it's Monday. Nobody goes to the Cape during the week. Plus, we really haven't been hanging out since Nelson came along. But you should know that, being me and all."

"This is a matter of life and death. It's time to reconcile. Take a couple days off, have her do the same. Hell, quit your job if need be. I know you hate it. Start writing again. Get away, and all will be well."

Surprised that I knew of his not so perfect employment situation, he started "I haven't written since…" before trailing off.

"Since the objection you never read. Don't worry about that now. There's still time."

10 A.M. Automatic

IT WASN'T THAT I DIDN'T TRUST MYSELF, but I needed to see what condition my condition was in. Thinking over what had just happened, I realized it was probably better to let myself believe it was just a dream. Even though I said I didn't believe in that type of prophetic omen, I knew that I really did. As long as I remembered the dream I was sure I'd at least try to act on it.

The walk across town was quite long. I didn't have to worry about traffic or crosswalks or jaywalking fines, but that isn't much of a positive when you have to walk 500 miles, much of it pseudo underground due to your holographic nature. (It was closer to five miles, but it certainly felt like more.) This is where the concept of a time "machine" would have really paid off, especially if that machine was a vehicle of some sort. I didn't even need or want a DeLorean. Just a time bicycle would have made me a happy camper.

Another concern was the elevation issue. The likelihood of my sister's place being exactly level with mine was slim at best, but since I had nothing better to do I figured the odds were in my favor that I'd still be able to at least observe from a few feet above or below. Easy come, easy go, little high, little low.

As for what I would do when I got to my sister's house, I still wasn't sure. Hopefully just confirm that she was with the other me and then blink back home to find that everything was now better. Had I screwed up, I could blink back a bit further and try again. I certainly wasn't going to stay around to watch her kill herself. That would be too hard to handle.

But wasn't letting her live a life with Nelson without saying anything watching her die in a way? I had made my initial objections, but it didn't do much good since we never really spoke again after that. Should I have attempted a reconciliation? Did my selfish and stubborn tough love tactics play a role in what was to eventually happen this evening?

When I reached the house I was walking on air about eight feet above the ground. After walking through the wall above the front door I was able to squat into an invisible crawlspace with a good vantage point of each room. I suddenly had a new appreciation for vaulted ceilings.

My sister's home was far nicer than my own. Rightfully so, as a dual income was involved in both the rent and the decor. As much as I disliked Nelson's personality, he did earn enough to lead a comfortable life. He wasn't rich by any means, and even if he were I don't think my sister would be in it for the money. That wasn't her style at all. It was more so that he showed up in the right place at the wrong time, found the right buttons to push regarding some of her insecurities at almost the exact point when she decided to drop her standards, and the rest was history. "Was" being the operative word, as now anything "was" possible for the new future.

I found my sister sitting at her dining room table grading papers while enjoying a glass of wine. She was just as I remembered her, but at the same time a little roadworn and weary. As I watched her focus on her work and smile at the joy the children she taught brought to her, I could see some of that old glow. The glow that said "I'm going to save the world one day, and nothing can stop me."

But something had stopped her. The glow was faded, dulled by the efforts she went through to make Nelson happy. By the sacrifices she made. They were killing her softly, and I was her only hope.

The kitchen timer buzzed. My sister checked her watch, then stood up quickly. The gas oven didn't appear to be on, but I now saw what she was up to. She shut off the timer and efficiently cleaned up her wine glass, hiding the bottle of blues in the back of a closet. She then put two pieces of spearmint gum in her mouth, rigorously exhaled, and returned to her schoolwork.

Less than a minute later Nelson arrived. He kissed my sister on the cheek, poured himself a glass of water and pulled up a chair across from her. She continued to work, leaving him to start the conversation.

"How was your day?"

"Fine," she replied quickly without looking up. "Yours?"

"The same, you know. Nothing wrong with that."

"No, not at all."

Nelson leaned back in his chair and took a loud gulp of water.

"Are you about ready to head out?"

My sister put down her red pen and looked at Nelson for the first time since his arrival.

"Actually, I had a different idea for tonight. My brother called…"

I smiled, proud of myself for following through on the "dream." I also tried to recall what I said since I now must have made that same call a year ago, but like before I was drawing a blank. I might have had it if I tried harder, but Nelson stopped my thoughts cold with the tone of his objection.

"Your brother?"

"Yes," said my sister. "I do still have a brother."

"What did *he* want?" he spat back, with heavy emphasis on the "he" accompanied by a theatrical dropping of his arms in a show of disapproval.

"He left a message. Said he was sorry and wanted to talk about some stuff. I haven't seen him for a long time and think it might be nice to give him a chance."

"But we're supposed to go visit my grandparents for dinner like always."

"All I'm saying…"

"He's not coming here! You two will just talk the night away like you used to, and I won't really be in on the conversation. Plus he'll want to drink beers, which will make me want to. You know I can't do that."

Grrrrr. I couldn't believe that he was still using that excuse. Yes, Nelson used to be an alcoholic. And I knew he had come a long way in recovering and had been sober for a good four years or so at this point, and I give him all the credit in the world for that. But he plays the card so much it's almost comical. Before their marriage my sister was more or less banned from any place that may have had alcohol on the premises because her boyfriend might have trouble keeping his demons at bay. It's one thing to seek support from people, but fight your own battles, pal.

My sister made me proud with a brief jump to my defense.

"He doesn't HAVE to drink, and I could always ask him not to. Though I was thinking of meeting him elsewhere. He suggested a night at the Cape house, just like we used to. You can still visit with your grandparents on your own this one time."

Nelson was getting red-faced now. "I forbid it! You don't need him. He wrote you off after the wedding—before the wedding for that matter. You'll be much happier at dinner with us. You know that, right?"

Then I saw the look in my sister's eyes. Not the glow, but the look. The same look I'd seen on and off for years. The look that said I don't like this, but I know the happiness of others is more important than my own, so I'll make the sacrifice just this once and next time will be for me.

But next time it was always the same.

And the next time.

And the next.

And the time after that.

I could see what this was leading to, and it looked real grim.

Even though the look said all of that in more than words could have conveyed, the single word that accompanied it spoke all that Nelson needed to believe to be the truth. "Fine."

Fine? Fine? Everything was moving along as before, making this far from fine. In the game of give and take, my sister was all give and Nelson all take.

I didn't know what to do next. I wanted to pop Nelson one in the jaw, to run back home and tell myself to get my ass over here, to take our sister away from this and back on her intended path to glory and greatness and sainthood.

But maybe all was not yet lost. Yes, she caved again. But I did one thing differently: She never got that phone call from me the first time around, which means they never had the small argument I just witnessed. Wishful thinking, but maybe that small gesture that said I still cared did the trick. It wouldn't have fixed everything, but I thought it could be the initial fissure required to cause their relationship to crumble. If nothing else it could have bought me more time to help fix things by giving myself a reason for being around. A few more olive branches could be just what I needed.

Maybe it was better to check the present before proceeding, as further action on this exact day wasn't necessary. And maybe if we think and wish and hope and pray it might come true. Yearning with all my heart that there would be no memorial mass to attend upon my return, I blinked back to the present.

Apparently I should have yearned harder.

Instead of the familiarity of my Mom's car, I was strapped to a chair with a series of electrodes covering my upper body, neck, and head. My right arm was immobilized by a set of braces pinning it to a metal plate. My head felt cold. Rubbing my scalp with my free left hand, I realized it had been shaved and coated with some sort of wet goo to allow a better grip for the machine monitoring my brain. A mild jolt of electrafixion radiated out of the metal plate and into my right hand, triggering a huge migraine as my mind was flooded with random bits of disconnected memories.

My sister died.

A lot of people died.

I could have and should have helped.

I'm being punished.

I tried, but nobody believed me.

I tried.

I really tried.

A man in a white lab coat suddenly stood before me mumbling to himself, empty syringe clutched tightly in his hand. The question en route to his lips was already apparent in his wild-eyed stare.

"Tell me, what did you see? Did it work? Is it safe?"

I didn't want to stay here long enough to answer. Closing my eyes as another flood of memories hit, I tried to grab hold of one that would get me out. But nothing seemed to fit, as most of what I was seeing was so new to me.

My mother crying.

An empty room with bright lights and men in suits.

A straight jacket.

This hospital room.

A syringe.

The syringe.

My headache multiplied exponentially until I wasn't really thinking of anything at all aside from the pain. I pulled my eyelids even tighter, altering my vision from black to red. Instead of darkness I could only see a big red tomato, which lit a candle of thought to the airplane conversation.

And then something changed. I opened my eyes. Mister MD man in front of me was gone. I had blinked back again, but I was still in the same little room. Two of us, actually.

"It's me! I mean, it's you! You're back! Tell them it wasn't a dream!"

This was certainly not good. I tried to calm my other self down.

"I might be able to get you out of here, but first I need to know where we are and how we got here."

He screamed again, directing his rant to some person or thing unseen by me. "It's me. I'm back! I'm not crazy! I know things! I want to help! It wasn't a dream! It hasn't happened yet, and I want to help!"

That was enough. I covered his/my mouth.

"I also need you to do it without drawing attention to the fact that I'm here. They can't see me, only you can."

My current time counterpart gave me a scared look but seemed to understand. As I had at our first meeting, I slowly took my hand away from our mouth. In summary, he told me how our sister had still killed herself by overdosing on sleeping pills and wine late that night. How he and her were supposed to meet, but she stood him up and never called to cancel. (What the fuck was this world coming to? She didn't leave a message? At least I could have heard her voice one last time.) How he got up the next morning and saw September 11th unfold before his eyes on the television screen and wished he had tried to stop it. He had the power, had the premonition, but did nothing with it. And then a momentary lapse of reason did him in.

"I told everyone that I knew it would happen because I told myself, but I thought it was a dream and didn't believe it. But one day I would come back from the future and tell myself something else, and I'd be ready."

Mom and Dad sent him/me to a psychiatrist when I wouldn't recant my story. The shrink reported me to the government. They wanted to ask a few questions about my foreknowledge, but the doctors from this hospital intervened and took me here. He wasn't particularly clear on where "here" was, just that it was a research facility of some kind studying the human brain, specifically memory and conscience. At this point they were still performing tests, none of which were having the results they anticipated. The scientists were always angry after he told them about dreams he'd have while under the influence of the assortment of injectable drugs they gave him. One doctor in particular just wouldn't let it go.

"But now that you're back they'll be happy. They'll know I'm not crazy, per se. They can study us together, and we can try to fix it again. This time I'm ready."

That, more or less, was all that I needed (or wanted) to hear. Time to give this another shot. If I went back to before I caused myself to be sent here, I should be able to "pinch away this whole ugly episode" to quote my future self. Which led to the next logical question: Did the old me who got this whole thing started still exist? I still remembered him, but that didn't mean I hadn't undone him by sending us here. But if he didn't exist, then I wouldn't exist, and…

A wave of fresh headaches hit me, again accompanied by a set of blurry new memories that were hard to make sense of. I'd almost rather have swiss cheese memory than runneth over memory. I still didn't have an answer to my question on how many gigabytes the human brain could hold, but I sensed that mine might be almost full.

Clearing my mind of this extraneous contemplation, I closed my eyes and thought back to my sister's wedding day. I remember the wedding day as opposed to the wedding since I wasn't at the actual wedding, my form of protest over her choice of a mate. I hoped that this passive display of my feelings would be enough for either her or my parents to call the whole thing off, but instead I was made to be the bad guy without ever playing my trump. A few months earlier, I had actually written out a scripted objection with the intent to read it to the entire congregation when asked to "speak now or forever hold your peace." I never did read it, and it wound up being the last thing I ever wrote.

But this time was different. This time around that's just what I'd do. I envisioned myself proudly walking down the aisle, objection held high over my head by an outstretched arm. The crowd looked on in anticipation. Eyes still closed, I backtracked from the wedding to have a few days of preparation. What could get me there? What happened before? I needed to ride a thought to the wedding, and nothing else mattered. Suddenly I had it, and then something changed.

Upon opening my eyes, the room was empty. Other me had disappeared. If I had gone back in time, it was good to know I didn't always have to pit stop in the present between trips. I wandered through the halls (and the walls) of the hospital in search of confirmation of when the hell I was, but reading material seemed to be off limits. I suppose they didn't want to give the mental patients any ideas to fuel their fantasies, and thus strictly monitored the flow of information in and out.

Eventually I managed to find my way out of the building. (Rather easy when you can just walk in one direction, passing through walls until the structure ends rather than have to navigate the maze of corridors for a proper exit.) The sun was shining, though most people were wearing heavy coats. After much wandering, I found a newspaper box. April 12th, 2000. It wouldn't be in the paper until tomorrow, but I remembered that this was the day Metallica sued Napster for copyright infringement, firing one of the first shots in the file sharing war. This lawsuit was a failure, but Napster's freeloading days were numbered.

In hindsight, covering the rise and fall of music sharing probably could have saved my career as a critic if I hadn't been so stubborn about my assignments. At least it was a good enough memory to time travel on. The wedding was three days away. Plenty of time. Somewhere out there, younger me was working on his wedding objection. This time he would read it.

Won One

MY ODYSSEY BACK TO THE OLD APARTMENT took the better part of two days including rest periods. It really shouldn't have taken so long, but my sense of direction isn't very good and I didn't plan it as well as I could have. At first I wandered around aimlessly, trying to stay above ground long enough to find a landmark I was familiar with. Then I tried chasing buses, assuming they'd eventually reach a terminal that connected to the subway or commuter rail and I could just follow the tracks.

Unfortunately the bus moved faster than I could on foot, and without knowing the routes I'd often get turned around amidst my guesswork. Other times I'd end up underground at such an angle that I could no longer see the bus I was following. Eventually I decided to take a clue from the Beatles and follow the sun. Actually walk away from the sun, to the east until I hit water, then north until I spotted a proper landmark, and finally back home.

I had garnered a few important learnings on the journey. First, I got dog tired when walking around. Not the kind of draining fatigue you get walking on a particularly hot or cold day, as I was immune to temperatures and quite comfortable all the time. But I still got just as tired as any multiple mile walk/jog/run will get you when you're a touch out of shape. Maybe even more tired than usual.

At least sleep came easily enough when I needed it. I no longer had the insomnia that often plagued me in the real world when I had too much things on bounce in my head. The thoughts were still on bounce, but they had slowed to a point where they resembled the pleasant static of a silver dream machine.

Another oddity was that I felt no need whatsoever to eat or drink. Not even the slightest twinge of hunger or thirst. With lots of time to ponder this, I was now leaning even more towards the theory that time travel was a mental exercise. The body needs nourishment, while the mind needs rest. I also decided that I wasn't so far off on my want for a bicycle when walking to my sister's place earlier (or from my current perspective, later), and made a mental note to try to pick up a skateboard at the very least when I was able to get back to a safe version of the present.

If and when that would happen was still up in the air by the time I got back to the studio apartment, for once again I wasn't home. The computer and desk were back in the corner where they belonged, the sale of the pair still a few months away. My bed was gone, replaced by the cot that preceded it. Everything else was more or less indistinguishable from my previous visit, except for slightly less clutter since I had slightly less stuff. I went over to the cot and collapsed over and through the top of it, effectively landing underneath. Content that I was hidden from view in the event I got home before I woke up, I settled in for some much needed rest.

The echo of the front door slamming shut killed my deep slumber. After stopping for a moment to realize where I was, I listened for sounds of movement in the apartment and took a tentative look around. Determining I was still alone, I ran to the door, sticking my head out in time to see my younger self walking away. I had slept through his return.

I tailed him for a couple of blocks, hoping that he wouldn't hail a taxi or take the subway. (I should have known better about the taxi, as I don't think I'd ever taken one before.) I also wished I wasn't such a fast walker, as it pained me to keep up with even my slightly younger self. Eventually I remembered where we were going and smiled. We had a date with the cute little redheaded girl.

Won One

The dive bar was exactly as I'd remembered it. A good old-fashioned beer hall with an ample selection of microbrews and eclectic yet rockin' tunes. This was certainly my kind of place. I've always found it much better to kick back with a pint or a pitcher while playing bowling or darts or shuffleboard than be bopping around to some ridiculous dance music that all sounds the same while spending ten dollars a pop on fancy watered down liquor drinks that will only make you black out and forget the majority of the evening. Sound familiar?

Tonight was our first date with the elusively flirtatious cute little red-headed girl. We were playing this one for the longer term since we really did like her. Don't be confused into thinking the longer term meant we were looking for "the one" to be "in love" with, as that wasn't the case at all. Marriage was the farthest thing from my mind. That being said, I certainly wanted to sleep with her. But younger me wasn't here to get laid on this particular evening. There'd be plenty of time for that later.

And would there ever be. She played the part of the good girl very well in public, but in about one week's time I'd learn how insatiable she really was in private. Erotic city, can't you see? Younger me was on the verge of the greatest sexual affair of his life, and current me had a front row seat into how it all started.

"Garbage Man" by G. Love & Special Sauce grooved out of the old school jukebox in the back between the his and her restrooms, ironically foreshadowing how I would indeed move, bruise, love, and lose. I just didn't expect that it would all happen in the next few hours.

As the weight of the lyrics set in I watched myself hug our ladyfriend hello, guide her to a darkened table in the corner with just the right angle for people watching, and finally head to the bar for round one of many. If I remembered correctly, we tied one on until closing, said our goodbyes, and that was that. Tomorrow she'd call late in the evening (of *the* day) to console me out of the funk I was in after skipping the wedding. We'd come to this same bar again to drink and talk and laugh, then make out a bit in the street after getting kicked out. I walked her home, tried unsuccessfully to finagle an invitation in, and then we kissed a little more before departing. Four days later we'd have another date that would end in a heavy petting sleepover. And two days after that the games would begin in earnest. We were extremely compatible in bed, and didn't explore too much of the out of bed part after this first week.

But I'm getting ahead of myself. From my position at the jukebox I watched me return with the beers. He had a schooner of something dark; she a smaller, fancier glass of something Belgian. Normally I'd be happy with any old watery domestic swill, but since this was a date it was appropriate to up the ante.

Younger me set down the beverages and gazed towards the jukebox. Not wanting to see me staring right back at me, I reached up to shield my face and looked down at my feet. Upon feeling my shaved head I figured I wouldn't be recognized and just waved while turning away slightly, still watching the scene play out in my peripheral vision. She laughed after I presumably said something either funny or stupid or both. Or maybe because I was waving to a nonexistent person at the jukebox. After a couple of sips and a few moments of conversation, I slid my hand across the table and awkwardly took her hand.

Wait. What the hell was I doing?

A sense of foreboding started to creep over me as a different memory took hold.

I come on too strong and try to kiss her at the table. She politely dodges and says not on the first date. Unfazed, I try again anyways and get a drink dumped on my lap. And we never speak again.

Which version was right? What about the sex? I'm sure I remember all of the sex. Most of those memories couldn't be made up, as I wouldn't have possibly thought of them on my own.

It dawns on me that this might be my fault. My mere presence in the room with myself could be having an effect on events of the past. But all I did was make eye contact and wave. Could that be enough to change history so dramatically?

Apparently so. I'm watching myself caress her hand and even from twenty feet away I can see the uncomfortable look on her face. She quickly finishes her beer and retreats to the restroom. I'm still uncertain as to whether or not I had anything to do with screwing this up, but I know for damn sure that I'm going to have a hand in getting it back on track. I walked to the table and tapped myself on the shoulder.

"Take this one slow, pal. You'll thank me later."

Younger me pretended not to hear, but his body language betrayed him. I hammered the point home.

"I'm serious. You can't hurry love. All in due time."

With that I walked back to the jukebox to observe. Younger me returned to the bar for two fresh drinks. Racking my brain to recall any differences was useless. I still had both ends of the memory spectrum in my head at more or less equivalent strengths.

The nightmare continued to play out before my eyes when the girl returned from powdering her nose. They talked a little more, with me glancing back every so often to get a better look at the mysterious dude at the jukebox watching my every move. At one point I seemed to ask my companion who I was, and twice pointed right at me while she just shook her head and shrugged.

After the second drink she picked up her purse and seemed ready to escape the young Casanova. He made his move, and just as I had predicted/remembered received a wet lap in a manner quite different than he was hoping for. As she walked out of the bar in a huff, younger me wouldn't leave well enough alone and followed her. I couldn't leave well enough alone either and followed them both.

Outside, the redheaded girl was insisting she did not need an escort while drunk me pleaded his case that she did. Eventually he caved and made a move towards her for a hug and a kiss goodbye. I let the hug play out, but forcibly twisted his head to the side of hers during the lean in to at least prevent part of the disaster. Surprised at the unexpected chivalry, the girl dropped her guard and once again said goodnight. My counterpart reached out to grab her arm, but I intercepted it with my free hand to prevent him from causing any more trouble. After about twenty hurried paces the girl took a nervous peek behind her, but her bad date was still firmly planted, politely waving goodbye with a little help from his older and wiser self with a hand inside the puppet head.

Once our girl was out of sight (though not quite out of mind), I let myself go. He promptly spun around and threw a punch, hitting me square in the jaw and knocking me backwards into a nearby dumpster. Although dazed, I had hoped that his seeing me vanish through solid metal like that would shock some sense back into him. Instead it had the opposite effect.

"I must be drunk, and I need to get drunker," he said aloud, pivoting on the heel of his Doc Marten boot. He caught his breath, then marched back into the bar to share in a drink they call loneliness.

Emerging from the garbage, I looked down the street towards the girl and then back to the bar. Should I stay or should I go? The decision should have been a simple one. Right now was my opportunity to convince myself to help. Following the girl wouldn't accomplish much of anything aside from stirring up old memories. I was unsure if I was ready for that just yet, but decided it wouldn't be a bad idea to make sure she made it home safely while I gave my other self some time to cool off before confronting him again. Unfortunately this plan was short lived, as she had barely gone two blocks before hailing a cab.

On the walk back, I once again tried to figure out why the scene in the bar was so drastically different from what I remembered. I hadn't been able to alter events based solely on my presence on previous trips, only the time when I interacted with myself. Is a glance an interaction? Everything with the redheaded girl was going as it had until my memories jumped ahead, at which point…

Suddenly it hit me. What if he was picking up on my thoughts of the redheaded girl? Did my foreknowledge become his foreknowledge, thus boosting our collective confidence level and changing what was happening in his present? And if so, why? We were the same person, but it wasn't like we were sharing a brain. *Or were we?* If anything, I should be the one picking up on his thoughts since I had already thunk them. Is thunk even a real word?

Thunk rhymes with drunk, and that's what I was when I returned to the bar. He was in rare form, zigging and zagging in the general direction of the jukebox. Apparently I had done some shots even though I can't handle them. They always lead to a blackout. A thunk was also the type of sound my younger head made as it veered left and hit the doorjamb en route to the bathroom. I rushed through the dwindling crowd, hoping to take care of myself before one of the bouncers intervened.

My younger version saw me in the mirror as soon as I entered the restroom. This caught me off guard as I didn't expect to have a reflection. At first he just stared at the emblem stitched onto the chest of my hospital shirt. Then a look of panic drained the color from his face.

"They found me. I don't know how, but they found me!"

He whirled and threw a balled up paper towel towards (and through) me while simultaneously charging forward in bullfight mode with his head down. In his inebriated state he couldn't quite coordinate the attack and was easily sidestepped. I caught him from behind and tried to pose him in a normal position before somebody came in to investigate the commotion.

"I think we'll go for a walk outside now. Don't draw any attention to us and you'll be fine." I moved to his right side and interlocked our arms. His pained expression was getting worse.

"How did you know I was here? It's not really a change when you think about it. I was just speeding up the inevitable."

Confused, I looked him over in search of context but found none. "I have no idea what you're talking about. Let's go outside."

His face kept the deer in headlights quality, but he managed to stop babbling and walk a relatively straight line to the exit. I was surprised that he wasn't acting more incoherently. Either I had scared him sober, or we were a better drunk then I had given us credit for.

Once outside, I sat him on the sidewalk and tried to continue our conversation. Before I could speak, he beat me to it.

"What did they tell you to do to me?"

"They who?"

"You know who they are. You obviously work for them."

He touched the logo emblazoned on my hospital shirt as he said this, running his fingers around the hairpin turn within the loops before tracing over the "LBDG" lettering across the bottom. My eyes followed his movements, examining the design closely for the first time.

"I assure you that you're in no danger. It's your sister. You can't let her marry Nelson."

His look of panic melted into one of confusion, then to realization before finally landing on annoyance.

"So it worked? It worked!"

Annoyance briefly flashed to joy before slipping into defiance.

"I refuse to undo what I've already done. And you can't make me if I'm not there."

That said, he passed out on the curb.

Rainy Day Women #12 & 35

THE WEDDING WAS A MODEST AFFAIR held in a lakeside lodge adjacent to the nearby state park. Sis had considered an outdoor wedding, but Nelson insisted on getting married in April, and a fifty-three degree New England day squashed that dream.

Wandering the grounds, I saw many of my sister's friends who had recruited me for the failed intervention a year ago (almost three years from my perspective). They would all put on their best fake smiles and make idle chitchat with Nelson's guests, then turn to each other and begin their vicious sewing circle of behind the back talk. We'd see how many stepped forward when it came time to ask those who objected to speak now or forever hold their peace.

I considered blinking home to outfit myself in proper wedding attire even though the traditional dress code didn't technically apply to me given my condition, but fear of turning up in that hospital again outweighed any awkwardness I felt being amongst the sharp dressed crowd. Either way it was too late now, as the same condition made blinking both forward and back with any expectation of landing on the same day an impossible dream, so I was forced to stay in the scrubs.

After dragging my drunken younger self home and letting him sleep off a portion (but not all) of his bender, I had slapped him awake and forced him to show me the objection speech. He hadn't remembered the fight, our late night conversation, passing out, or even getting home. But since we had managed to arrive there safely, he believed me when I told him he had asked for my help with his objection. He also seemed excited to have the validation that somebody else agreed it was a good idea.

We edited his draft, transposed it onto some four by six index cards, and rehearsed the exact point in the ceremony to be ready for when presenting the priest with our objection. Editing went much easier than expected. The initial draft was fine—I primarily just peppered the rewrite with bits and pieces thought up in the next year that I wish I would have said originally. Being that we're the same person, my younger self and I tended to be on the same page regarding style and word choice. Still, it was refreshing to have a deep conversation with myself while actually vocalizing thoughts without seeming crazy. We could relate on just about anything, though I chose not to reintroduce the fact that I was him. The jilted sister suitor angle seemed to work better as long as I applied incesticide to the undertones. By the end of the night he was so groggy I figured he'd forget everything else as well. I actually made him pin the objection to the inside of his front door and leave himself a note to read it at the wedding as insurance.

Most of the guests were in their seats as the appointed time drew near. I worried that I should have stuck around to make sure younger me dragged himself out of bed and was in attendance for his own performance. It looked like I would once again not be visibly attending, though this time it wouldn't be exclusively out of protest. Where was that damn kid?

Finally I saw him stagger in. He was a bit disheveled in his wrinkled blue suit, but at least he was here. Since I was a late addition to the guest list and hadn't been to rehearsal, I wasn't actually in the ceremony. A seat had been assigned for me in the second row of the lodge where I would sit behind my parents with the ushers and other nonessential members of the wedding party. In the original history my father had called and offered me a last minute ushership, but in this case it appeared that other me had wisely turned it down as I had. Probably for the best, as it would be rather hypocritical for a member of the wedding party to stage a coup mid-ceremony.

The early stages of the service leading up to the reunion of the in-tended were painful to watch, so I mainly focused on the crowd. Careless whispers, fake smiles, real smiles, tears of joy, tears of dread. Emotions ran the full gamut, but it was easy to discern the difference between the allies of the bride and the groom. The groom's relations and guests beamed as if they had won the lottery, and in a way they had. Their man Nelson was way out of his league. In the other corner, we've already been over the notion of settling down, so I won't rehash it here.

Instead, let's discuss my pet peeve of people who won't stand up for what they believe in. Who elect to adhere to the traditional rules of good manners set down by society so scrupulously that they would allow an abomination such as this to occur unchallenged. We've all experienced and/or participated in it time and time again.

"Is she really going out with him?"

"Her boyfriend is a real tool shed."

"That bitch has him whipped."

"I don't know why he stays with her."

"Good thing she's pretty."

Etc, etc.

When the lights go up and the curtains go down and the couple in question is around, not a single derogatory comment is uttered. It's all but-tons and bows, nice to meet you, good to see you, how you doing, let's all get together again real soon. Seldom is heard a discouraging word. But as soon as the couple departs for the evening the stories of disaster, humili-ation, and ridicule follow in full force before the echo of the door closing behind them has softened.

Why not speak up? Isn't that what friends are for? Isn't keeping the people you care about amused and out of trouble a primary tenet of ca-maraderie? What ever happened to making a pact to bring salvation back? Aren't the tougher curves life throws at someone the most important times for friends to step in? As soon as a relationship ends, friends will line up to say things such as:

"It just wasn't meant to be."

"I never really thought you two were that good together."

"Goodbye to you girl. She's skanky anyways."

"You could have done better."

Etc, etc.

After finally breaking the silence and the metaphorical ice, both shunned lover and friend will engage in a bashfest of the dearly departed for the rest of their lives now that it's the proper thing to do. All memories of the "good" times will be soon forgotten, and badmouthing will be almost encouraged from this point onwards.

I think my reaction would be "Why the hell didn't you say anything? You could have given me back two years of my life!" Or, in this case, maybe a lot more…

Of course, there is usually a brave soul who will try to intervene if an affair or some kind of abuse is going on, but these extreme cases are the exception. Why not just object on the basis that one's significant other is a schmuck who only wants a wife so he can feel like a normally functioning member of society? Or because he couldn't give a damn which lucky girl filled the role so long as someone did?

And if the couple in question ends up married, there's usually not a peep before or during the wedding ceremony. Afterwards the silent haters can always fall back on the "forever hold your peace" line to justify their inaction, but that's just a cop out. You can't have it both ways, adhering to "forever hold your peace" but ignoring the more important preceding "speak now."

Which brings us to the part of the program you've been waiting for.

"Do you, Nelson, take this woman to be your lawfully wedded wife?"

"I do," was his obvious reply.

Wait! What happened to my cue? You can't have a wedding without asking for objections. But it seems that they had. The church had failed me again. I must have missed the memo on the change in wedding procedures. Why can't the church leave well enough alone and honor the sense of tradition they were allegedly built on? You could say I lost my belief due to modernizing stunts like this. I might actually still believe if that hadn't been the case.

The priest continued. "And do you…"

Our plan hadn't taken this twist into account. Unsure of what to do next, I knew it had to be quick. So I screamed at the top of my lungs, knowing only one person would hear me.

"SPEAK NOW!!"

Up in the front row, I saw my father tense his shoulders an instant before young me stepped forward to interrupt the ceremony. With his arm outstretched high and in an intonation even louder than mine, he voiced the two magic words that could stop time:

"I OBJECT!!"

The crowd was stunned for differing reasons. The groom's side could hardly believe this was happening and began to chatter amongst themselves. That is, everyone except for an attractive older woman and her escort in the front row, whose actions led me to correctly presume they were Nelson's parents. They were dumbfounded, but not quite speechless. His mother tried to get an explanation from anyone in her vicinity, but her protests fell on deaf ears. Meanwhile, the bride's team buzzed with anticipation, somewhat shocked that I actually had the balls to go through with this. I wondered if this had ever actually happened before, half proud of myself for bringing an old wives' tale to life.

My mother had one hand over her mouth while the other squeezed my father's arm so tightly it was impeding his circulation. I had a good look at my dad as he surveyed the room. As his eyes scanned past mine I could see his expression was close to neutral, but definitely ready to turn if the situation got too far out of line.

As younger me strutted his way past the stunned trio of bride, groom, and clergyman, I briefly wondered if this stunt would positively or negatively influence any chance I had of scoring with the maid of honor. Previously my sister's roommate, she was one of the girls who went behind her back to confide in me that I needed to put an end to this. She was also one of my botched infatuations from days gone by. Maybe a single gallant gesture would be all that was needed to win her over. Or maybe the curse already ruled her out since Mom knew her name prior to the start of my crush, sealing the predestiny from the start. (I know my younger self was technically attached to the redheaded girl at this point, but she was so far removed from my modern brain that I was free to consider rekindling other possibilities. Besides, your mind gets dirty as you get closer to thirty.)

I watched myself reach the podium and fish out the index cards. Tapping the microphone before he spoke, I realized it wasn't working at the same time he did. Undeterred, he turned to the priest.

"Can we turn this thing on? I'm trying to object here, and I have a prepared statement."

"I didn't ask for any objections," was the stern reply from his holiness.

"Under the circumstances, you really should have. Could I please have a microphone before I…" he trailed off, whispering something he didn't want the crowd to hear.

Our backup plan involved telling the priest he knew of some alter boys ready to make a confession to the local authorities. The scandal in question wouldn't break in earnest for a few years and I had no evidence regarding this particular priest, but I figured the odds were good that the cover-up had already started by now and was common knowledge among the insiders of the religious community. Younger me had already started his break from the church and had no problem stating the threat.

It worked like a charm, as the priest slowly and deliberately plucked the wireless microphone from the collar of his robe and handed it to his accuser. Love the sinner, hate the sin, keep it quiet, swallow everything. Younger me walked back to the podium to start his speech.

"I'd like to begin with a quote by Edmund Burke. 'All that is needed for evil to triumph is for good men to stand by and do nothing.' Though I'm not here today to tell you that Nelson is evil in a devilish or antichrist sense, I do think that I'd be letting evil win if I did nothing. So being a good man I've decided to act."

I nodded in agreement and encouragement from the back. He took a deep breath and continued.

"Although I stand alone here, there are others in this room who share my sentiment yet choose to keep it to themselves, to forever hold their peace as it may be. Forever is a long time, so I am in part speaking out and casting the first stone to show that there is no shame in the truth and only good may come of it."

Though the crowd remained silent, they were certainly paying attention. Nelson's father stood up to comment but couldn't find the words or the voice and sat back down. His wife whispered something to him, then folded her arms and slid her chair slightly away from his in a very Nelsonian manner.

Young me went on: "I'll admit that I don't know the groom very well. But I do know the effect he has had on my sister, and it hasn't been very positive. Her usually high spirits are withdrawn, she barely speaks with her best friends, and her giving soul has been smothered to the point where it's nearly undetectable. A candle cannot continue to burn under these circumstances, and I would hate to think that one that once burned so bright could possibly be extinguished in a few years time if these circumstances were to continue."

I tried to convince myself to change that last line to read "Seventeen months time," but refused to give him my reasoning. "A few years" was close enough to get the point across.

"Many of you are wondering how I could have the nerve to stand here knowing that my outburst will blemish this day. I have no problem making one day seemingly horrible if over time it will serve to make the next nineteen thousand days to follow that much brighter for my sister and the rest of the world, which will be a far better place with her in it.

"I'll now relinquish the floor for a supporting statement if any are willing to stand by me. I trust there won't be any honest rebuttals from anyone who has ever seen the couple together, so please don't waste my time with a half-hearted and transparent lie. The choice is yours, sis. I do what I do because I love you."

With that, he walked off stage and out the back door.

—⁂—

"I think we got the message across," younger me said through an ear-to-ear grin.

The two of us were standing in a field between the wedding site and the access road to the park, maybe fifty yards from the lodge that housed the main event. My counterpart wanted to walk and talk since he was cold, but I insisted we stay in one general area because it was relatively flat and the first spot I had found where the level of my feet and the ground were on par with each other. I doubted much attention would be paid to my feet, but walking down a hill or in higher grass could require some explaining.

"We definitely gave them something to talk about," was my reply.

I hadn't focused on the faces of the crowd while making my hasty exit, but now the moment of truth was approaching—literally. One of those faces was storming towards us with an expression of anger rather than wonderment. As the face got closer, it took on enough form to be identified as "she." Both versions of me recognized her at the same time. It was the mother of the groom.

Nelson's Mom wasted no time, immediately taking a swing at me with her right hand. The blow traveled through my head and slapped the me she could see across the face with a painful sounding thwack.

"How dare you ruin this day! Your sister is very good for my son, and all that will be accomplished by your foolish stunt is…is…" she struggled to unpack the adjectives to finish with, finally settling for "Well, nothing good!" followed by another slap to the face, this time to the opposite cheek with her left hand. Gauging the look of pain in my eyes, she must have been ambidextrous.

Young me paused for a beat to compose himself before calmly addressing his attacker with a reprise of his objection speech.

"Ma'am, I completely agree that my sister is very good for your son. He likely couldn't do better. But she certainly could. He's taken her life away, ruining everything, and in turn taking the life out of everyone she knows and loves. Is that what a good marriage should be based on?"

Midway through this speech I had walked behind and prepared to restrain my other self in case I did something stupid like take a swing at Nelson's Mom. It appeared that cooler heads were prevailing, so I backed off slightly while staying on guard.

You couldn't really blame the lady for her feelings. I'm sure there was a lot of "because I'm the mother" sentiment behind it, along with some "my children are infallible so I can't see the forest for the trees." Surely if Nelson's Mom was linked to him in a capacity other than blood she would also see him as the jackass he was. (And when I say jackass, that's just a euphemism for fuckhead.) He was certainly a boy that only a mother could love. Or only a mother and a lonely brainwashed sister.

The confrontation between my doppelganger and mamma Nelson had devolved into a standoff. Both just stared at each other red-faced searching for something else to say. A new voice broke the silence.

"There you are!"

My father had spotted the screaming match and wandered over to intervene. I'd been so caught up in the show that I hadn't noticed his arrival until now.

Dad turned to the lovely mother of the groom and began doling out the charm. "Ma'am, I'm terribly sorry for my son's behavior. He's always been protective of his sister and thought he was doing the right thing. If the kids choose to continue the wedding, your son will certainly be a welcome member of our family."

"Bullshit!" I chimed in even though I thought that only I could hear myself speak. "He's going to kill her."

Younger me repeated a paraphrased version of my line. "That's right. He's going to kill her."

I wished he had kept the swear in there for emphasis.

What happened next shocked and confused everyone, albeit for differing reasons. Dad turned and faced real, phantom time traveling me directly. Looking me in the eye, he said, "Nobody is going to kill anyone, and I'd appreciate it if you'd stop putting ideas into my son's head."

I looked around dumbfounded, as did Mrs. Nelson. Young me thought nothing strange of it, as he thought everyone could see me. All eyes were on Dad.

"Yeah, I'm talking to you," he said emphatically. "First you yell out during the ceremony, and now this."

Mrs. Nelson didn't know what to do with herself. "I never even suggested that my son would kill your daughter, and I'm offended by the accusation!"

Dad brushed her off.

"No ma'am, not you. I'm talking to this nosy park worker," giving me a shove for emphasis.

I say he gave me a shove rather than tried to give me a shove because he really did. His arm didn't travel through me as the blow from the mom did, but landed square on my shoulder and caused me to stumble back a few paces before falling to the ground.

"Did you put him up to this? Are you in love with my daughter?"

"Don't blame him, Dad," other me said in my defense. "I've been planning this for a while."

"Whomever are you talking about?" said a still confused Nelson's Mom.

Amidst the hullabaloo, Nelson's father had also reached our circle.

"They've decided to have a private ceremony back at the house. Immediate family only."

He turned slightly to face younger me. "That is, except for you. I forbid you and your shenanigans from my home!"

Like father, like son I suppose with all the "forbidding" going on. Nelson's father took his wife's hand and marched away with nary another word to my father nor my visible self. When they were far enough away to be out of earshot, Dad put an arm around younger me.

"Let me take you home. I have to go give your sister away, then we can talk about why you did what you did. That wasn't a very good first meeting with the in-laws."

They both smiled at the joke. Dad continued. "Also, I don't think you should associate with this guy anymore," motioning to real me, still on the ground.

Young me turned his head back towards me for help, but I waved him off. A new plan was already forming.

Dad was right that it wasn't a very good first meeting with the in-laws. What I really needed to stop was a different first meeting. I'd have to head the relationship off at the source. If they can't meet they can't kiss, and if they can't kiss they can't get together, and if they don't get together they don't get married, and if they don't get married my sister lives.

Piece of cake.

No, For The 13th Time

SEEING THE MAID OF HONOR REMINDED ME of the Hearts tournament. If a moment could be pinpointed where the world had turned on my sister, this would be it. Innocently enough at the time, but I should have known better. By this time I had already learned my lesson on setting up my sister with my friends, but the opposite lesson was not yet true.

Yes, I was a hypocrite.

My sister was living in an apartment with a girl she knew from somewhere. All of my friends were enamored with her hot roommate in some way or another, making every attempt to fish for an invite whenever possible. I didn't particularly mind, as I shared their fancy to a degree and liked hanging out with sis. It soon became routine that a rotating cast of characters would hang out and play cards a couple of times a week.

One night, after a particularly fierce game, the conversation shifted to who was the best card player among our little tribe. Everybody was entitled to their own opinion, with most statements ending with a cocky "...besides me" in an effort to impress the object of our affection. Unable to reach a consensus, we decided to organize a tournament to answer the question once and for all.

Turning the tournament into a social event was my sister's idea. Rather than the typical stand around and drink cocktail gathering, she was always fond of theme parties and enjoyed the planning and preparation that went into the festivities. The game of choice would be Hearts, with an elimination format that was so confusing it was a wonder we were even able to get people interested in participating. (Of course, most weren't coming over for the tournament...)

We needed sixteen players for this to work effectively. My sister had eleven lined up; I was tasked with filling the remaining five slots. I found four without any problem (dangling the roommate as bait didn't hurt) and asked around to learn if anyone knew a serious card player for the last seat. That player ended up being Nelson. I wish that I knew what I know now when I was younger.

But how could I have? Friend of a friend, liked playing cards, seemed harmless enough. How much of a screening process did I need? An extensive background check and three references from former lovers? I wasn't even trying to set them up. It was just one of those things that happens when you least expect it.

In actuality, my most vivid memory of that day wasn't Nelson and my sister meeting. I really didn't give it much thought when it happened. Instead I remember being bounced from the tournament in the first "real" round after a misguided strategy in the qualifier backfired on me. I can usually play decent defense when it's every man for himself, but a three against one conspiracy is hard to overcome without having a lot of luck in the deal. And luck was certainly not on my side on this day.

Harnessing those feelings of embarrassment, shame, and anger allowed me to blink back to 1998. It was still midday, giving me plenty of time to walk over to my sister's place from the future wedding site. Again I wished that I was able to go home first to change out of my hospital scrubs, but I still had a bad feeling. I may have undone the trip that led me to the hospital by going back to the wedding, but what if I hadn't? Or what if I had both undone and redone it in yet another attempt to coerce myself? In the end I had to trust my instinct that it wasn't a risk worth taking.

I made the trip to my sister's apartment without getting too spectacularly lost. Normally I took the subway when I visited, and thus knew the last leg quite well as a pedestrian. Getting there entirely by foot would have been more difficult had I not learned from my previous blunders and followed the train tracks to a place I was familiar with.

Upon my arrival I immediately discovered a flaw in my plan. Although my sister lived on the first floor, the building was raised from ground level. Three steps led up to her front door. Combined with the fact that I was already wading in the earth due to elevation differences between the park and the city, it left me just head and shoulders above the hardwood floor upon entering. Interacting with myself might be out of the question this time around.

My sister and her roommate were in the kitchen preparing snacks for the main event. The roommate was wearing a t-shirt, a new pair of fitted jeans, and open toed red shoes that showed off her pedicured feet but not much else. My sister wore a thin sweater and a long, loose skirt. With my lower perspective and invisibility I started to wish their outfits were reversed, but my nice guy instinct overrode my sex drive and forced me to stay focused.

They talked as they cooked, expertly moving around the kitchen without getting in the way of each other in a choreographed routine they had performed a million times before.

"How many people did you say were coming?" asked the roommate.

"Sixteen for the tournament, though you never know who else will show up to watch."

"You didn't count me as a player, did you? I hate cards."

Hates cards? I suddenly liked her roommate a lot less.

"What do you mean you hate cards? You play with my brother and I every week."

"You haven't noticed that I'm terrible and lose every time? I just play because I like the attention. Especially from your brother."

Likes me? I suddenly liked her roommate a lot more. My sister didn't seem to feel the same way.

"My brother?" she laughed. "You can't."

"Why not? It's not like you're about to go after him in an incestual affair."

Sis made a face. "Of course not. But he's like…your roommate-in-law. It would be incest for you too. Plus we share a wall."

"Enough. I get it. It's not like anything will come of it anyways. Don't say anything to him, okay?"

My sister just smiled as she put her magic nacho casserole into the oven.

"I'm serious. Promise you won't tell him."

"I promise I won't tell my brother that you have the hots for him."

Not that the promise would matter, as now I did know. That would have been good information to have a few years ago. I was actually a little upset that my sister hadn't told me. If she was screening I couldn't really blame her, as I was fairly certain who she learned that trick from.

Dual memory syndrome started to have its way with my mind again. Only this time, the second memory was better than the first. I began to recall a series of harmless trysts with her roommate over the years. Nothing too serious, just an occasional roll in the hay without any strings. As a matter of fact, I was starting to realize that the first of these was going to be today.

Was it real life or just fantasy? Bounced from the Hearts tournament early, everyone else still occupied by the games, she and I on the living room floor. *"Consider me your consolation prize."* Although I was fairly sure that never happened, a vivid landslide of memories were tumbling through my mind. Or were they? I couldn't even remember if we were lovers or if I just wanted to.

The door buzzer sounded as I pondered this conundrum. My daydream breezed into the hallway and pressed the unlock button without first using the intercom to identify the entrant.

"Who's here early?" my sister asked.

"Don't know. We'll find out."

"I really wish you wouldn't open the door without knowing who it is first."

"What's the big deal? Our apartment door is always locked."

The words weren't even completely out of her mouth yet when the always locked apartment door opened with neither effort nor knock and my younger self walked in.

"Always locked, eh?" started my sister. "And don't you ever knock?"

I maneuvered into a position behind a chair so as not to startle myself with the image of his lifelike bust on the floor of the apartment.

"Sorry," said younger me. "Being buzzed in and then knocking on top of that seems pointless. It's like getting double permission to enter."

"What if we were naked?" asked the roommate. I could tell she was flirting based on the conversation I had just eavesdropped, but younger me was oblivious.

"Um. I'm sorry," he said, hiding behind his long dyed hair and inspecting the ground in front of him.

Why was I acting so shy? Inexperience? I realized that the cute little redheaded girl hadn't came into my life at this point, and thus the confidence she instilled in me was also missing. I always recalled feeling more confident when my sister was around, but maybe the effect was cancelled out by the presence of a (presumably) unobtainable crush.

My sister had had enough. "Alrighty then. Who wants a drink?"

So there we were, just we three, continuing to prepare for the party. Different playing areas were set up, along with March Madness style brackets drawn up in the living room on a chalkboard that my sister had borrowed from the school she was student teaching at. From my enlightened perspective I could tell my sister's roommate was paying a lot of attention to me, but again my younger self was oblivious. Or at least he did a good job of playing it off that way. For our sister's sake of course. He probably considered her to be off limits by the same roommate-in-law reasoning. Or maybe it was just to keep my hypocritical side hidden so as not to give my sister ammunition when I criticized her boyfriends. Or maybe I was just a wimp. Along with having trouble remembering if we had or not, I also wasn't completely certain of why not if we hadn't.

The arrivals began in typical party fashion, where someone shows up ahead of time (in this case me), followed by a block where you aren't sure if people are being fashionably late or just not coming to your lame party at all. By the time you convince yourself that the latter is true, a few single guests arrive in quick succession. This leads to a few more awkward moments where you try too hard to be a good host or hostess to overcompensate for the lacking attendance. Then the floodgates open when a large group arrives together, and you're rockity rolling from there. Everything's fine until the end of the night when the reverse happens and you're stuck with the final guest who just can't take the hint that it's time to go. This party would have one of those as well. I'll trust you can guess who if you've been paying attention.

We were in the period just after the floodgates where there is a flurry of small talk and the guests are getting comfortably numb with the surroundings. (The drinks didn't hurt this process any.) At first I was constantly on edge and flinching whenever a shoe-clad foot came dangerously close to my floating head, but once I turned off my peripheral vision the crowd ended up being a good smokescreen to conceal my disembodied state. I felt far more comfortable drifting around a full room avoiding only myself than I did when it was nearly empty.

The last to arrive was a friend of mine from the music 'zine I was writing for, accompanied by his infamous friend.

"This is Nelson," he said upon arriving. And that was the start of it.

Sis dove right in as hostess, taking their coats and offering them hot snacks and cold beverages. Nelson offered to help himself if she just pointed him in the right direction, but she declined and practically insisted that she do all the work. I could see how he may have misconstrued her actions as a special privilege of sorts, but I knew she was like that with everyone.

My younger self and his colleague chatted away about the articles they were working on, the shows they had recently seen, and what forthcoming albums they were most looking forward to. I left them to their own devices and followed my sister and Nelson into the kitchen where she was serving him for the first time.

As I've already said, it was innocent enough. He wasn't particularly aggressive or negative or mean. And she was just caught in the act of being herself. I can't really fault anyone here. Who wouldn't love her right now? He took his food, thanked her, and was gone to scope out the competition as she freshened up drinks and discretely signaled me to let the games begin.

The tournament started with a qualifying bracket to neutralize skill level differences. Everyone played in a semi-randomly assigned group designed to separate the skilled and unskilled players initially in hopes that it would set up some more meaningful showdowns early on, before everyone got drunk and lost interest. After the qualifier, the next rounds would be all winners in one group, all second places in another, etc. The losers would be eliminated leaving three to move on from each group, narrowing the field from sixteen to twelve. (The format doesn't make much sense to me now either, but it seemed to be an excellent idea at the time.)

My strategy in the first round was to play conservatively enough not to lose, but still take a few heart-laden tricks here and there to prevent myself from winning. That way I would theoretically have an easier go of it in the rounds that mattered as part of a lower pool rather than getting thrown into a cutthroat match with the other winners right away.

That plan failed on many levels. The first hand was a breeze. I had a nearly foolproof moon shooting hand with all of the royal spades, all the aces, and six high hearts but opted to control the flow of the queen of spades and broke up the hand on the pass. It worked like a charm as I managed to come in a very calculated third place, just two points behind second and five off the lead. My sister's roommate was not so coincidentally in my group, and not so coincidentally the loser.

I was teeming with cocky confidence when I entered my third place match looking like a tough luck loser until I made my big mistake. Because of my ego I didn't see the conspiracy against me. Everyone knew I was favored, so they all stuck me with points whenever possible. They were all out to get me. I took the queen of spades on the second trick three different times and narrowly missed a moon shoot early, leaving me dead in the water from square one.

Leaving my younger self to enjoy his new miserable experience, I drifted over (actually under) to the second place group where both my sister and Nelson were part of the foursome. Although I couldn't see the table from my subterranean position, the sighs and banter from up above it indicated that my sister had just ambushed Nelson with the black mariah.

"I see how it goes around here. Gang up on the new guy," said Nelson as he angrily collected his trick and flopped it face down in front of him. The force of his drop caused the cards to skid off of the table and into his lap, where I had a prime view to Nelson slipping the queen under his leg and replacing it with a card from his hand before returning the quartet to the table as if nothing had happened.

"All's fair when you play cutthroat," replied my sister, "unless you can't stand the heat."

She didn't know the half of it.

Nelson ended up bowing out next despite his sticky fingers, and he wasn't too good of a sport about it. Everyone was adopting the easy strategy of ganging up on whomever took the first queen in order to advance to the next round. I wish I had thought of that ahead of time, as it was much simpler than my ill-advised sandbagging scam.

Since my sister was advancing and Nelson was not, I felt safe enough checking up on my younger self. My secondary memory now recalled sulking in the corner after my loss and eventually hanging out with the roommate. She alternated between consoling me and giving me the business regarding my big choke. Not that she was one to talk having lost even earlier.

When I reached their corner of the room I still couldn't believe how thickly she was laying it on and how proportionally thick my sweet oblivion was. I wasn't catching sparks off her, though in the other memory I still recalled her pre-kiss line about being my consolation prize. I racked my brain to figure out what was happening to my love life. First tree house girl, then the cute little redhead, and now hot maid of honor roommate. Something was definitely not right.

In the meantime I made my way back to the gaming area. Nelson was sulking in the kitchen while my sister was still at the card table. She was on her way to shooting the moon but got burnt at the end, taking all but one point and eliminating herself. Rare for her to miss a moon shoot, as she never went for it unless she knew she had it. A better loser than Nelson, she took her defeat gracefully and went looking for me to arrange the finals.

Seconds later younger me followed my sister back into the room and began scribbling on the chalkboard. She tried to assist, but he told her he had it under control and sent her to the kitchen, which was the very room that Nelson had entered moments before.

It was my own damn fault. Not only was I not hooking up with the roommate as I should have been, I was pushing my sister towards Nelson without even realizing it!

Angry with both of my selves and the world, I rushed towards the kitchen, ducking down below the floor and pausing only to give my younger self a punch in the Achilles as I passed by.

I found my sister preparing more hors d'oeuvres for the party, with Nelson leaning casually against the counter talking to her. Like before it was harmless chitchat, though now it was a conversation I had provoked. Other people made their way in and out of the kitchen for alcohol refills and attempted conversation, but Nelson always managed to forcefully keep her attention focused on him by butting in whether he had an appropriate opening or not. I couldn't outright fault him for it. Even though he was being a jerk he was giving it a much better try than my younger self had given the roommate. But it still made him look rather needy, especially in hindsight.

Figuring this would be my only shot, I threw my hail mary.

"Help! Help!" I yelled in a high-pitched voice that was more comical than urgent before retreating into the cabinet below the sink. Knowing that only my younger self would hear me, my only real option was to lure him into the kitchen to break Nelson's spell. With a lot of luck he may bring his gal as a reinforcement, though part of me worried she may serve to encourage rather than discourage.

Younger me did come running in, and gave a confused look upon seeing nothing out of the ordinary.

"What's going on?"

"Nothing," replied my sister. "What's going on with you?"

He started to answer, but Nelson jumped in immediately.

"Do you need any help cooking?" he asked, stepping between my sister and I while reaching towards the oven.

"I thought I heard you calling for help," said younger me.

Nelson gave him a glance that seemed to say get lost, then verbalized the same. "We've got it under control, all right?"

I watched helplessly from the floor as I gave Nelson a skeptical look, made brief eye contact with my sister, then shrugged and left the room.

Fourteen Rivers
Fourteen Floods

BLINK.

The kitchen was gone. I was sprawled out on the ground in a field watching two different dynamic duos walk away. My father and myself were closest to me, with Nelson's parents about fifty yards in front of them. I was still at the wedding site, which meant nothing had changed at all.

But how could I be here now? Older me had said I couldn't visit the same day twice, but here I was. Not only was it the same day, but the exact instant I had left from. Maybe he was oversimplifying it for me and meant I couldn't revisit the same event. Since I hadn't seen this part of the day yet it was still fair game, and as the last place I remembered it was an easy enough time to will myself back to.

The revelation that it all started in the kitchen had me reeling. I had pushed my sister towards her doom with Nelson. What was I thinking? I tried to remember, but my recollection continued to be hazy at best. The Hearts tournament had been a misstep in more ways than one, both past and present.

The four figures in front of me continued their walk. Nelson's parents veered off to the right, presumably heading home on foot. Younger me and our father were about to get into a car parallel parked alongside the field. Vehicles of other guests peeled off one by one. My counterpart gave an over the shoulder look towards me, almost being hit by a tan van that screeched to an abrupt stop in front of him. Dad continued to scold as he ushered me into the car, waving an apology to the driver of the van before giving a final long glare back at real me. The burn from his eyes could be felt from even a full football field away.

Again I wondered if he could really see me. It seemed pretty obvious by this point, but how? Not that the question really needed an answer, but I was curious. Was it a bloodline thing? No, because Mom and sis would be able to do the same. Well, sis at least. Mom had different blood than Dad, but partially the same as me. Maybe a y-chromosome, gender related anomaly? That didn't make any sense on the surface, but it was the only piece of genetics I remembered from all the crap I learned in high school biology. If Sam Beckett could leap into his great grandfather during the Civil War, maybe I could interact with all of my male ancestors too.

I know I said before that I was going to start grounding my baseless theories in the real world rather than the fictional lands of television and cinema, but sometimes those are the only concepts I have to work from. I often wonder if there are hidden messages in good time travel stories—things only a real time traveler would pick up on included as a signal to other displaced blinkers so they can seek each other out or at the very least know they are not alone in the multiverse.

As Dad's car drove away, I recalled his comment about this not being a good first meeting with the in-laws. Those in-laws were as good of a lead as any, so I got up and followed Nelson's parents four or five blocks back to their homestead. My mother was waiting on the porch when we arrived. She was alone, as my Dad was taking the other me home. I hoped that other me could handle it. In a perfect world he might have even convinced Dad to object to the union as well. That was wishful thinking, but I could keep on dreaming.

I entered the house through a side wall and joined my Mom for the grand tour. Nelson's parents' house had been in his mother's family for years. She had grown up here, and although the family was well off enough to have bought or built a place of their own the sentimental value and some persuasion by the Mrs. over the Mr. had them instead decide to add on to and refurbish portions of the old family residence.

"Although I don't condone your son's behavior," started Nelson's Mom, "it is nice that we get to have the wedding here. I was married in this very house."

My mom tried not to turn red as she changed the subject. "We're very sorry things had to end like that. It's a lovely home to be wed in. How many years have you been married for?"

"We'll be celebrating our thirtieth wedding anniversary next year. And you?"

"We're a little behind you. We'll hit thirty in 2003. Some would have liked us to wait, but we met and married in the same year. Only knew each other a few months. Nobody thought it would last, but it did."

Mom's answer provided yet another tidbit about her past that I never knew before, causing me to do some quick bowling math to determine if I had a stain on my shirt. (Not that it mattered, as I'd be insane to complain about it.)

Mrs. Nelson wore an exaggerated look of horror on her face. "Our parents insisted on us having a proper courtship before settling down. We met in the summer of 1969."

Mom giggled. "Standing on your mama's porch, you knew that it was now or never?"

Nelson's parents both stared back at her blankly, not getting the joke. It goes without saying that I was quite amused by my mother's musical trivia.

"I'm sorry. It's a song. I guess you don't know that one."

Nelson's Dad hadn't said a word since I'd been here. I started to wonder if he was the one settling down in this scenario. He was rather stoic—I actually hadn't heard him speak since his outburst at younger me after the wedding. But I supposed that speech was more required than anything else. Now he just stood by the window staring off into space.

Imagine being stuck with a son like Nelson. How could you love him? I'd think even "because I'm the mother" would be tough to justify. And what about the poor father? His wife was a bitch, but at least she was a bit of a looker, especially considering the fifty some years she had under her belt. But was that enough? I'd never thought too much about the concept of a trophy wife before, but this seemed to be a prime example of one.

Nelson's father broke his silence with just one sentence.

"The kids are here."

A limousine was parked out front, delivering the betrothed and enabling this sham of a wedding to conclude as soon as my father returned. The smug look on Nelson's face as he helped my sister out of the car was enough to make me want to kill him. The only thing that saved him was my transparent existence and morally grounded upbringing. But suddenly I realized that neither of those reasons would necessarily stop me.

At this point I hadn't really seen anything that would justify Nelson's elimination. Although surly, he wasn't all that bad of a guy except for the cheating at cards bit. But was that really any worse than my attempt at backing my way into the championship? In all fairness he probably wasn't one hundred percent responsible for my sister's suicide. Some of the blame should fall on her, as well as on me for not noticing the extent of the problem before it was too late. But Nelson ended up at the wrong place at the wrong time, and if I was certain of anything it was that if he had not married my sister she would still be alive today. And for that reason alone I wanted him dead.

Or did I?

I knew that murder was wrong, and no matter how much grief he had or would cause my family he didn't actually deserve to die. Maybe what I was really hoping for was the slightly less malicious wish that he had never been born to begin with.

And what if he hadn't? What if I could go back, break up his parents with a little help from Dad, and thus leave no chance of him ending up with my sister? He can't hurt her if he doesn't exist. Would it be murder if he were never conceived?

I suppose it was similar to abortion in a way, but not directly. Part of that argument focuses on whether life begins at conception or birth or somewhere in between, so if there wasn't a fetus involved at all I shouldn't take any heat from neither Roe nor Wade. I'd be the only one that knew about it, and I would be doing society a favor. He was forgettable enough that no one would really miss him. And if he really was meant to be I was sure I'd fail in my attempts. He'd still come around by some other means and I'd be off the hook. It was the perfect crime in theory. The biggest question was whether or not Dad would help.

I looked at Nelson's Mom standing near her husband as they watched their son and his bride-to-be approach the house. Both were focused on the children, with not so much as a sideways glance of happiness or a loving caress of shared joy between them. Were they really happy? Could Dad split them up?

My Mom was different. She gazed towards her daughter and smiled, then checked her watch, wondering where her man was. That's how it should be when it's real. She would wait a million years for Dad and walk a thousand miles to fall down at his door if she had to. If I borrowed him for a few months before they ever met it wouldn't hurt anything in the long run. At least not anything I couldn't fix.

Plan in hand, I just needed an event to send me back. Something that happened between Nelson's parents meeting in the summer of '69 and their wedding in 1971.

The answer was simple: "Paul is dead."

—⚬—

October 12, 1969. WKNR DJ Russ Gibb airs a story during a phone-in show that Beatle Paul McCartney had died three years earlier in a car crash and clues to his death had been appearing on each subsequent Beatles release since then. Many claim the hoax actually originated in print form much earlier than this, but the radio broadcast is widely regarded as the match that set the rumor ablaze like wildfire. I had always been fascinated by the story and wrote a paper about it in high school. Thinking back, that was probably the first inkling of my future career.

Despite my predilection for conspiracy theories, I never actually believed Paul was dead. I did always suspect that the Beatles either or-chestrated this plot from the outset, or at least heard the early theories and decided to run with it by planting more clues. When Ringo is the sole surviving Beatle, I've got a feeling he'll spill the beans.

Not long after my thought process hit the Paul segue I found myself outside of Nelson's family estate. Apparently the room I had been standing in while concocting this plan was part of the new addition Nelson's mom described. Without bothering to check inside the house, I headed further on down the road. My grandparents lived in the same neighborhood, and I needed to track down my father.

With the last few time trips I had developed an overboard and self-assured confidence that I'd always find the right memory to blink back to. It seemed that time travel was much like any other skill: if you believe you can do it, most likely you can. But if you overanalyze too much, you haven't got a chance in hell. That applies to just about everything. School, sports, work, writing, dating, etc. Practice plays a part too, but confidence is key. Life would be so much easier if I could keep that doubting little voice out of my head. If you put your mind to it, you can accomplish anything.

Embarrassingly enough, I had trouble finding my grandparents' house. Even though I'd been there hundreds of times over the course of the past twenty-eight (or, future thirty-three) years, it had always been a part of a family outing that I didn't drive to. My sense of direction is bad enough as it is, so when I'm occupied by something else as the passenger in a car (conversation, reading, sleeping, music, overanalyzing some little thing that I don't really know enough about to really do so, etc) my internal navigation system shuts down. A few landmarks here and there looked familiar, but I couldn't remember what I was supposed to do when I saw them. Left or right? Straight or stop? The memories of coming and going were fused together into one blurry, circular map with no natural placement of cardinal points and no direction home.

After an hour of wandering I finally found my way to what should have been a walk of less than fifteen minutes. A buzzing noise filled the air as I approached the house. A neighborhood teen was in the side yard, mowing the lawn barefoot and shirtless despite the October chill, wearing only a pair of basketball shorts that were a bit too short for my liking. On the front stoop sat another young man, this one modded out in a sharkskin jacket with a velvet collar. He was noodling on his guitar while wearing a bulky pair of padded headphones. It had to be Dad.

I paced in front of the house, making a point of clearing my throat while stomping and shuffling my feet to get his attention. But he was so engrossed in what he was doing he barely looked up. I'm not certain, but he may have been stoned. Trying to learn a lesson from my past hesitations, I verified the distance between my feet and the lawn was negligible and marched up to the house to confront him.

The quality of his jam left a lot to be desired, causing my critical ear to cringe as I approached. My intended strategy was to kick off a conversation by asking him what he was playing, but I wasn't sure I'd be able to feign interest.

"Excuse me mister."

"Nice song."

"Pleased to meet you. Won't you guess my name?"

"Hey, what's that sound?"

Between the headphones, the guitar, and the lawnmower he was otherwise deaf to the world, including me. I reached out to tap him on the shoulder and was startled by the result. It was the last thing I expected to happen, though I should have been prepared for it by now.

My arm went right through him.

Why? What was different about young Dad vs. old Dad? Maybe it was because I blinked back to before I was injected? No, because then he wouldn't have seen me at the wedding. Or because it was before I was born? Maybe he never really saw me at all? But the park worker comment had to come from somewhere. Plus he pushed me. Real, undeniable physical interaction. I racked my brain for an explanation, but came up with none. The only answer was another question, and a rhetorical one at that. There was still so much I didn't know about time travel.

A horn honked. Several sweater clad girls ogled and whistled as they leaned out of the back of a pickup truck, trying to gain the attention of the mower who was now moving on to the front yard. He pretended not to notice, but I could detect a sly smile forming on his face as they passed. A few minutes later the same flatbed of girls did a slower drive-by, again accompanied by horns and leers. Unfazed, the yard boy stopped mowing, wiped the sweat from his brow, and pulled a bottle of beer from his back pocket. He opened it with his teeth, spat the cap into his hand, and took a long sip.

Screams of ecstasy were heard from the Ford. He was showboating, and the girls loved every second of it. I laughed to myself, took one look back at my mod squad wannabe Dad, then started towards the street to figure out what use I could make of this side trip to 1969 if I was unable to interact with anyone. En route, the boy silenced the mower and waved me over.

Which meant he could see me.

Which meant he wasn't just any young man from the block. I had the wrong guy before. *Here* was my father.

I composed myself, checked my feet again, and shifted direction across the lawn to make my proposition.

"Can I help you?"

"Um, yeah. I was going to talk to that guy..."

He laughed. "My cousin isn't very friendly. I am, but I'm not sure I can help you either. My parents aren't home, but if you come back later they may want to make a donation."

This caught me off guard. "Donation?"

"Yeah. I figured you were from the hospital when I saw that outfit on you. Never heard of LBDG though. What's that stand for?"

I had forgotten about my attire again and for the 250th time wished I could go back to the present for something new to wear. At least he thought I looked like a hospital employee rather than the escaped mental patient that I really was. And what did LBDG stand for?

"Um, hospital. Yeah. The Lyndon B. Disease…something. I forget what G was for. I just work there. But I wanted to talk to you. Ask a favor actually."

"Never heard of that. I'd have guessed Lyndon B's Democratic Great Society if there had been an S, but that wouldn't be a very good name for a hospital."

I changed the subject and introduced myself, telling him I saw the girls cooing and knew quite a bit about his reputation. That was why I wanted to talk to him. There was one girl in particular…

"Hold on," he interrupted. "I don't know if I'm freaked out or flattered, but I don't have much trouble getting my own dates. So if you're here to set me up or sell me an aphrodisiac that can double my dating…"

"You've got me wrong. It's more of a challenge. This girl has a boyfriend. A few of us who know your style have a little wager on whether or not you'd be able to break up the happy couple. Are you up for it? We'll all chip in and give you the whole pot."

He paused and thought about it for a minute. "What's the catch?"

"No catch, why?"

"Are you pulling my chain? Because if you are…"

"Absolutely not," I interrupted. "It's all on the level. We just want to see if you can pull it off, and then learn from the master. You'd be teaching us a lesson in the art of seduction."

He thought about it again, his smile widening with each passing second. Finally, he spoke.

"Does this girl have a name?"

—m—

Scouting and/or stalking the woman who wouldn't be Nelson's mother kept me occupied for the next few days. She worked as a secretary in a local law office. Each afternoon at exactly one o'clock she would go out to run errands for the three lawyers at the firm. Dropping off dry cleaning, stopping at the post office, and finally picking up lunch before returning to the office. She ran all of these errands on foot, making it that much easier for Dad to intercept her. From there it was just a matter of having him be at the right place at the right time to work his magic. I could stay nearby to play Cyrano if needed, though I was fairly confident that wouldn't be necessary. Hopefully I was right, as playing Cyrano would open a whole can of worms I wasn't ready for. The only risk I could see was whether or not she'd fall for an unemployed deadbeat like my Dad.

I had been careful in my few meetings with my father to act like a normal, solid, flesh and blood person. My true identity was my ace in the hole just in case something went awry and I needed to scare Dad into performing a task. Other cards in my backup deck included walking through walls as a scare tactic, bribing him with gambling advice or other beneficial future knowledge, or threatening to melt his brain if he didn't do what I requested. I kept our meetings brief and private, fading into the background or choosing to "excuse" myself if anyone approached my father for a conversation. I always timed things so we would meet in the early early morning or the early early night to explain why I was still wearing this lame hospital uniform. Dad didn't seem to mind. He had a bit of a fascination with the loopy aspects of the logo, but I was again starting to feel like a cartoon character since I hadn't changed outfits since God only knows when.

From past interactions with myself I knew that the truth was dangerous to lead with, especially over thirty years earlier. At least my younger selves had a predisposition to time travel from media saturation and the unrealized potential of modern technology. I found it rather easy to believe and accept because I really wanted to. The Dad I knew wouldn't want any part of that nonsense, and thus would have a much harder time dealing with the gravity of the situation. Since those feelings had to start somewhere, it was safe to say his younger self would feel the same way.

Watching Dad go in for the kill was nothing short of amazing. Disturbing given the circumstances, but still amazing. I couldn't hear the conversation starter as I had to be far enough away so as not to have to explain why he could see me and she could not, but it went a little something like this: Within ten seconds of introducing himself he was carrying her parcels for her, and sixty seconds after that had her phone number. They hadn't even arrived at her destination yet when her belongings were back in her hands and my father was on his way back to rendezvous with me. And this girl had a boyfriend—a boyfriend that I knew she would go on to marry.

If it was this easy I may have changed history already. I didn't know enough about Nelson's Mom to know if she always had a wandering eye like this. But wow, go Dad!

Maybe that's just the way it is for a trophy wife. She doesn't really care who she ends up with. If someone better comes along, so be it. That probably explained where her son learned his dating strategy. No offense to Mr. Nelson, but after that performance my Dad could run circles around the conquests of both Mick Jagger and Wilt Chamberlain, possibly even beating their combined total. Roll over Beethoven, and tell Don Juan the news. I shudder to think…

Dad and I met up later at the park behind his house. I asked him how the introduction went, and he responded with a big old shit-eating grin painted on his face.

"I'm supposed to call her tomorrow for a date on Saturday night."

"Did she even mention her boyfriend?"

"Not a word. Are you sure she has one?"

"Pretty sure," I said, knowing I couldn't have changed her current relationship status as I hadn't been back this far before. "What did you say to her?"

"None of your business. Old family secret."

I know I couldn't tell him this, but if it was a family secret, then I should be privy to the information, shouldn't I? "The talk" when I was a kid was as brief and awkward as I'd imagine it was for you. This does this, that goes there, don't be stupid, treat her with respect, don't go around breaking young girls' hearts, etc, etc, the end. I understand why it isn't appropriate to give your thirteen year old son seduction lessons, but a little helpful hint now and again wouldn't have hurt matters, would it?

I had to say something, so I gave it a try. "We'll double your fee if you let us in on your secret. I told you we wanted to learn from the master."

"No way. I'm not really in it for the bet. It's all about the love of the chase. After a few rounds in the sack I get bored and move on to the next one. But the chase never gets old, never goes the same way twice, and always has a rush of adrenaline with it. If I ever found a girl who kept things compelling enough after the chase I might stick around, but otherwise, the hunt goes on."

Mom had certainly gotten that part right.

My anticipation was difficult to contain over the next few days. When morning arrived I planned on jumping forward forty-eight hours (to October 19 if you're keeping track) to ask how the date went, but since I had absolutely no idea of anything important happening on that day I couldn't blink there. So wait I did, biding my time with some sightseeing.

I checked in on my Mom, who wasn't scheduled to even meet my father for another four years. She was sixteen years old and in school during the weekdays. Her free nights and weekends were interesting, leaving me with the impression that I needn't have worried about her discovering my tree house action of years ago/years from now. The majority of her nocturnal hours were spent sneaking beers and smoking pot with her hoodlum friends outside. I found out she had a secret date on Friday night, but decided it best not to chaperone for fear of what I might discover. Although my father having a good love life was crucial to my plan, I still didn't really want to witness a live performance from either of my creators.

I also started to ponder if this was a stupid move that may be endangering my own existence. I was setting my father up with a woman that was not a part of his original dating history, and doing so before he ever met my mother. What if he decided that this was the woman who intrigued him enough to retire from the game? Or what if he saw a quality in her that he liked, and started to seek that in a partner? Or if he saw something that he hated, and it happened to be a trait my mother shared? Technically I would have succeeded in stopping my sister's suicide, but at what cost? Would I still exist? Would I be able to return to the present? Was this really worth the risk?

Rationalizing (or justifying), I figured I wasn't in too much trouble just yet. Based on my Mom's offhanded comment and my own observations, Dad was quite a womanizer. For all I knew Nelson's Mom may have even been one of his conquests the first time around. They hadn't let on at the wedding, but that didn't mean anything. I wished I had a scorecard to refer to.

Yes, my plan was crazy. But if I made sure to break their relationship up and to give him a push towards Mom, I was confident it could still be made to work out. It might mean having to live in the past for a few years to make sure everything stays on course, but even that would be worth it to serve the greater good in the end if needed.

Sunday morning finally arrived and I caught up with my father.

"How'd the date end?"

"Fine," he replied, with the return of his beaming grin indicating it was likely much more than fine.

"That's great!"

"Why are you so interested? It seems to be more than just a silly little bet."

"I might have more of a vested interest than that, but mainly I'm just looking out for you," I replied, which wasn't a total lie. "Are you seeing her again?"

"But of course. I kinda like her in some bizarre, forced upon way. It won't last though. Awab will see to that."

"Awab?"

"You've never heard of AWAB, Mr. LBDG? It stands for All Women Are Bitches."

Dad grinned at his acronym. I couldn't believe that those words had just come out of his mouth.

Prophet 15

THE COURTSHIP OF MY FATHER AND NELSON'S MOTHER continued for a few more dates over the course of the next week. I kept a low profile so as not to seem like a lonely pervert who needed to live vicariously through my stud friend. Checking in on Mom and discovering more revelations of her revolution helped me bide my time. I also watched quite a few high school football practices at the field behind Dad's house, studying the players for any sign of a future superstar. Unfortunately it seemed that this small town just didn't breed them.

It was at this field that I eventually met up with my father again. I was lying on the sidelines (no danger of being hit by a ball for me) when he came running up and kicked me.

"I've been looking all over for you. Aren't you cold? It's freezing out here."

He tightened up his jacket and put his arms around himself. I'd been so worried about avoiding crowds and keeping my feet on the ground that my immunity from temperatures had slipped my mind. It was October after all, and one single day where Dad could mow the lawn shirtless and flexing did not constitute a heat wave.

"Don't worry about me. I'm cold blooded."

"At least come up to the house with me. I need your help."

"You need my help?"

"She told me about the boyfriend. She goes for musicians. He's a classical pianist."

"Musicians?" I asked in confusion. I could hardly believe that the stuck up woman who yelled at us after the wedding was a groupie. Though I suppose ending up with a classical pianist may account for some of her arrogance, stereotypical as it was.

That train of thought came to a screeching halt with my next realization.

"You play the guitar!" I exclaimed, excited to see this come full circle. "So what's the problem?"

"How do you know I play?"

Oops. "I saw a guitar. I mean … I saw your cousin with one. He wasn't all that good though."

"No, he isn't. That's my guitar. He just fools around with it when he hangs out here. Drives me crazy. At least he tries. I can play, but just cover songs. She wants me to write a song for her."

I laughed. "A battle of the bands for the hand of the fair maiden?"

"Something like that. What am I going to do?"

"Why not use your suave charm?"

"Charm has gotten me this far, but I'll need to show some skills to keep it up."

"We could just call the whole thing off right now," I bluffed.

"No way. I'm gonna win this one on principle if nothing else. I told you, I don't care about the money. You have to help me."

I knew I had him. "Let's go write a song."

—⁓—

Dad had perched himself on the edge of his bed, guitar in hand. I stood in the corner trying to keep my feet obscured. He wanted to play in the basement, but I made some excuses about mildew and allergies and a desire to peek at the football game through his window so as not to have to explain my true inability to go downstairs.

"Don't you want to sit down?" he asked.

"It's fine. I prefer to stand when I hear live music."

"You can at least come a little closer."

Actually I couldn't, as I needed to stand behind the pile of laundry on the floor to distract his attention from the fact that I was ankle deep in the floorboards.

"The acoustics will be better from this angle."

"What do you want to hear?"

"I don't care. Play whatever."

"Anything?"

"Anything you want. Just play."

And play he did. His setlist that afternoon:

People Are Strange
We Can Work It Out
Everyday
Piece of My Heart
All Along the Watchtower

All cover songs, each one with a distinct treatment and pop sensibility that made it his own. His guitar playing was very skilled, and his vocal style comfortable yet oddly hypnotic. After hearing this much raw talent from my young father, it amazed me he hadn't become a professional musician. Maybe his inability to write his own songs held him back, but even a session musician could make a decent wage and obtain a little bit of new found glory.

I beamed when he was done. "When I asked you to 'play whatever,' I didn't expect that. That was fantastic!"

I should admit here that even though I'm a musical connoisseur of sorts, I'm not a songwriter. I've tried, but it's a very difficult craft to perfect. I know a great song when I hear one and understand the basic concepts behind a solid hit single, but authoring one just isn't a skill I have. Let the critics critique, the artists create, and the singers sing.

Dad blushed. "Thanks. It's not all that special. I'm just copying. What's so funny?"

He had caught me in the middle of some laugh, as I thought to myself it would have been amusing if he had actually played the song "Whatever" by Oasis when I invited him to "play whatever." But he couldn't have, since it wouldn't be recorded for another twenty-five years.

But maybe we could borrow it, and a few others…

Teaching the song to Dad was much easier than expected, mainly because of his remarkable mimicry skills. We started with the lyrics as a poem, letting him get a feel for the language. Then I'd hum a few bars of the melody for him to play back. By the second or third try he had the chords and rhythm down. The process could have gone much faster if I was able to play him a tape, as my humming wasn't what they call pitch perfect. But this turned out to be a good thing, as it made the song one step closer to his own. The same was true for the delivery of the lyrics, as my lack of melody also allowed Dad's "cover" to deviate from the originals.

Wanting more, I threw "Lounge Act" by Nirvana at him next, trying to emulate *Unplugged* but ending up somewhere between *Nevermind* and *Rubber Soul*. Kurt would have been proud.

The whole scenario brought back memories of nights spent with my former college roommate when he would write songs in my presence and I'd give an immediate thumbs up or thumbs down as he tried various sets of lyrics and chord progressions. Inspired, I taught my Dad one of his unreleased numbers that I always loved, but my roommate thought sounded "too '60s." I'd even come up with the clever title of "Won One" as a play on a repeated homophone in the chorus, my one claim to songwriting (ok, song titling) fame. It also took away some of my guilt in this plagiarism exercise, as my friend always refused to play it at his shows in college even though I insisted it was great. That argument would be ended soon enough.

As I recited the lyrics for Dad to transcribe, it struck me for the first time that they seemed to eerily foretell my current situation. Was the author a prophet of sorts? Or possibly from the future? Probably not, but you be the judge:

Come on in you might as well hear this too
One day your mind took flight and it flew
Around the trees you thought were waving at you
No things just don't seem like they used to

So turn up the rain and turn down the sun
As I lift my hand from yours girl I assure you no one won
Turn up the sun and turn down the rain
The clouds they came but they were not the same

Come on in you might as well hear this too
Well it's slipping away but hey it's just a part of you
These are all things I thought you knew
Oh things just don't seem like they used to

(Great solo here: duh doo doo doo doo doo, di doo doo…)

So turn up the rain and turn down the sun
As I lift my head from yours girl I assure you no one won
Turn up the sun and turn down the rain
The clouds they came, swelled with their pain

Dad paused briefly after finishing his first full run-through of our tri-fecta. "You wrote these?"

"With a little help from my friends, but they won't mind if you use them."

Dad took my lyrical bait and had a glow in his eyes when he made his next proposal.

"You and I should become a songwriting team. Like Lennon and McCartney. It'll be great."

"Let's just see how these three songs go over first, okay?"

Dad played those three songs at a coffeehouse open mike night on Halloween and they went over brilliantly. He won the girl, blowing Mr. Classical Pianist off the stage with his dangerous folk rock appeal. I feigned an illness caught from too much time in the cold without a jacket and boy-cotted when I realized it was in a basement cafe, but I did peek my head in through a back corner of the ceiling and saw the entire set. It was quite a high to see the joy and adulation the crowd bestowed upon my father.

Based on his open mike success, the venue wanted to book Dad for his own forty minute set the following week. I agreed, figuring a few more songs wouldn't hurt.

"Stealing" music was about to be taken to an entirely new level. File sharing was a hole in the bucket compared to actually claiming authorship. Was it wrong to teach my Dad some future hits, intercepting potential roy-alties from the artists who created them? I can justify downloading since it creates hype, selling concert tickets and increasing album sales when fans truly want to support the bands. But if someone stole the song from the artist before it was ever created, that was much worse. The potential for profit was gone. One single can make or break a band's career. And I'm not even talking about one hit wonders. Even perennial chart toppers need an initial spark to kick-start a career. Would Nirvana have been as big as they were without "Smells Like Teen Spirit" to start the phenomenon?

I knew I'd never get caught, but is it right for a lover of music to undermine the creation, arguably the most important part of the process? I recognize the irony in the fact that I had no problem eliminating Nelson from existence, but had a real moral dilemma over potentially denying Huey Lewis credit for "The Power of Love" under similar circumstances. Am I really that bad of a person? I suppose everything's relative.

The plan wasn't foolproof. Lyrics and melody are a big part of the equation, but the actual performance is equally important—perhaps even more so. There are hours upon hours of bad covers (and even bad originals) to prove that point. Attempting this was almost as much experimental as it was necessary. I thought I was into something good combining my father's skill, personality, and charm with my future knowledge and critical ear. We were three for three so far...

Weighing the pros and cons, I eventually settled on a reasonable compromise in my head. I'd only teach my Dad one song per artist, and it wouldn't be their biggest hit. When all was said and all was done, I'd steer him away from a musical career, leaving my meddling as an undocumented footnote in the college of musical knowledge.

We followed the same writing process as before. This time I backed off a little after providing lyrics and any notable intros or solos to see what Dad could do on his own, only jumping in with hints of the original if his interpretation lacked a can't miss hook or seemed to go too far astray. The end results were what good covers should be: distant cousins once removed rather than blatant carbon copies of the source. We spent about an hour on each song, hammering out a workable set in just two sessions.

The setlist we came up with:

> **We Can Work It Out** (our 'known' cover)
> **Won One** (Roommate)
> **Whatever** (Oasis)
> **Piece of Sky** (The Wonder Stuff)

> **Lounge Act** (Nirvana)
> **Only** (Anthrax)
> **Nowhere Fast** (Carter USM)
> **Captain Jack** (Billy Joel)
> **O Lonely Soul, It's a Hard Road** (Mary's Danish)
> **Martyr** (The Mr. T Experience)

He was a big hit again. Nelson's Mom officially dumped Nelson's Dad and my dad became her absolute ultimate shortly after this show. Most amazing to me was how Dad could not only learn but truly master nine new songs in less than a week. My mission was accomplished and I was ecstatic, which is probably why I caved when Dad asked for a fresh setlist. Since steering him away from a musical career already seemed far-fetched, I decided to at least humor him for now. I abandoned all of the rules regarding artist rights this time around and went for the jugular with a barrage of hits from the future.

The new additions to his repertoire:

> **Sunshine** (Jonathan Edwards)
> **Cats in the Cradle** (Harry Chapin)
> **Alive** (Pearl Jam)
> **I Want A New Drug** (Huey Lewis & The News)
> **Summer of '69** (Bryan Adams)
> **Missing You** (John Waite)
> **Start Choppin'** (Dinosaur Jr)
> **Your Wildest Dreams** (The Moody Blues)
> **White Wedding** (Billy Idol)
> **Straight Up** (Paula Abdul)
> **Baby One More Time** (Britney Spears)
> **Debonair** (Afghan Whigs)

I admit I was living dangerously on some of the choices by deviating from the relative safety of music from the distant future. Some of the songs were only a couple years from release and could very well have already been written and performed by now, but I was feeling invincible based on our past successes. If anything came of it there could be trouble, but since this was a local show at a no-name venue it was unlikely to be an issue. If Dad went on to record an album (which was quickly moving from remote possibility to forgone conclusion based on the buzz he was generating), I'd try to make sure he either kept those songs off or at least didn't credit himself as songwriter.

At one of our rehearsal/writing sessions we had just finished balladizing "Dead Horse" by Guns N' Roses when we decided to call it a night. I took the opportunity to broach a more important subject. It was time to take away his ball and chain.

"Absolutely not," he objected. "I know this started out as a game, but I've grown attached. That's never happened before. She's going to be my manager. And she wants to meet you too. My mysterious songwriting partner who's too superstitious to go to my shows."

"Very superstitious. Writing's on the wall," I sang back.

"That's good. Let's use it."

This was a conundrum. My very existence was somewhat in jeopardy. I say "somewhat" since I had already considered this possibility and knew I could just go back further and undo what I had done. I wasn't sure how much time I had to play with if I really screwed things up, but my best estimate was that I would probably continue to exist at least up to the point in time where I should have been conceived.

For a backup plan I could always have my Dad beat up Nelson's Dad and tell him to keep his damn hands away from his future wife. But I wanted to have it both ways; to somehow find a way to let my Dad keep his fledgling stardom, keep myself in the picture and keep my sister alive all in one fell swoop. Perhaps I was getting a bit greedy, but this folk rock star stuff was just too much fun.

It was time to play the Yoko card. "She's holding you back artistically. If you had the time you were focusing on the relationship to focus on your music, we might be able to come up with some original tunes."

"What are you talking about? We just wrote two albums worth of original songs in a week. Or you have. I'm your mouthpiece to the world, and I don't mind at all. The writing is your department, I'm just the frontman."

I sighed. "You're a regular Johnny Bravo."

"Johnny who?" said Dad, not catching the Brady Bunch reference that was still at least a half dozen years ahead of its time.

I wasn't quite ready to trump in and reveal the true nature of my involvement, so I had one more chord to play.

"I can't meet her, because she already knows me. I'm … in love with her. That's why I wanted you to break them up, so I could have my revenge."

Although it made no sense, that comment had the shock value I intended, but not the end result.

"I don't know what to say." He paused as he searched for the right words. "I'm sorry, but I can't do it. If the choice is you and the music or her, I choose her."

"But don't you see? She only wants you for the music and the fame. When she walks out that door you'll come looking for me. Like you said before, AWAB, right?"

As I said this, the doorbell rang.

"That should be her. Wait here, and we can all talk about this."

Dad exited the bedroom before I could vocalize a response. Even Mr. Awab couldn't help me now.

Not wanting to explain myself here, I left via the bedroom wall to blink ahead to a time when I could get Dad's undivided attention again. I'd have to throw everything on the table, and hope that he handled it better than my younger selves had.

Christine Sixteen

SEPTEMBER 18, 1970. JIMI HENDRIX IS FOUND DEAD in the basement apartment of a London hotel at the age of 27. Officially deemed a drug overdose, though as with Kurt Cobain conspiracy theories came in droves and ranged from ambulatory malpractice to a mob hit to straight suicide.

I effortlessly blinked forward to this date soon after leaving my father's house in 1969. Since I wasn't scheduled to be born until 1974 I would still be within my theoretical existence window, and thus still had time to see how the matchmaking events I set into motion had played out. Ideally Dad would have parlayed our stolen songs into fame, lost the girl, and be ready to accept the persuasion that would set him on his path towards Mom, me, and eventually a Nelson-free sister.

Dad had moved out of his parents' house since I was last here. From the looks of things, my grandparents had moved on as well. The house was missing, replaced by a parking lot and a record store. Even though I sometimes had trouble finding it, this was a house I had known all my life. Now it was gone before my time. The area behind the house had changed as well. A large red barnlike structure stood where the field once was. I wondered how I managed to cause such a major ripple.

"Who Knows?" from Jimi's *Band of Gypsys* live album played as I entered the record shop, hinting at the right year. The employees listening in silence with glum looks on their faces confirmed the rest. The store was an obvious enough first step to figuring out what went astray with it being new and all. Locating Dad was my first logical task. Browsing the bins of vinyl proved to be out of the question with my inability to physically touch any objects, and the few potential record-buying customers in the store weren't in the right alphabetical section for me to read over their shoulders. Not that reading over their shoulders would be a valid option unless the person browsing decided Dad's album was one they wanted to purchase. Otherwise I'd just see a brief glimpse of the cover as it flipped by like a forgotten page of a photo album. And this assumed he even recorded an album in the year I'd skipped over.

The featured items on display didn't help much either. I stopped for a moment when I saw a poster advertising Don McLean's *Tapestry* album. I wondered why I hadn't thought to teach my Dad "American Pie" when I had my chance, and also if the follow-up album would still exist at all without that staple hit song as the title track. Granted, Don McLean would likely still be making music, but he's more or less only known to the masses for that one extended classic. He'd still have "Castles In The Air," "Vincent," and the notoriety of being the inspiration for "Killing Me Softly," but in the scheme of things *American Pie and Other Hits* was a bit of an oxymoron.

Another display showed "brand new" sixty-minute Memorex recordable audiocassettes. Is it real, or…?

Just as I was beginning to long for the convenience of online shopping—or at least the days of clearly labeled CDs with white stickers on top—I noticed a small section of wall racks holding cassette tapes. Unfortunately the selection was quite limited. It only took a couple of minutes to determine that an album by my father was not here, unless in a daze he found God, changed genres and took up gospel while I was out. Scanning the room I noticed another, wider set of wall racks in the back of the store that held more cassette tapes. Closer inspection revealed they were not cassette tapes, but eight tracks.

The evolution of music formats has always fascinated me. It's always bigger, better, faster, more! Striving for the largest capacity in the smallest possible space without sacrificing aural quality. Vinyl to eight tracks to cassettes to compact discs to mp3s. A man made example of natural selection and survival of the fittest at work. All the way back in the seventies, advances in noise reduction had cassettes on the cusp of breaking through as a viable competitor, but the eight track was still entrenched as the format of choice.

I browsed the stack-o-tracks in earnest, but still found no sign of an album by my father. It also dawned on me that just knowing his name might not be the right approach. He could be using a band name or even a pseudonym, and discovering what that may be would require more snooping. I might have already passed him by without realizing it. It was even possible for him to have been discovered for his mimicry skills and be utilized exclusively as a backup or touring musician, in which case he wouldn't have a record of his own.

Discouraged, I headed for the exit to wander around and figure out my next plan of attack. Maybe the coffee house he used to play at would hold a clue. En route to the door I remembered I could exit any way I wanted and veered off through a bulletin board of promos, advertisements, and other announcements hanging near the eight track racks. Something caught my eye as I passed through, and the only way to find what I left behind was to double back again.

Exactly where my eyes had entered the wall was a poster featuring the logo from the hospital—the same logo that adorned the scrubs I'd been perpetually wanting to change out of. The poster advertised a concert at a local venue, headlined with:

See Local Boy
author of the hit singles
WON ONE and IF ONLY
in his own backyard!

Excited, I ran back to the eight tracks and scoured the 'L' section. Resting on top was one Local Boy album left unpurchased, entitled *Local Boy Done Good*. The simple cover included nothing more than the logo and the abbreviated title—LBDG.

The three slots immediately up above it were empty, allowing me a clear view of the track listings.

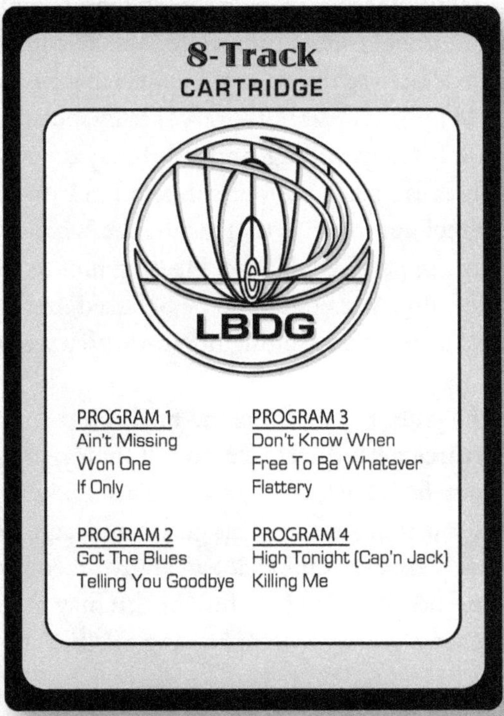

I could hardly believe it. The titles were a little bit off, but our songs remained the same. (Ok, maybe not *our* songs.) His inclusion of the acoustic Anthrax cover was hilarious. It was a well-timed bout of musical tourette's that put the song in my head, and then curiosity more than anything else that had me teach it to Dad in the first place. His treatment of it was so hauntingly beautiful it shouldn't have come as a surprise that it made the album and was one of the hit singles. I wondered if we could have done as well with Pantera or Megadeth.

According to the poster the concert was to be held that night at a venue called The Barnstormer. Based on a crude drawing and map, I was able to discern that this was the "barn" built on the site formerly occupied by the athletic field behind Dad's home. Now that I knew where to find him, I just needed to figure out what I was going to say.

I was perfectly willing to lay out all of my cards this time, and expected that I would have to. Even if I could convince Dad to break off the relationship with Nelson's Mom, I'd be crazy to expect him to immediately allow me to set him up with another woman. Maybe my parents had a higher love that was meant to be, and nature would take its course if I could just get them introduced. Then again, my crash course in time travel as it relates to dating seemed to indicate that nothing was truly meant to be.

When I say I was ready, willing, and able to lay down all of my cards, I didn't necessarily mean all. "I'm your son and I'm from the future," was fine, but it didn't feel appropriate to get into the whole "Your daughter will die, that's why I'm here" angle of it. Helping him to realize his musical dreams sounded altruistic enough to be believed, but I'd have to work out a whopper of a lie to justify setting him up with a woman who wasn't Mom.

I arrived at the club in time for some final setup and the load-in for sound check. The three performers were to test their gear in reverse order, meaning Dad was up first. He took the stage in a sharkskin jacket reminiscent of the one his cousin wore, tuned his guitar, and launched straight into "Ain't Missing," aka "Missing You." That had always been his favorite of the songs I taught him, and I couldn't help but think it may be dedicated to my abrupt disappearance a year ago when he sang the line about "wondering why you left."

One song was all he needed to be prepared. With the closing chord still reverberating, he handed his guitar to a roadie (who may have actually been his cousin) and wandered off stage. I hadn't noticed her before, but Nelson's Mom was in the wings waiting for him. I wasn't missing her at all.

She kissed him on the cheek and slinked her arm around him as they walked towards an exit just beyond stage right. They were still together, and it set my blood boiling. My hatred for Nelson had bled into a feud with his entire family. I had to get his Mom away from my Dad as soon as possible.

The door they used led outside, but by the time I reached it they were nowhere to be found. I circled the building and came upon a Winnebago parked in a fenced in area near the back. Entering the wall of the trailer, my vision was obscured by billows of whiteness. At first I thought the wall was thicker than I had gauged and I was still inside it. But the obstruction began to thin and I realized it was smoke. Though I couldn't smell it myself, I was pretty sure I knew what was going on. The next thing I saw provided some insight into why they were still together.

On the bed my Dad and Nelson's Mom were stoned and making out. Even though they had only been inside for less than a minute, she was topless and he was about to follow suit as she tugged at his shirt. I tried to speak up before it progressed any further, but had trouble finding the words to express myself.

"Ahem," I coughed before beginning, "Let me clear my throat. Sorry to interrupt, but we need to talk."

Dad opened his eyes mid-kiss and turned to face me, still groping the ample bosom before him. Instead of seeming angry, he smiled wide and propositioned me.

"Hey, partner. Welcome back! I was wondering if you'd turn up today. Care to join us?"

I was too shocked for words. Before I could formulate a response, Nelson's Mom chimed in.

"Let's start out with just you and me. I can give your cousin a ride later on."

Stoned, Dad laughed and temporarily released his lover from his embrace. "No babe, it's my song writing partner. The one who made all of this possible."

"The one who said he used to love me?" She was now reaching for my father's belt without even so much as a glance around to room to locate me. "He can have a go too if he wants, but he never wanted to before. Saving himself for marriage. Does he even know what year this is?"

Dad replied, "No, not the pianist. The one before." He then gave me a funny look, and asked if I had shrunk.

Glancing down, I realized that the floor of the trailer only came up to my knees. Thank god for altered perception, though I knew my secret would have to be revealed soon enough.

"I don't remember," she moaned back, eyes still closed. "But keep touching me and I'll do anything with anyone." Those last sultry words were followed by her thrusting her breasts back into Dad's waiting hands.

Scarred for life, I had to stop this now. I reached over and pried Dad's right hand off her boob and used his arm to push her fingers away from his belt. Covering my father's wet mouth with my free hand, I whispered in his ear.

"Listen carefully. She can't see me, only you can. Get her out of here so we can talk."

Dad jumped up off the bed with a sudden start, trying to shake me off his back.

Nelson's Mom was annoyed, but still proposed a compromise. "Ménage-à-trois again? We can if that's what you really want. But sometimes I just want you."

Dad looked at her and then back to me.

"Get her dressed and out of here, then we can talk," I repeated, passing my arm through the door for both emphasis and to frighten him a bit.

"Whoa!" said Dad.

"What's wrong? You look as if you've seen a ghost."

"I…I have. He's here."

Nelson's Mom was thankfully in the midst of putting her shirt back on (though it shouldn't have taken this long, as she didn't seem to have a bra to replace). "You know I don't like it when the drugs hit you this way. I'll get what I need somewhere else."

She straightened her blouse and buttoned her skirt in a silent, exaggerated manner before continuing.

"Jeez. You'd better get your act together before the show starts. Sleep it off. I'll come back before your set."

Dad had moved back to the vacant space on the bed and sat down. "But…he is here. He's mmph…"

I had covered his mouth again, forcing his cooperation.

"This is not a hallucination. Get rid of her and I'll explain. Tell her she's right, you need to sleep it off. Sorry to be so stern, but we need to talk now."

Dad closed his eyes as I released my hand from the front of his face. "Yes. I'm sorry. Come back later. Much later."

Now fully dressed, Nelson's Mom checked her hair in a mirror, grunted something inaudible, and left in a huff. Dad kept his eyes closed for a few minutes, then rubbed and opened them to see if I was still there.

"Are you dead like Jimi?" he asked.

"No. At least not yet."

I told him I was a time traveler from the future that only he could see and hear. That I didn't fully understand what was going on or the implications of it, but I knew he wanted to be a musician and wanted to help him fulfill that dream.

Although skeptical, the marijuana racing around his brain made this proposition really resonate with him. It seemed I had underestimated his ability to believe in the supernatural, though had I factored in the era and a penchant for psychedelics I should have expected this.

He caught me up on what had happened since I last left him. His local performances kept packing them in. Scores of A&R guys were turning up every night, setting up a bidding war that eventually got him his album deal and a national tour. He bought a new house for his parents and hit the road with Nelson's Mom. Today was his homecoming show.

He often wondered where I had gone to and if I'd ever forgive him for stealing her away, although she still claimed to have no idea who I was. But that troubled water was all under the bridge for him now that I was back. They had an open relationship, and he said we could share the girl if I wanted to (a bit more literally than the traditional Betty and Veronica sharing of Archie). He was also excited for me to help work out some songs for the new album he was being hounded to record but kept putting off due to his chronic writer's block. He had enough left in our vault for a single record, but his label wanted a double set.

Happy to stop talking about sharing Nelson's Mom with my father, I latched on to the change of subject even though I suspected Dad wasn't going to like it.

"About those songs," started my confession, "we sort of…borrowed them."

He didn't take the news well, and actually made me dictate a list of the artists we had pilfered from for him to write down. I reluctantly complied with his request, simultaneously ashamed of myself and proud of my father. Though he did like his women, he was still a man of honor and didn't like to lie, cheat, and steal his way through anything. Even the multiple sex partner thing was consensual and out in the open, though I wished he hadn't told me about that.

"Why are you so appalled by my sex life? Are things that much different where you come from?"

Although AIDS and other sexually transmitted diseases led to historians proclaiming the death of the free love era, I never thought that it had completely died out. People may have fewer simultaneous partners, but sex was still a major part of any dating relationship. Casual sex was not only accepted but practically canonized and woven into the plots of movies, television shows, and even songs. The concept of being like a virgin on a wedding night was an extremely rare exception in my time, especially in a world where the "normal" chain of courtship included cohabiting well before the wedding.

"It's not so much a difference in my generation as it is an old traditional principle. You don't want to know about your parents' sex life."

He looked dumbfounded. "We're your parents?"

"Not quite. You're my father, but she isn't my mother."

"But you set us up! I've read enough about time travel to know that you shouldn't go messing around with your own conception for crissakes. Who are you really?"

I assured him that I really was his son, and shared my theory that I would likely continue to exist up to the point of my conception. Since that was three years away I still had time, but I needed to get him back on the path to Mom before it was too late. As for Nelson's Mom, I lied and said she was a girl he had a pre-Mom fling with later in life that I decided to accelerate to get him into my confidence and down the path to musical stardom. When it went on longer than it should have I had to make excuses so he would end it, but he wouldn't budge. Finally I decided to jump ahead a bit and hope that the relationship had faltered under its own weight. When it hadn't, it was time to resort to the truth.

"You mean I never taught you to always be truthful?" he asked with a hurt look. "And I just got caught fooling around and smoking dope by my own kid. Some father I am." I couldn't tell if he actually believed me or was just humoring me.

"What was I supposed to say? Hey, I'm your future son, let's make you a rock and roll star to help pay for college?"

"Okay, Future Boy. If you really are my son, who am I supposed to marry?"

Finally I had a chance to convince him. I told him about my mother, but he had no idea who she was since he wouldn't even meet her for a few more years. I also told him that he'd have a son and a daughter, when we were born and, more importantly, approximately when we were conceived.

"Presuming this is true, you basically want me to find this woman, get married on this date, and start having children on these dates. If my life is already planned for me, what am I supposed to do in the meantime?"

"Whatever you would normally do."

"But what's the point if I have to follow this plan? If everything is already written?"

I thought this over for a moment, then realized that he wouldn't necessarily have to follow the plan to a T. He needed to get together with Mom, and he had to keep the conception dates of my sister and myself relatively the same. Just the same menstrual cycle ought to do the trick, giving him a reasonably large window of opportunity. Also, I could care less if he had twelve kids this time around, so long as two of them were the same.

As for meeting my Mom, would accelerating the timetable really matter? It was possible, but this could be a special circumstance. Mom did say they met and married in the same year, and with Dad so gifted in the art of seduction I was fairly certain he could pull it off. Parents are the same no matter time nor place. Even though I doubted it both logically and experientially, part of me still looked to find a reason to believe that fate had a hand in some aspects of life. Maybe once the course was resumed things would work out relatively close to how they did initially with the exception of a little bit of foreknowledge. He might follow the right path whether I told him to or not.

I explained all of this to Dad. Although he was taking it with a shaker of salt, I felt that I was getting to him.

"I want to believe you, really I do. But I don't see what's in it for me. Hendrix just died today, and they're already calling him a legend. What if I think that's more important than settling down?"

I bit the inside of my lip. Though it pained me to have to debate in favor of settling down and lie to my father again, it had to be done.

"That's not what you want. All the rock stars die at twenty-seven. First Hendrix, then Joplin, then Jim Morrison. The music world is changing, and it's not a club you want to be a part of for the long haul."

I hoped that would put him over the edge. If nothing else he might check in on the name I gave him for his future wife out of curiosity once my predicted dominos started falling. If fate were still in play, I could theoretically be home free from there. I was starting to sound like my older self more and more. We were just a smile, a nod, and a few decades apart.

Our conversation ended with me channeling my older self by providing a warning.

"Don't tell anyone about this, not even me after I'm born. We don't want to alter my life so much that this chat never happens. I'll bring it up to you when I get back if the time is right."

That type of implication really seemed to sink in. Hell, what did he have to lose? I may have actually scared him into following through on it. I wondered once more if I really had already been through this before in my version of real life. It seemed to explain why he stopped womanizing for Mom, why he stuck with her no matter what, and why he often seemed to be holding something back in any conversation he had with me. Maybe I wasn't too far off in thinking that fate had a plan for everyone to follow.

Satisfied that I had done all I could, I bid him farewell and blinked out in plain sight, hoping to leave him with a lasting impression to think about for the next few years.

Wounded Kite At :17

I REALIZE I'VE WRITTEN QUITE A BIT about the occasional difficulty in finding the right memory to ride back in time on, but I haven't described the reverse process of blinking back to the future in any detail. You might think the two would be similar, but in actuality they are not. Rather than relying on a specific event, returning to from whence you came is a simple feeling that shouts "This has all been wonderful, but now I'm on my way."

It can be part boredom, part panic, part satisfaction, and part curiosity all at once. Thinking about it, I figured that made some sense. If you had to use a memory to get back to your real time you'd never quite get there, because your most recent memory would be of the instant before you left. At least that's how I thought it was supposed to work, but this time I didn't make it all the way back.

One moment I'm in Dad's trailer, the next I'm outside my grandparents' house walking towards the football field. The barn was gone, the house was back, and everything appeared to be just as I remembered it.

Although it didn't make any logical sense, I wasn't particularly shocked. At least I wasn't in that hospital again. Part of me hoped to land next to Mom's car outside my old apartment, but the rest of me knew that anticipated ending would be the most unlikely of scenarios since I'd no longer have a reason to make that drive. With Nelson effectively eliminated, I could have turned up anywhere.

But was *here* a valid *anywhere*? If Local Boy killed Nelson, this house shouldn't be here since Dad bought his parents a new place with his stolen royalties. But if the record store wasn't here, I shouldn't even remember Local Boy since that's where I discovered him. Confused? Me too.

Stuck in the moment, I kept walking and absentmindedly lifted my arm to grab at a low hanging tree branch blowing in the wind. My hand went right through it.

I couldn't grab the tree. The wind was blowing, but I couldn't feel it. Checking my clothing, I still had the hospital scrubs on. Scratching my head, I felt that it was still shaved. Why wouldn't my hair keep growing since I'd been back in time for a good month and a half by now? And that's where I still was, somewhere in time.

I cautiously returned to the house to find out when I was and what was going on. The voice of my younger father drew me to an open window.

"He's right in here," I heard him say. "Word of warning though, you might be surprised by who it is."

He entered the bedroom holding hands with the prim and proper Nelson's Mom from 1969, then gave a quizzical look upon realizing they were alone. I ducked away from the window and decided to just listen rather than risk being spotted.

Nelson's Mom sighed. "Your mysterious imaginary songwriting partner, gone again. Can't you just take credit for what you've done on your own and drop the modesty act?"

"But he was here. And you know him. Or he knows you. He said he had a thing for you."

The conversation continued, but I had stopped listening. For some reason I had blinked back to where I had left from before my most recent blink to the Barnstormer show. This didn't deviate from any of my past experiences, as I'd always returned to the same exact moment I'd departed from previously. It also explained why I returned to the wedding after the Hearts tournament. It wasn't because I wanted to; it was because I had to. A simple law of time travel forcing me to retrace my steps on my way back home.

If I was right, my next attempted blink home should take me to the living room of Nelson's parent's house…

…and that's exactly where I landed. The house seemed to be more or less as I had remembered it from my brief stay last time, except that nobody was home. Checking outside, there was no limousine, indicative of the fact that I had eliminated Nelson and thus the wedding. Do re me so far so good.

I left the porch for the next scheduled stop at that awful hospital. I wanted to get it over with as fast as possible, so I prepared myself to blink twice in rapid succession, stopping just long enough to confirm the vacancy of the room, which set me up to land in the real world of my present.

The headache that hit me was more excruciating than before, leaving me half unconscious from the pain. Imagine the worst migraine you've ever had, combined with a terrible wine hangover plus the nausea of a bad concussion. Multiply that by infinity and you'll almost ache like I ached. It turned my world to black. My eyes were forced shut so tightly from the pain that I still had no concept of when or where I was. Or if I even was at all.

Was I dead? Or maybe worse, erased? What had gone wrong? If I was dead I probably wouldn't be thinking about it. But if I had gone back to a present that I was no longer a part of, maybe I would be somewhere like here. Everywhere and nowhere, thinking about the sun and the moon and the spinning of the room and a million other things all at once. Brain exploding or imploding, not knowing where it is supposed to be. Was this the same fate I had subjected Nelson to? So many thoughts, but not a single one was stable enough to support another blink.

A voice broke through the darkness. "Are you okay, honey?"

I fought my eyes open and found myself at the kitchen table across from my mother. A cribbage board was between us. What was presumably my six-card hand was flopped on top of it, partly face up and partly face down.

"I asked if you were doing okay."

"Yeah. Just a bad headache."

"All of a sudden? We don't have to play anymore. Do you want to take an aspirin and lay down for a bit?"

"Yes," I managed to utter through the pain.

Mom led me downstairs to the couch. She said something about Dad being here for dinner that I didn't quite hear, but I couldn't be bothered with asking her to repeat it. Rest was all I needed or wanted.

After what seemed like hours of trying to sleep but was actually closer to seven minutes, I realized that a big part of this headache might be malnutrition. My stomach was growling and also in pain, but I had failed to notice with the mosh pit rocking and rolling in my head. I hadn't eaten for over a month because I wasn't able to, but I probably wouldn't have even if I could as I never felt the need. Even though my body had theoretically never left, it was screaming for nourishment now that my brain was back.

Weakly I crawled up the stairs (I hadn't climbed stairs in so long I had taken for granted how much effort they really took) and stumbled into the kitchen. My head still a blur, I found a ham and cheese croissant in the freezer and tossed it into the microwave. Upon closing the microwave door, I caught my reflection in the glass and almost fell over.

The problem wasn't in what I looked like so much as that it wasn't what *I* looked like. The man in the mirror was a stranger. I couldn't quite place the specifics at first, just that my hair seemed darker, my eyebrows thinner, and my face narrower. Forgetting about my aching body, I ran to the bathroom to get a better, full color look in a proper mirror.

My normally straight blonde hair was now red and somewhat curly. Not the dyed red I experimented with on occasion in my younger days, but a natural hue closer to Glitzy's color. I also had to be at least three inches taller, and upon closer inspection saw that I lost at least an inch down below as well. A wide goatee engulfed my chin and upper lip in a darker shade than the red locks on my head.

I felt my entire face to confirm what I was seeing, and noticed that my sense of touch was in perfect synchronicity with what I saw in the reflection. As I was trying to recall if Sam Beckett felt his own face or that of the person he leapt into, my mother knocked on the door.

"Is everything alright in there?"

"Yes. Fine."

"Is that thing in the microwave yours?"

I'd already forgotten about my starvation, but the very mention of food brought the aches in both my stomach and my head to the forefront of my consciousness again.

"Yes. I'll get it in a second."

"Don't eat too much now. Your father and brother will be back with dinner in ten minutes."

"Ok."

Wait, brother?

"What did you say? I can't hear you."

Mom screamed back, "I'll tell you when you come out. You're frozen thing is on the table waiting for you. Do you want something to drink with that?"

After splashing water on my face and taking about five aspirin I got my composure together enough to be somewhat presentable and walked into the kitchen. Mom was wiping down the microwave with a dishtowel, trying in vain to eliminate the smell of my junk food. Undeterred, I scarfed down the croissant in two bites.

"What's for dinner?" I asked, my mouth still half full.

"Town Spa Pizza. Your favorite."

Mmmm…Town Spa. "And who did you say is coming?"

"Your father is picking up the pizza and coming over with your brother. He should be here any minute. Will you set the table?"

"Don't you mean my sister?"

Mom threw down the towel.

"Jesus! You know I don't like it when you call him that. It's not nice, and it's really immature. There's nothing wrong with it so long as it's his choice."

I wanted to ask what there was nothing wrong with, but decided to just see for myself.

After setting the table as penance and drinking a gallon of water my stomach was somewhat normal. My body still felt weak, but at least the aspirin had toned my head down to a single alarm quake rather than the raging death hangover it had been before. Or at least it had toned it down until the creaking of the storm door sent another shockwave up the expressway to my skull.

The front door opened, and in walked my older father as I had always remembered him. Behind him was the brother I'd never had before. And behind the two of them was Nelson, same as he ever was.

Stomach churning, I immediately vomited a mixture of water and snack before collapsing onto the floor.

—⧟—

Still groggy, aching, and starving, I woke up on the couch with a figure hovering above me.

"Mom? Mom is that you?"

This seemed oddly familiar. Was it all a dream?

"There there honey. Are you okay? Should I call the doctor?"

"No doctor, I'm fine. Just a stomach thing."

"I knew it. You shouldn't eat that junk anyways. There's still plenty of pizza left whenever you're ready. Your brother and Nelson are out back helping your father with something in the shed."

Nope, not a dream.

"Thanks, Mom. Can you bring the food to me?" I asked, confused as to the real difference between microwaved junk food and bar style pizza but not wanting to start a lengthy debate. She retreated upstairs to the kitchen, returning moments later with the familiar white and blue box.

"While I've got you cornered, look here and smile!"

I turned my head away as the flashbulb exploded, sending another shooting pain through my brain.

"No flash photography!"

—⁂—

Finally my headache started to dull. I inhaled the pizza fast enough to win any type of eating contest, then turned my thoughts back to what I had witnessed so far.

I wasn't really me, and my sister was now my brother. But my parents were the same, as was Nelson. Nelson had no discernable physical differences based on my cursory inspection of him, which should mean that absolutely nothing had changed regarding his conception. Was Nelson's father not the father I stopped his Mom from marrying? That would have been a good thing to know before I started meddling.

If Nelson had the same parents, why were both myself and my sister/brother different? Same parents should give the same results. Or would they? The best theory I could come up with is the following. I call it my simplified dissertation on sex ed as it applies to time travel.

A woman is born with all of her eggs readymade, whereas a man makes his sperm on the go and as needed. Individual sperm cells contain randomly selected bits of genetic code designating the specific traits that will be passed on, as do the eggs.

Factoring time travel into the equation, let's suppose that every woman releases her eggs in the same order with each menstrual cycle in all possible replays of the timeline. Let's also assume that a man will generate his individual sperm in the same order. If conception occurred at the same time in two different versions of a timeline, the egg would still be the same. The sperm would also be the same, but there are millions of the little guys. Since only about one thousand actually reach the egg, we can assume that the fast ones will still win the race and select the proper path to reach their destination. Chances are now only one in one-thousand that the same sperm will fertilize the egg. These aren't very good odds that the same child will be born, but it's probably safe to extend our time travel induced leap of faith and assume that if the same single sperm makes it to the final destination, it will again claim victory. Thus you end up with the same offspring every time…theoretically.

Now let's assume the sex life of the male was thrown off track somewhere previous to the conception of his children. (For example, maybe his idiot son set him up with an extra partner somewhere along the way, and possibly even eliminated other lovers during the same period.) If the sperm creation remained on the same cycle, but the male in question was either running ahead or running behind his original schedule at the time of intercourse, then the correct sperm isn't even running in the race and thus can't win.

And that would mean different kids!

One extra ejaculation along the way could have been all it took to erase the real me from existence. If Nelson was exactly the same person, it meant that there would have been no changes to the sex schedule of his father (whomever that may be), and the same timing for his coupling with the mother. So much for keeping Mom and Dad's first meeting on track.

This theory explained most of the changes to my physical characteristics, but not why I knew that I was the same person. And since I was still the same person mentally as far as I could tell, would my sister still be there in my brother somewhere? My head was spinning in both confusion and anger for not thinking this through before setting my father loose as an American gigolo. I had to track down Dad and have a very bizarre version of "the talk" in order to figure this out.

Outside, the shed and the surrounding dog shrine area were empty. Digging around at the corner of the doghouse for my stash proved unsuccessful. The dirt was tightly packed, as if the hole was never there to begin with. I decided to have a peek in the tree house. After climbing the ladder and lifting the trap door, I was greeted by the sight of my brother and Nelson entwined in a full on make out embrace.

I slammed the trap door shut and ran like hell down the ladder, kicking the roof of the doghouse in frustration before turning back towards the house.

What had I done? What could this mean? Was Nelson gay all along, and his repressed feelings were taken out on my sister causing her suicide? Or was this fate telling me they were star-crossed lovers, meant to be no matter what happened to the flow of time? At least (s)he was still alive. That could mean that the out of the closet Nelson was new and improved, kinder and gentler, a lover not a fighter.

I found it ironic that I hadn't actually changed the sexual preference of my sibling, as it was the same right down to the significant other. I had only changed the gender, appearance, and longevity. But was the conclusion of this relationship inevitable regardless of the form taken by the participants?

I wished that I could move forward and check, but I had no memories of a future beyond this present. *My* future didn't actually exist as of yet. Perhaps if my older self were to tell me something that would happen to me in the future I'd be able to blink to it, but if he was still three thousand miles away a trip west seemed unwise at the moment. Not to mention more than likely unnecessary, since that presumed there still was an old me to meet up with after the changes I'd made.

Back inside, I snacked on some leftovers and noticed that my stamina was just about back to normal, albeit still a little weak. My brother eventually joined me at the kitchen table.

"How's the pizza?" he asked.

"Fine."

"Look. I'm sorry you had to see that. I know it makes you uncomfortable."

"No it doesn't. What makes you say that?"

"Well, your reaction for one. Plus you've always addressed me by feminine pronouns, especially growing up. And we haven't been very close since I came out."

Was this new me a homophobe? Real me never would have acted that way. It was time to nip this in the bud.

"I don't have any issue with the life you choose to lead. It's more in who you choose to lead it with. I mean, I'm sure there's a better man for you than him."

My brother got angry in the same way my sister did when we had our similar conversation. "You're unbelievable. You live in your own little world where you get to spin things however you want. Nelson's great. He understands me and I feel like I've known him forever. And no matter what you think, he isn't the reason I am who I am, he just helped me realize it. I'm so right about this."

He stormed out of the house before I could reply. Searching for him would be a waste of time, so I decided to let him cool off.

Downstairs in my makeshift living quarters I noticed that the room had changed. It was now a shrine to my father's musical legacy. Three gold records for Local Boy adorned the wall where the clocks once hung, framing the poster from the record store mounted between them. On top was the *Done Good* record with the LBDG hospital logo I had found. To the left was *Live At The Barnstormer*, and the one on the right was entitled *Quits* and contained most of the live songs I had helped him work out that did not appear on the first release.

A photo album was left on a shelf just below the wall hangings. Inside were the original lyric sheets Dad had taken from my dictation. They also had chord annotations he must have added on his own to help remember his guitar parts. Subsequent pages included magazine articles (he was on the cover of Newsweek and on the cover of the Rolling Stone), photos from the road, reviews, ticket stubs, and other memorabilia. The critics gave consistently high praise, honing in on the diversity and eclectic mix of topics and styles covered. One even called the songs "ahead of their time" and "from a future age."

The most amusing of the clippings was an angry letter from Harry Chapin's lawyer asking that Mr. Chapin's wife be given proper credit and royalties for writing "Don't Know When," along with a title change to "Cats in the Cradle" on future pressings. This was followed with some pompous and sarcastic lawyer speak insinuating that if this was more than just a simple oversight in citations there would be further damages sought.

The last page had an article chronicling Dad's final show and sudden announcement of retirement. It included quotes from his resignation speech, with his handwritten text of the same on the facing page.

Ladies and gentlemen, you have just witnessed my final per—formance. I have decided to retire from the music business and try my hand at real life. I might even raise a family and have a couple of kids. Something tells me now is the right time, and I'd like to go out on a high note. It's been great fun making the albums and playing for all of you, and I sincerely appreciate the support you've given to me.

Although this is my swan song, I hope that the spirit of my music will live on with other artists. To facilitate this, I will be donating all of my royalties to up and coming musicians whom I deem worthy. My hope is that these artists will perform and record these songs as their own.

Thank you again for your support. Here's one more for you to remember me by, and for me to remember you by.

Though missing from the handwritten notes, the article said the speech ended with: "Harry, you can have this back after I play it one more time." Then he closed with a rousing version of "Cats in the Cradle," with the final line about the return of the narrator's son being repeated over and over at the ending, becoming more powerful each time. He never played another show or gave another interview again.

"Since when do you care about my musical past?"

My father had entered without me hearing him.

"Since always. I made it happen, remember?"

Dad slowly sat down on the couch. A look of distress overtook his mouth as the smile ran away from his face. Eventually he found words to speak again.

"So it was real. Oh boy."

We had a lengthy conversation regarding the years I had missed. A few days after the Barnstormer show he began recording sessions for a second album of our leftovers with the working title of *Coverville*. He still had no true originals, causing me to wonder if Izzy Stradlin was from the future, as Guns N' Roses never recorded another original song after his departure, just covers. Dad had mostly written off all that I had said and thought it was just a drug-induced dream. That is, until Janis Joplin died.

Work on the new album was scrapped and Local Boy went into seclusion, with the live album released by the label in time for the holidays to fill the gap. Mrs. Nelson continued to be his groupie gal pal and fan club president for a little while, but things were tense between them now that he was trying to be a regular guy. After a few months she convinced him to embark on a short acoustic tour to build on the buzz of his second coming. The tour seemed to revitalize him. He returned to the studio in late June of 1971 to finish up work on *Coverville*, intending to discretely thank the original artists in the acknowledgements using the list I had given him—just in case.

And then Jim Morrison died.

That was it. He confirmed that the future mother of his children actually existed, gave Nelson's Mom the Heisman, renamed the album *Quits*, played one final show, and abruptly left the music business behind to seek out his ~~density~~ destiny with my real mother. In the end he couldn't stand the guilt of potentially killing his child through his own ignorance.

Nelson's parents reconciled and became a rebound couple, eventually marrying on schedule. And since Nelson's old-fashioned father had saved himself for marriage, everything went exactly as it had the first time around, at least from a genetic standpoint. I smiled a bit that my reproduction theory seemed on target, then frowned when I realized I was smiling while thinking of Nelson and his origins, flashing back to the scene in the trailer. That in turn led to an image of my brother in the tree house, which begged the next question I asked my father.

"You do know that your other son's lover is your former lover's son, don't you?"

Dad looked at me sternly for a moment. "Yes, I'm aware."

"But…that's incest."

"Technically no, since she and I were never married. And just calling her my former lover doesn't really do the story justice…"

I had a grim inkling as to where this was heading, but I let him continue in sequence. He went on to say how he and Mom hit it off pretty well. She resisted him due to his prior reputation, but eventually gave in and they also wed on schedule. He was careful to use extra birth control up until the times I told him his children were to be conceived. Everything was fine until my brother came along.

"What did that change?" I asked.

"It made me think you were just a vision, and I had thrown it all away for nothing. I had invented you as a reason to settle down, but reality was setting in. Or maybe it was denial. A couple of messed up rockers died, but in hindsight anyone could have predicted that. For five years I believed in you, but now I had doubts. And once the nagging doubts come to you…" he trailed off and looked at the ceiling.

Since I had told Dad he'd have a child of each gender, when the second child was another male my credibility was shot. I explained my reproduction theory and he seemed to accept it, but it didn't really make him any happier. All of this was proof that no one should know too much about his or her own future. Had I not told him of how his life was supposed to turn out, he wouldn't have pegged me as a liar when things didn't happen as predicted. Then again, if I hadn't told him anything at all he just as likely could have stayed with Nelson's Mom and negated my existence altogether. Would you have done it differently? I can't win for losing.

He kept going, recounting how he met up with Nelson's Mom again a few years later and they resumed their affair, eventually leading to the two of them leaving their respective spouses. He couldn't bear to tell Mom to her face, and instead left a note on the kitchen table. She got custody of both me and the house. Dad got my brother, and they both moved in with Nelson and his mom. She wanted Dad to record a third album, but he didn't have enough material. He tried to appease her by resurrecting the abandoned Coverville moniker for a set entitled: *Coverville: A Collection of Other People's Songs by Local Boy*, but the lack of new material caused another rift between them. Eventually she left, taking both boys with her. That was nineteen years ago. He later re-entered Mom's life for the sake of us kids, but they never truly reconciled.

His story didn't really explain the Local Boy museum in Mom's basement (unless that was my creation), but I figured it was a better question for her than for him. Instead I asked about the brotherly love.

"Living together as brothers, they developed a fondness for each other. That fondness led to experimentation, and the rest…" Again he trailed off before finishing. "I presume that wasn't the way it was supposed to be? Is this better or worse?"

Supposed to be was a relative term, though the answer was the same from both perspectives. If he meant how it was supposed to go the first time I lived it, this wasn't even close. If he meant did it go as I had intended when I set out to change things, again it was no. And as to which result was better? Take your pick. At least there hadn't been a suicide the second time around. But a broken marriage, a musical career cut short, a me that wasn't me, my sibling still dating a Nelson who now had my father as a guardian, and a partridge in a pear tree wasn't much to write home about either.

I declined getting into specifics. "That's not how it used to be. Back to the drawing board I guess."

It was time for a different approach and a clean slate. I tried to blink back to before I created this alternate bizarro world by thinking of Woodstock, but nothing happened.

I tried again, still nothing.

Hendrix plays the Star Spangled Banner.

(blink)

They put a man on the moon.

(blink blink)

My father just stared at me as I squinted in deep concentration. "What on earth are you doing?"

"Trying to make everything right again. Tell me something that happened before October 12, 1969."

He remained silent.

"C'mon, anything at all."

"Ok, um … the birth of Christ."

I laughed. "A bit too far away for my liking. It has to be something in your lifetime. And something known to have really happened."

"You don't believe in Christ?"

"Do we really have to talk about this now?"

"How about Woodstock?"

"Already tried, no luck."

He smiled. "You already tried to get me to play at Woodstock?"

"No, no. I already tried to go back to Woodstock to stop you from playing anything at all. Give me something else."

I closed my eyes and concentrated, rubbing my temples to stay focused.

"Richard Nixon's inauguration."

Nothing.

"Sirhan Sirhan confesses to killing RFK."

Nope.

"Vietnam. The Apollo space program." Dad was really chucking the history at me. For what it was worth, I was quite impressed.

"Too vague. It needs to be tied to a specific date."

"Who the hell came up with these rules? You?"

"Maybe. I'm not sure. Most of them I just figured out on my own. It's somewhat inconsistent, but this is what works best."

Dad continued "Charles Manson. Midnight Cowboy. Tiny Tim gets married. Eisenhower dies."

I started chanting to myself, "Lawrence of Arabia, British Beatlemania, Ole Miss, John Glenn, Liston beats Patterson."

Dad smiled. "That would make a great song."

"It is a song."

He gave me a doubtful look. "From the future?"

"I'm not from the future," I explained again. "I'm from the present, just not this present. It's a Billy Joel song."

"The Cap'n Jack guy?"

"Exactly," I answered impatiently despite Dad's confusion. "Can we talk about this later too?"

We kept trying to find the right memory, but nothing would do the trick. Panic started to set in. Although I failed to use it once I got the hang of things, I decided it was worth a try to rub a finger across my neck bruise.

But it wasn't there. It must have healed.

Or…

"Fuck!!!!" I yelled when I came to the ultimate realization.

"What? What?" asked Dad, ignoring my language as he felt it was justified by my frustration.

"This body never got injected to begin with. I can't time travel. I might be stuck here forever."

18 And Life

Thinking it through further, I came to the conclusion that I probably wouldn't be stuck here forever. The fact that I could remember all of the time traveling done so far seemed to indicate that it would still happen. Thus I was likely to take the path of my older self, who would obtain the ability to time travel at some point in his life and subsequently go on the mission to inject me and set the chain of events I've been detailing here into motion.

I had no idea how or when this would happen. And in cases such as this, it always seemed that the harder you looked for something the harder it was to find. Step up to bat trying to hit the game winning home run and ground out. Go out to the club looking to take a girl home and get slapped. Sit down to write the great American novel and end up with some pompous trash. Instruct your father on how to conceive you and lose your identity. Try to save your sister from an untimely demise, and…

You get the picture. Things just need to happen without being forced. Under those conditions, I changed my mind again. I had to prepare myself for the possibility that I would be here forever.

—⁂—

Over the next several weeks I fell into the routine of my new life. I had never moved out west, which made sense since I didn't have a dead sister to trigger the migration. I was a lifestyle reporter for the local newspaper, writing articles covering small town events that weren't nearly as much fun as my past music magazine experiences. I never took that path in this life for some reason. Living at home with my mother was a possible cause, as I had my hands full trying to help her maintain her sanity after the separation. She never really recovered from it emotionally. Never remarried, hardly dated for as much as I could remember or figure out. Her interactions with Dad were limited to custodial formalities, though I hoped that the existence of the Local Boy artifacts in the basement were a sign she still cared. Why I allowed them to be in my bedroom was a mystery, especially since this me never really acquired a taste for music. Maybe the lack of interest stemmed from resenting Dad for leaving and blaming his past career as the underlying reason. I sounded like a parent scolding their teen for listening to heavy metal. "If it wasn't for that damn music you listen to…"

Speaking of music, Dad not knowing "We Didn't Start the Fire" wasn't just early senility. The song was never written. Nor were any of Billy Joel's other hits. But he still existed. I found a copy of his *Cold Spring Harbor* debut album at a record store. It was a flop, and the only record he ever released. He was still the piano man though. I tracked him down selling baby grands at a shop in Poughkeepsie.

The strangest part was that all I had borrowed was "Captain Jack," a song that was never a single and more of a cult favorite (and a funny song to hear my father sing) than anything else. But for some reason it erased *Piano Man* and everything else that would follow. Though I wasn't a huge Billy Joel fan to begin with, I wondered if never being exposed to the magic of *The Stranger* contributed to my musical apathy in this life.

Now and again I would still try to blink back to another time, but it was becoming more and more clear that I had lost the touch. I now know that it was the missing injection that prevented controlled time travel, but it was almost as if the part of my brain that knew how to harness the memories had been closed off, forgotten, or otherwise detained.

My memory was weird in general, as bits and pieces from this life overlapped or combined with things from my "real" life. It was sort of a cross between an alcohol blackout and trying to remember a dream. Some parts are so vividly clear that you swore they actually happened, but the whole sequence of events is out of context with major lapses in continuity at certain moments. Sometimes the gaps fall during unimportant junctures such as how you got from one room to another or one building to another. Other times they are more major issues. Why am I writing this article? What is my relationship with this person? Which bedroom is mine? Who was in my room last night? Do you remember the first time? Where is my mind?

To top it off, I was plagued by nightmares of that creepy hospital, presumably suppressed memories from the other reality where I was committed. Electrodes, gowns, doctors, shots, shocks, syringes, injections, blood, defibrillators, heart monitors, clocks, puddles, clouds, shadows, and lots and lots of questions. I'm often getting injected in these dreams, and wake up just after seeing the face of the person administering the shot. Sometimes it's the doctor, sometimes older me, sometimes former me, sometimes Dad, and most often Nelson. Wide-awake, I shake in a panic until the illusion dissipates and my new life takes center stage. I had to make a concerted effort to keep my original existence from getting completely suppressed for fear I'll do some damage one fine day that causes it to fade away altogether.

My new brother was a lot like my old sister, making me think that maybe she was still in there somewhere. To clarify, he was a lot like the later, post-Nelson version of my sister. We didn't speak much after the kitchen confrontation (a sad little bit of history repeating), but would have dinner together with one or both of our parents from time to time despite the protests from his other half. There was still a spark of life in his eyes that came out on occasion, but for the most part it was completely smothered by Nelson's domineering persona.

That was the root of the problem I hadn't been able to outright identify before. Nelson was a huge control freak. Since he didn't have control over many things in his life, he latched on to my sibling as his pet. He may have meant well, but this overprotectiveness was to such a high degree that it bordered on the ridiculous. It was so heavy-handed that my younger self's alleged overprotecting of our sister in his youth was nothing in comparison. Nelson's strategy also followed no real logic. If you're so insecure that you think you might lose your lover when he has dinner with his Mom, imagine how you'd be when he was out among the general population with a very legitimate shot at finding somebody better. Don't start me up again.

I was actually beginning to doubt if Nelson was really a homosexual at all, but instead just adapted into it when the opportunity to be a dominant player in any relationship presented itself to him. Dad seemed to feel guilty and partially to blame for this aspect of the turn of events. This was further complicated by a paternal soft spot he seemed to have for Nelson. I hadn't filled him in on any of the old Nelson backstory, especially not the suicide. But he clearly knew that I didn't like the guy and was sharp enough to see that the hatred was strong enough to have transcended both of my lifetimes.

He was having regrets over his relationship with Nelson's mother for the same reasons. Though that topic was off limits as well, he had to know that I was setting them up for more of a reason than I let on, and that my disgust in the result reflected on him to some degree.

There was also a part of him that may have blamed me for his woes. How did I get him into this? And why? And at what cost? But he was doing his fatherly duty and taking most of the rap on behalf of his son, with few questions and no complaints.

My new life wasn't all doom and gloom. My relationship woes were finally on the upswing. Just when I thought our chance had passed, it turned out that this tall redheaded version of me was still dating the cute redheaded girl. That seemed to give credence to my theory that the death of my sister was what broke us up, meaning that I've been correctly blaming Nelson for that all along.

To say I was shocked when I discovered this would be an understatement. I was absolutely thunderstruck. One day I returned home from work to find her in my bed. She attributed my confused excitement to a bad day and took good care of me for a few hours before cooking a late dinner for us when Mom got home. It seemed that this version of me didn't believe in Mom's curse, though I had a feeling that might be a mistake. Some things never change.

It was about six weeks into this new life when I found the advertisement. Daily tasks were becoming routine instead of new, and the deception of pretending to know about my own past was steadily replaced with solid knowledge of the standard things one should remember. There was even more boredom than normal at the newspaper, allowing me the necessary time to get my act together and start having a normal afternoon life that included out of the office lunches. En route to my car before meeting the cute redheaded girl (now my cute redheaded girlfriend; how I loved the sound of that), I found a note under my windscreen wiper blade:

> *Ever wonder what could have been? Better still, does the little voice inside your head insist you already know?*
>
> *Test subjects wanted for experiments on the subconscious powers of the mind. Top $$$ to those who qualify.*
>
> *Call 310-779-5234 to register.*

I read the ad at least five times in disbelief, then twice more just to make sure I understood it. Although the little voice inside your head was a juvenile way of putting it, it certainly fit the bill. Finally pulling my eyes away from the paper, I scanned the rest of the cars in the parking lot. Not a single one had the same flyer. I was taking an early lunch, so there wasn't really much of a possibility that the others had already been found and disposed of. The note had to be meant for me.

I wondered if it might be a message from my future self. That's why I couldn't see any other messages, because nobody else would be able to see this one. Relieved, I drove to my lunch date with a new confidence that I may be getting out of this situation after all.

That confidence was quickly shaken at the restaurant. I set the paper next to my plate so I could continue pondering it during the meal unbeknownst to my companion.

"What's this?" asked my gal as she immediately snatched it up and started reading.

"You can see…I mean…you can read that?"

"Yeah. It's in English," she replied with a look of half sarcasm and half concern, not sure if I was joking or not. "Sounds like a scam." She dropped it back onto the table, having already dismissed the contents. "Why are you keeping it? For a story?"

"That's right. Figured it might make a good piece for a slow news day. We've been having quite a few of those lately."

So it was just a regular, real note. I should have known, as if it was a phantom object from another time it wouldn't have stayed on the car or on the table but instead just passed right through to the ground as the bowling ball had. My remedial grasp of time travel science was slip sliding away from me. I guess I just wanted to believe older me was still out there. But this could be just as good. Maybe an even older older me had perfected sending objects through time? I felt that I was grasping for something that wasn't really there and reading too much into the note. But what if I wasn't?

Playing devil's advocate, what if this was more of an investigation than an experiment? Maybe someone was trying to smoke out the person who caused these changes in time. Was I just being paranoid? The only major difference that would have any bearing on the world was the music we stole, but if someone were actually monitoring this they should have suspected that Dad was the culprit from the start. No need to resort to the classifieds. And what would a time patrol do if they couldn't interact with anyone? Recruit my older self to come back and arrest me? And if he did stop me, wouldn't he have done it before now so this never would have happened anyways? I wasn't sure if I should be worried, excited, or if it was just my imagination running away with me.

The rest of our lunch date was uneventful. Or at least it seemed that way to me, as I barely paid attention. I wanted to get back to the office now that I had this new lead to follow. If nothing else I could pad my bank account a bit by participating in the study, since my job as local interest beat reporter wasn't making me a rich man. I was slightly better off than before without any rent to pay, but living with Mom was starting to get to me even with the perks of free room and board. Apparently this new me was a bit more of a mama's boy than the real me. This real me (if you could still call me that) wanted to move in with the redheaded girl, but I knew that being a mooch wasn't the best approach.

I rattled off a quick and abrupt farewell along with some excuse about a forgotten deadline and sped back to the office, dialing the number printed on the flyer from my cellphone as soon as I pulled out of the lot. A recording picked up before the phone even rang once, instructing me to leave a name and address or phone number to which a questionnaire would be mailed or faxed to determine eligibility. Mailed or faxed? Hadn't these guys ever heard of email? I opted for fax so as to have some form of instant gratification, albeit about fifteen years out of date.

Since I hadn't yet learned the fax number at work, I had to track that down upon returning to the office. I wasn't even sure if we had a fax. I asked the office manager, who immediately laughed at me and asked if I needed help with the Internet. I told her I had a lead on a story and faxing was the only available contact method. After a few more barbs she relented and gave me the info I needed, promising to bring the fax to my cubicle when it arrived.

Forty minutes had passed since I had left the number on the recording, but there was still no sign of the office manager. I emailed her and tried her extension, both without any luck. Finally I went back to her end of the building to find four coworkers around her desk laughing.

"What's so funny?" I asked upon entering.

"We were following up on your lead," someone said. The comment spawned a deafening laugh track of obnoxious guffaws.

I didn't get the joke. "Did my fax arrive?"

More laughter.

"Yeah, it's here. Does your lady know about this?"

"We haven't been able to figure out if it's for a regular dating service or a mail order bride."

"What the hell are you guys talking about? It's a questionnaire for a psychology experiment." I grabbed the form off of the desk and stormed out of the room, leaving the peanut gallery behind.

Back at my cube I flipped through the thick stack of papers hoping to find a clue as to its purpose. At first perusal it offered no answers, only hundreds of questions on various topics. The front page happened to be the ones about romance. No wonder the busybodied lovemongers mistook it for a dating application.

Hair color of the first person you kissed. Hair color of the first person you remember kissing. Have you ever been married? Were you ever married in another life? Estimated length of longest relationship in days. Should it have been longer or shorter? Where did you first make love? etc, etc.

Each page of questions was prefaced with instructions that multiple answers were okay, and to mark a special box next to any question if you weren't absolutely certain of the answer. There was also a passage advising that this was a serious study and fatuous answers would not be appreciated. (Don't worry; I didn't know what fatuous meant either, but from the context I had an idea.)

After the romance portion were similar sections on family, friends, and self-awareness, followed by a psychological profile that seemed to summarize and revisit some of the previous categories. What was the coldest you've ever been? Who was your second best friend in college? What had the most positive impact on you in high school? How often do you talk to yourself? Do you feel that you're conscience is strong or weak? Have you ever personified your conscience? Have you ever had an out of body experience?

I answered the questions as best I could, but often had to mark the unsure box or all of the boxes when memories of my disparate lives overlapped. As I pondered some of the options, I seemed to remember always having multiple memories of incidents when I was younger, even before the blinking started. People always said I had an overactive imagination that never let the truth get in the way of a good story, but maybe they had it all wrong. Everything was truth to me, though some truths couldn't be validated by traditional means. For all I knew I could have been through this time altering cycle innumerable times before. I might have even been the one who wrote the questionnaire I'd just finished answering.

Part of me felt a sense of déjà vu that I was on a circular, Leonard Shelby type quest that repeated again and again, setting up clues for myself to find in each phase that would point back to another place (or time) and start the cycle anew. Another part of me agreed with those who said my imagination had trouble separating fact from fiction. The only thing I knew for sure was that there wasn't anywhere in my wildest dreams that I could have invented everything that had happened since the injection. It was all too real.

That evening I stayed with the cute redheaded girl at her place. At the conclusion of our nightly duet she decided it was time to have a talk.

"Are you planning on breaking up with me?"

"Of course not," I mumbled while awakening.

"Why were you in such a hurry to leave lunch today?"

"I told you, it was a deadline I had forgotten." My lies were starting to catch up with me.

"Then what's this about a dating service?"

How the hell had she already heard that gossip? There had to be a mole at my office. I couldn't trust anyone.

"That's research for a story. It's not what it seems like."

"Then what has been wrong with you lately? Are you on drugs?"

"Um, no." I hadn't so much as thought about smoking weed in my newest incarnation since checking the doghouse, and I wouldn't have been surprised if I never had in this lifetime. "But now that you mention it…"

Her eyes widened.

"Don't worry, I'm kidding."

"You're scaring me," she continued, sitting up and nervously pulling at the duvet in front of her. "You walk around like the world is new to you. You sleep far more than you used to. Your memory is terrible. And it seems like you're trying to keep me away from your mother for some reason. Now you deny shopping around, even though it's flying through the rumor mill at the paper."

Stuck for something to say, I blurted out the first words to come to mind. "Would you rather be sleeping with my mother?"

From her reaction, I'd guess the inappropriate comment didn't go over so well. She immediately pulled the covers up over my head in disgust.

"Of course not. I just can't figure out why you've changed so much."

"You've changed too."

"I've changed? I haven't changed."

"Oh, you've changed."

"This isn't about me right now. You're not the same anymore."

"So why do you blame me for it? What's so different?"

She thought for a second, clutching the comforter tighter and lifting it up between us in a latent show of our impending separation.

"You always used to speak so romantically of the time we first met, and you never do anymore."

That shouldn't be hard. I laid back down on my side and draped an arm over her. She tentatively accepted the gesture as I began my story. "I had just been recruited by this new music magazine…"

A look of confused horror came over her face as she moved my hand away. "What the hell are you talking about?"

"The night we met. We…"

"You never worked for a music magazine. You don't even like music."

"But I…"

"This is exactly what I mean." She sat up and clutched the covers again. "Lately you just make stuff up that you think is funny when it's really scary."

"But you said…"

She said, "You don't understand what I said!"

"I said no, no, no you're wrong."

"And that too! Quit it with the song lyrics! It's like you're speaking in tongues and I can't deal with it anymore."

She paused in a silence that was as much thoughtful as awkward, then finished. "I think we should spend some time apart."

"Let me get this straight: You want to break up with me because I'm a womanizing liar, I like music too much, we don't hang out with my Mom anymore, and you think I'm doing drugs?"

She answered in the affirmative without hesitation.

More unwise words from me. So much for my laying the blame on Nelson for this. I didn't have a chance to finish my thought internally before she finished hers aloud.

"I think you should leave now."

"Right now? It's the middle of the night."

"I'm sorry. Maybe I'll call you later. But please go."

I was somewhat shocked, but I didn't see any sense in arguing. Once that kind of decision is made you're only fooling yourself if you think it can be undone. *Unless you have the ability to go back and fix it.*

"You made your decision. Here's hoping it's the right one…"

I got out bed and found my pants, only finishing my sentence when I was nearly out the door and fairly sure she couldn't hear me.

"…this time."

19-2000

THE DAYS FOLLOWING THE BREAKUP were spent in that all too common haze of poorly hidden depression, second guessing, what ifs, anger, and booze. Lots and lots of booze, with a heaping helping of sour grapes on the side.

I had given up on the fabled attempts to win back exes years ago. When it's over, it's over. No point in putting in the effort after you've been dumped to show you've changed. You both know you haven't, and the second set will just be one of torture that prolongs the agony. It may have some good times, but the fissures are seldom overcome.

Maybe new me and her were a good match, but it was becoming clear that former me and her were not. Instead of dwelling, I wondered how different her relationship with other me had been, which led me to wondering what happened to other me when I blinked in. Was he just a placeholder awaiting my return? Did we meld into one person upon my arrival, causing the headaches and the scattered memory fragments that were more annoying than useful? Or maybe he was in the waiting room being analyzed by Ziggy while Gooshie and Al tried to find where I was lost in time? (I know, I did it again. Shame on me. I just can't help it sometimes.)

It was in the midst of one of these self-analytical dump days when I got the phone call. My preliminary questionnaire had been approved, but the doctors running the study wanted me to undergo three days of testing before being officially accepted into the program. They assured me it was just a routine physical exam followed by a few endurance and memory exercises. I told them I'd be ready anytime. They offered to send a car right away.

My editor was a bit of an unreasonable man from what I'd seen so far in this life, so I was glad to get his voicemail when calling in to let him know. I told him I was following a lead on a big story and would check in when I could. You usually have to call your boss in these situations, though I'd prefer to exclusively use email. It's just not accepted for some reason, especially if you're sick. Email looks like you're trying to get away with something by avoiding any chance of cross-examination. There's never a need to add fake coughs or a nasally voice to an email message.

I also called my Dad to let him know I may be close to fixing the trouble I'd caused. Left a message on his end as well, though it was on an old-fashioned analog answering machine rather than more modern voice-mail. As for Dad, I would have preferred to send him a text message, but he didn't have a cellphone and was confused by modern technology for the most part. He still favored cassette tapes over CDs.

A tan van came to pick me up. I hesitated before boarding. Something about it was familiar, but I couldn't quite put my finger on it at the time. In the end I made the mistake of writing it off as nothing more than ridiculous déjà vu.

The physical exam at the hospital wasn't anything out of the ordinary from what I could tell, though I hadn't been to the doctor in ages so I wasn't quite sure. Pee in a cup, pin prick, blood, blood pressure, eyes, ears, nose, throat, deep breath, deep breath, reflex kick, reflex kick, cough, squeeze, cough, walk this way, rubber glove, touch your toes, get dressed.

With that out of the way, I was led to a claustrophobic little cube of a room for the memory testing. Match the pictures under the squares, find the differences in two photos, memorize a list of words, and other fancy stuff that made me feel like a child. Though I was making a joke of it, I admit it was a bit tougher than it probably should have been. This body of mine had been marijuana free to the best of my knowledge, but I seemed to retain my old stoner brain.

I had a college professor who once told our class that marijuana was actually safer than alcohol as far as the brain went. Alcohol kills brain cells, and once a brain cell dies it ain't coming back. Weed, on the other hand, just coats the synapses that send the signals through your brain, making the connections a bit sluggish. Abstinence and heavy thinking are all it takes to knock the guck free and regain your sharpness. The concept sounded reasonable enough, although my inability to remember that professor's name seems to be a direct contradiction of his theory.

After memory testing came the infamous Rorschach inkblots. I was actually kind of excited for this, as I'd never tried this type of test and considered the premise to be rather neat. Really just a bunch of psychological/psychic interpretive bullshit, but still interesting.

Most of the inkblots seemed to portray dragonfly type insects, aliens, circles, or sex. Or maybe not sex, but I suppose anything can look dirty if you really want it to. All of the imagery was intentionally vague and debatable, as the questions asked during the test seemed designed to elicit a specific response.

What do you see? How does it make you feel? Did you see a type of animal, machine, or insect? Did you see anything sexual in it? Does the image seem to be ancient, contemporary, futuristic, don't know, or none of these? Did it make you think of life on other planets? Are they masculine or feminine? Hot or cold? Do they make you feel nostalgic? Were you aroused?

So far these seemed to be aimed at a time traveling repressed pervert, or maybe that's just me. But near the end of the process, the real question came.

"What does this one remind you of?"

The doctor flipped over the card and fixed his eyes on mine to gauge my reaction. Printed in black ink was a badly drawn version of the hospital logo that inspired the cover of *Local Boy Done Good*, minus the LBDG lettering.

Did they know? The logo practically advertised both the thievery and ability of my past. It all happened so fast I wasn't able to hide my perplexity, but I tried to talk my way out of it.

"I'm not sure. Looks like the emblem of a club or an organization. Maybe Lady Bird's Democratic Greatness?"

The doctor asked if I was sure, then smiled and dismissed me.

Next on the agenda was endurance testing. I was mentally spent from the inkblots, but they wanted to move on immediately. It started with doing as many pull-ups as possible until I couldn't go anymore. I was actually surprised at how well I did. Pushups were a different story, primarily because my arms were still tired from the pull-ups and I didn't have ample rest time. Sit-ups were just as bad. My stamina was fine, but the actual strength required was lacking. Even after weeks of recovery, my body was still out of shape from the lack of exertion during my displacement.

The above activities took the better part of the day, so I wondered what we needed the next two days for. When I asked the doctor he just smiled and turned away. I asked another doctor the same question. He said he wasn't allowed to reveal what was next, but he would advise me strongly to have something to eat or drink and take a nap if I'd like. It was about seven o'clock now. Testing was to resume at midnight. I was free to do whatever I wanted in the interim so long as I didn't leave the premises.

After eating I still had about four hours to kill. I tried to crash out on the exam table but it wasn't particularly conducive to sleep. I'd almost prefer a nice divan or a cot to the sterile, paper covered soft plastic. At the moment it didn't matter, as my unfamiliar surroundings ensured I wouldn't sleep even if they gave me a custom fitted waterbed with lots of fluffy pillows. The insomnia was starting to kick in, but this time it wasn't so much thoughts in my heads but images. One image in particular: LBDG.

What didn't quite fit was the absence of the logo at the hospital this time around. Aside from the thinly veiled version on the inkblot, I hadn't seen it anywhere else. My current scrubs were logoless, as were those worn by the doctors. The logo originally came from my alternate present, but my younger self also seemed to recognize it the night before the wedding, and that was before I should have ever encountered it. Dad's subsequent use of it for his album cover would now chronologically be its first appearance. Did he copy it from the hospital, or did the hospital copy it from him? Did the earlier appearance now proscribe the hospital from using it? Shouldn't negating the inspiration of the album cover make it cease to exist? And taking Dad out of the equation, what did the initials LBDG really mean? Which came first, the chicken or the egg? I ate the chicken, and then I ate his leg.

The smiling face of the doctor popped into my head, and I realized my error. The inkblot didn't have any letters, but my LBJ cover story told him everything he needed to know. He wasn't looking for what it was so much as what was missing. The inclusion of the logo (and the exclusion of the letters) among the inkblots wasn't a coincidence. This was the right place; the real deal that would hold the answer to my questions and possibly get me home. Maybe my slip-up wasn't a mistake after all.

Comforted with this glimmer of hope, I drifted off to sleep without realizing it and dreamt of the evil inkblot dragonflies smiling the doctor's toothy grin while circling the Local Boy album like vultures investigating fresh kills.

—⁓—

Although I didn't remember falling asleep, I definitely remember waking up at midnight to the anarchy of sirens, bells, whistles, and bass drums all at once. I fell from the exam table and ran around the small room in a disoriented stupor. Seeing my new self in the wall length mirror helped me to gather my bearings, and as soon as I was standing fully upright and away from the sleeping table the awful racket subsided.

The door was locked. I dealt it a couple of blows with my shoulder, but it wouldn't budge. Before paranoia could set in reason got the better of me and I figured out that this wakeup call was the start of the next test.

"What's going on?" I asked nobody in particular, presuming I'd be observed for every waking hour from this point forward.

After a few seconds of silence, I spoke again.

"Hello? Is anybody in there?"

More silence. Not even my own echo. And then the crackle of an intercom…

"Sleep deprivation. Forty-eight hours. Starting now."

Oh, excellent.

I laughed at the prospect of being watched for forty-eight continuous hours. Even just twenty-four hours stuck here again would be less than amusing. 24 as a reality show set in a single room with a camera in each corner. There's a real ratings juggernaut for you. I'd almost rather they follow me around outside on a documentary style adventure.

I've probably had around ten days or so where I stayed awake for a full twenty-four hours. Granted, lots of them would be boring slices of normal life followed by cramming for a college exam or trying to make a deadline for the magazine. Also a few nights of insomniatic tossing and turning, which is essentially what these doctors should be expecting out of me this evening.

On the far side of the room was a sink with cabinets above it and three drawers below it. I splashed some water on my face and found a cup in the cabinet to drink from. The drawers didn't have externally visible locks, yet only the bottom one would open. It contained just one item: A solitary deck of playing cards resting in a disorganized pile. At least I had some entertainment to help me rock around the clock.

Playing cards are one of the greatest entertainment inventions ever. Simple and complex at the same time, with so many possibilities out of just fifty-two pieces of laminated paper. Technically many of the games are just repeated variations on the same five themes: gambling, bidding, rummy, drinking, and solitaire. It's not really fun to play cards by yourself, but with a little creativity it's certainly possible. Since I was just killing time, I decided to run through every game I could think of. And since I presume you also have time to kill, I'll recount them all for you here.

Poker, Blackjack, Let it Ride (aka: Live Video Poker), Pai Gow, Baccarat, Caribbean Stud, Acey Deucey, Indian Feather (yes, I was that bored), Spades, Whist, Euchre, Pitch, Forty-Fives (all regular and honeymoon style), Rummy (Gin and Classic), Crazy Eights, Hearts (though short lived, as it gave me flashbacks to that day…), War (What is it good for? Nothing), Canasta, Egyptian Ratscrew (or Ratfuck, depending on whether you learned it from a parent or a friend), Golf, Old Maid, Go Fish, Cribbage (boardless), Spoons (spoonless), Pinochle, and Cassino.

Drinking games were out of the question. They all tend to be more about the drinking than the strategic enjoyment of playing them, plus there was the small problem of not actually having anything to drink. Unless one of the locked drawers concealed a mini-bar, I was out of luck. (I realize that a lack of money didn't stop me from trying my hand at the gambling games, but this was a different matter altogether.) A by the rulebook version of Asshole may have been worth trying, but it's so associated with getting blasted in my mind that I just couldn't allow myself to cheapen it. Besides, does anybody really know the "official" rules to Asshole? Does anybody really care?

A reprise of the whistles and bells snapped me out of the trance of the hearts and spades. Again I didn't remember dozing off, though I may have had a case of the head bobs. The doctors must have been playing it safe. It had only been five hours so far.

Of all the possible milestones of the wee hours, reaching 5 AM was always the hardest part of an all night thing for me. 3 AM and 4 AM aren't too much of a problem as you often see that side of evening after a night on the town, a poker game, or a late night club show. But as you cross the 4 AM threshold and approach 5 AM, you start to understand this is no man's land where normal people just aren't supposed to be awake.

When it's this late, solitaire's the only game in town. I had never really understand how old people can play this all day for hours on end until now. It must just be something to fight loneliness. Traditional solitaire really bores me now in a hundred different ways, but I had to keep my mind active just to stay awake. Of all the possible variations I like the simplicity of Aces, where the only object is to end up with all four aces left on the board. It's mindless enough to keep you occupied on an airplane and doesn't take up much space. It also plays fairly well against an opponent as a drinking game. Each person has a deck, and you play it out on your own as "Aces Races" until someone emerges victorious.

After Aces, I thought of the old fortune telling game my sister taught me. I don't know what it's called, but essentially it's a card based version of "she loves you, she loves you not" with a few interesting rules. The whole thing is a crock, but like solitaire, it's something to do.

Shuffle the cards while thinking of someone you're attracted to (for example, the cute little redheaded girl). Deal the cards into four equal piles. Starting with the first pile, flip each card face up until you reach either the King or Queen of Hearts or Spades. When you find one, put it back on top of the pile it came from, discard the previously flipped cards, and move on to the next stack. If you find the King or Queen there, put it back on top, put that pile on top of the first pile, and continue. After going through all four piles, redeal your remaining cards into three piles and repeat, this time ending with two piles. Do it all one last time to end with a single pile. Keep the remaining cards in order and fan them out like a poker hand. The distance between the Kings of Hearts and Spades represents your feelings for the person you were thinking of during the deal; the distance between the Queens of the same suits represents her feelings. The distance between the Hearts represents romance; the distance between the Spades represents geographic location. The fewer cards you're holding, the better your chances are. Any other cards in the middle represent potential problems for that aspect of your relationship. Any extra people (Jacks, Queens, Kings) represent that your other woman's got another man.

At least that's how you're supposed to play, but as soon as I finished dealing out the first sets of four I noticed something was wrong. I ended on the first pile rather than the last, which meant I either misdealt or had too many cards. Assuming I was delusional with the lack of sleep (it was now almost seven in the morning, and I had little more than a power nap before starting this exercise), I figured it was my error and decided to reshuffle and redeal. Same problem. I fanned out the cards looking for the joker I had likely left in by accident. Nope.

I found the extra card by sorting the deck into suits. There were two Kings of Hearts. I thought it was strange that I hadn't noticed this before, especially with the irony of it being the suicide king. Pinching the extra king between my index and middle fingers, I flipped it frisbee style towards the full-length mirror. It spun forward with pretty good speed, clanged off the shiny surface after colliding with itself, and fell to the floor landing face up. Amused, I practiced flipping the remaining cards towards the wall. In the midst of this I realized I was dealing one of the games I had forgotten about: Fifty-two Pickup.

One by one the cards ricocheted off the mirror and onto the floor. About half landed face up and half face down, probability doing the job it was entrusted with. My aim wasn't perfect, but if I had another day and a half to practice I could see myself developing some expertise. Reaching the bottom of the deck, I was down to my last card: the other King of Hearts. It was fitting enough that this would be both first and last. I wound up for a mighty heave and flung the card for the mirror. Perfect spiral, good altitude, reasonable velocity...

...and then it was gone. Passed right through the window as if it wasn't even there.

Energized, I ran towards the wall that the card had just vanished into. I was certain that I had blinked back in time off of some card playing memory, and I was getting out of there while I still could.

My body hit the wall at full speed. The mirror cracked, my face bled, and I was knocked down onto the cold linoleum below.

20ft Halo

Hours later, I awoke strapped to a chair in the same room as my first trip back to the alternate present. A bandage clung to my injured cheek. Electrodes were taped to my chest again, though this time they hadn't shaved my head and instead had wired just one electrode to each of my temples. Also new this time around were two IVs protruding from a bulky machine. A rush of blood was extracted from my left arm, spiraled through the tubing and into the machine, then exited out the other end, rejoining me via my right arm.

A familiar face stood before me: the doctor from the original hospital. As he finalized some settings on the machine, my mind raced to come up with an explanation for the logo and the album cover his cohort had shown me. The doctor noticed that I had awoken, but said nothing. He calmly checked my pulse and blood pressure, then flipped a switch on the machine and left.

I expected him to return with a syringe to give me the time travel injection at this point, but he didn't. Instead I listened to the hum of the strange machine as I watched my blood circle the loop de loop and speed back to me on the other side, like a rollercoaster running in perpetuity.

After a few moments that were probably really seconds, a green LED light started flashing strobe-like on the machine's control panel. At first I thought it was a warning light indicating a problem, then remembered that green is typically a good thing, so I quickly let that thought slide as I became entranced by its rhythmic pulsations. Mesmerized by the coded signals embedded in the emissions, I stared at the light until it consumed my vision and was the only thing that I saw. No longer a light on a machine, my eyes just saw green black green black green black green. Faster and faster the light flashed until it abruptly stopped, cutting me loose and leaving only the blackness. The ambient noises of the room and the machine had also stopped. Sound slowly returned before sight did.

Chirping birds.

A horn.

The quiet whoosh of passing cars.

Idling engines.

Footsteps.

Then the world started to fade in again. I wasn't in the room anymore. I was outside.

Someone was dragging me somewhere. No, not dragging me, but moving me. Almost like a conveyor belt or an airport people mover, but with a little more of the bounce associated with natural human motion. From my perspective I was moving myself and just walking, but I had no awareness of physically engaging my legs into the positions necessary for motion. Not that I normally have to think very hard about walking since it's an ingrained reflex, but usually I know when I'm making myself walk, and I clearly wasn't in control here. I concentrated all of my telekinetic energy on stopping, but still continued to travel at the same pace. Tried to turn my head to look at my feet but could not.

This was dreamlike. But it was more than a dream in some ways, as I was very aware. In this lucid state I walked down the street, stopping at crosswalks and waiting for white flashing hands like every good boy should. I still didn't know I was walking, and I also couldn't tell when I was stopping except for noticing that the flow of images to my vision would become static. Same with turning my head to look both ways before crossing. My eyes told me I was doing it, but I couldn't tell you whether I was going to look left, right, or straight at any given moment. Confused, I tried to lift my arm to rub my eyes but had no control over its mobility either.

Clearly I could use it, as I had a bottle of water in one hand and would take a sip from it every now and again. It was almost as if I was a passenger inside somebody else's body, or a character in someone else's song.

I continued walking down the street, seemingly without a care in the world. A girl walked by in a low cut top, and my eyes caught a fleeting glimpse as they moved on their own as she passed. The next intersection only had the regular red, yellow, and green traffic light rather than white and red hands for pedestrians. The light turned green, then blinked green. Green black green black green black green black green black green black green, shrinking in size as it increased in speed. The blinking got faster and faster and smaller and smaller until it wasn't a traffic light anymore, but instead the green LED of the hospital machine.

I was back in the chair. The doctor stood before me, leaning inches from my face.

"Tell me, what did you see? Did it work?" he asked, getting closer with each word. This was almost exactly the same as our first meeting, minus the syringe and the LBDG logo, both digitally erased from this remastered version. Was I the artist or the producer?

He repeated the question. "What did you see?"

"I was walking. Down a one way street."

The doctor backed off a bit to ponder my response. "Where was this street?"

I thought for a second. "I'm not sure."

"Why were you there?"

"Don't know. Maybe I was looking for someone to meet?"

The doctor furrowed his brow and gave a stern look. Apparently he wasn't a Huey Lewis fan.

"This is a breakthrough. You're the first that this has worked on. You have to take this seriously!"

Here was my opening. "Maybe I could take it more seriously if you told me exactly why I'm being held here."

"Memory research. The intent of the experiment is to send you into the memory storage portion of your brain via hypnotherapy to replay events from your past. A trip down memory lane, so to speak. So tell me, did it work?"

Just as he said this, a man walked through the window wall and into the room I was in. Not just any man, but me. The same old me from the bowling alley who started this with the injection. But how?

This old man was the spitting image of the one I had met before. Since that me didn't exist here anymore, shouldn't the new old me look more like the new young me than the old young me? Or should he even exist at all since I hadn't yet happened to lived that long?

Although I recognized him, he didn't seem to recognize me. He looked around the room, and was turning to leave when he noticed my shell-shocked stare. He cautiously pointed to himself and then at me. I nodded in agreement.

The doctor noticed the shift in my attention and gave a glance in the direction of other me. Seeing nothing, he turned back.

"What's wrong? Is someone there?"

Older me had walked over and cautiously touched me on the shoulder. Upon feeling that I was real to him, he spoke. "Just tell him what he wants to hear so we can be rid of him. We need to talk."

I complied and recounted my brief jaunt down the street to the doctor, trying unsuccessfully to avert my eyes from myself as I spoke. The best analogy I could use to describe the experience was that I was a stowaway inside my own head. He seemed to like that word and underlined it in his notes. Excitement filled his face. He couldn't seem to write the words on the page fast enough. My older self also became visibly animated by my tale.

After going over the full story twice and answering questions, I asked if I could have a breather. He agreed and brought me back to the hospital room where the sleep deprivation experiment was held. Old me followed.

The playing cards were still scattered around on the floor. Cleaning up didn't seem to be a priority after seeing me presumably lose it and go bouncing around the room. Old me saw the pile on the floor and tried to pick up a card unsuccessfully. He then stuck his head through the wall with the window, vanishing after seeing something he liked. He returned holding the extra King of Hearts in his right hand.

"You found the calling card I left for you," he said with a grin as he skillfully flipped the card towards me, hitting a bullseye on the center of my bandaged right cheek. "Did you know it was from me?"

I actually hadn't got the connection, but now I saw it clearly meant that a time traveler had been here. Had I thought it through I should have realized it was me, as only I should be able to interact with an object like that. Maybe Dad could too, but we hadn't tried.

"Yeah, I've been waiting for you to show up."

He didn't buy my lie. "You know when they say you can't fool yourself? They're right. What happened? You look like hell. I didn't even recognize you."

"I think I took things too far. Nothing is fixed, everything is worse, and I can't travel back to change it anymore."

"You can't travel back? Then what are you doing here now? You shouldn't find out about this place for another thirty years or so."

"You knew about this place?" I asked.

My elder counterpart took a deep breath. "This was the place I was trying to erase when I gave you the time travel injection. I was trying to keep you out of here, and away from him." He motioned towards the mirror.

"What is this place?"

"We'll get to that. I think you need to catch me up on what's happened to you, and why you look like someone else."

We sat on the floor of the examination room and had a full heart to heart regarding my misadventures. Since I've already recounted most of those details here I won't rehash them again, but I will mention his important observations and reactions.

Regarding blinking back in general: "It just takes practice and not trying so hard. I could have told you more, but I knew you'd get a kick out of figuring it out on your own. All that useless music trivia is good for something."

Regarding the girl in the tree house: "You were young and your heart was an open book. I turned the page."

Regarding giving myself the subliminal messages while napping on the couch: Smile, nod. "Doing it the old-fashioned way."

Regarding the botched date with the cute redheaded girl: "Selfish and sad. We'll get to her later."

Regarding the wedding objection: "That's why I needed you." (Nod, smile.)

Regarding my revelation at the Hearts tournament: "We'll get to that during my side of the story. I know it seems funny trying to understand, it's just that things don't always go the way you planned."

His biggest reaction of all came with the realization that Dad could see me and we could fully interact.

"What do you mean Dad could see you?"

"Dad could see me, just like I can see you."

"But if you met your dad…" he stopped, putting a hand on my head and looking me over again from head to toe. He immediately seemed to comprehend.

"I knew something was different when things started changing around me, but I was having trouble tracing what it was since I wasn't looking before our lifetime. You're extremely lucky to still exist at all. I have no idea how this happened. It's as if your old brain found its way into the body of the new offspring your parents created instead of you."

It was time for me to ask some questions of myself. "Why are you still the same old me as before, and not the new older version of me now?"

"I'm not really sure. It could be because I haven't been back to the present—my present—since I last met up with you. Generally speaking, you're protected from paradox while displaced in time."

Light dawned on me. "Hence the headaches."

"Hence the headaches. Your mind tries to catch up quickly, but also tries to suppress a lot of the memories as if they were part of a dream. Too much rattling around in your head at once."

"The redheaded girl?"

"She was my first wife. But I told you, we'll get into that later."

"Wife? But…"

"No buts. I'll explain it all in good time. I think the best starting point would be…"

"…this hospital place?" I said, once again finishing my own sentence.

"Exactly. Some of this will shock you, so please let me get through my whole narrative before interrupting. It's time I told you the whole truth from the beginning."

Now We Are Twenty-One

Years from now and years ago, my older counterpart had come to this hospital to participate in an experiment on memory, dreams, conscience, and superego. He underwent a barrage of testing similar to what I had experienced, upon completion of which he was paid up front for a monthlong study. He was to have no contact with the outside world, but he hardly gave it a thought since the money was good. The possibility that this exercise might turn into captivity never occurred to him.

He was hooked up to a sleeker, more compact version of the machine with the two IVs and suddenly found himself outside of the room and walking down a city street, just as I had experienced. He agreed that stowaway was the perfect word. Observing and along for the ride yet unable to drive, his body was a big free willed robot and he was in the passenger seat looking out the eyes as his window to the earth and sky.

Several of these trips down memory lane were made each day. At first they displayed random snippets from his personal history, but through gentle hypnotic persuasion the doctors could more specifically select his destinations. Via this method he revisited his birth, his first steps, and his first day of school as an internal observer. Though jarring at first, he came to enjoy living in these moments from such a unique perspective.

The prevailing theory at the hospital speculated that he was tapping into the memories stored inside his brain. Even though most people don't remember day-to-day events of their infancy and early childhood, the brain has everything locked away somewhere. Accessing that stored data was similar to playing a videotape or a DVD of a certain moment from the perspective of a specific camera. Figuring out how to rouse any memory in perfect detail and at will was the purpose of this particular study.

On one of these trips back, older me ended up in the tree house with the neighborhood girl. It was replaying just as it had originally. They used to laugh a lot, hanging out, smoking pot and talking. He had always had a crush on her but was too shy to do anything about it until nearly two months into this nightly ritual. While riding along in his head, he started reminiscing about the stoned make out sessions still to come. He wished he could re-experience one of those good times on a future trip. Then, almost on a whim, he thought to himself *Don't talk, just kiss her! Kiss her!* And right before his eyes, he did.

Or at least he tried. She pushed him away and ran off crying into the night. He didn't understand what had happened. It was the first instance where what he had seen had deviated from what he had known. The doctors were intrigued by this and tried to return him to the same memory again, but it wouldn't work. Since he still had total recall of numerous later occurrences with the same girl they tried to place him in a similar memory, but for some reason he couldn't get there either.

Having no shame, the doctors even went so far as to track down the girl in the name of science. She was quite offended by both the call and the gossip, and said she never wanted to hear the name of that liar again. They accused me of attempting to sabotage the study by substituting fantasies for memories, but he couldn't get back to those memories because they were no longer real. His confusion allowed them to entertain the possibility that this experiment was bigger than they originally thought. If altering a memory also altered the experience, maybe it was more than just a memory.

It was time for a new hypothesis. The experiment was extended another month, older me was given the benefit of the doubt, and the next several rounds of memory trips focused on attempts to recreate a similar change. It didn't take long for him to accomplish that, but gaining acceptance was another story.

Driving to his old part time job after school. He had never missed a day of work and was always punctual, but today he convinced himself that he was craving a Town Spa pizza and watched as the driver veered off course to pick one up, causing him to be thirty minutes late. Upon arriving he was promptly fired by the new manager. But the way he remembered it, he'd kept that job on and off for years, right through college.

Final game of the little league season. Extra innings. Bases loaded, down by two runs, full count. He vividly remembered the shame and embarrassment of striking out looking on a perfect meatball straight down the middle. *Swing, dammit, swing!* Game winning triple off the top of the chain link fence in right field.

Oasis concert at a small club in Providence near the start of the *Morning Glory* tour. A triumphant show that lasted over two hours and kicked off the buzz that arguably allowed the band to equal their stadium rock status from across the pond. *Noel is a wanker* said the voice in his head. He took off his shoe and threw it on stage, striking Noel's guitar just a handful of songs into the performance and pissing him off enough to cut the set short.

The doctors would try to verify each of these events. All records and memories of interviewed witnesses would show that things happened the way they played out the second time, not the way older me had remembered them. Or at least not one of the ways he remembered. He still remembered both versions of each and every instance.

But at the same time, he didn't remember everything. The aftermath of his changes never caught up to him. He could remember both the triple and the strikeout, but didn't remember that the team then cruised through the playoffs and won the championship. He remembered being fired, but couldn't remember his subsequent job search or next employer. He remembered throwing the shoe, but not the scuffle he got into with other fans on the way out of the club.

"That was me," I interrupted. "The triple and the firing and the shoe, they all happened to me. I don't remember the alternatives."

"It may have been you they happened to, but they happened because of me. We didn't realize it at the time, but I was shaping your life by altering mine."

"But what about the girl. Why do I remember both sides of that one?"

He didn't have an answer. The only new memories he had were the ones he experienced firsthand. Everything else was a hazy dream that he couldn't quite put his finger on. Most of the doctors thought it was nothing more than a dream he kept having that didn't seem to mean anything. But one doctor sensed they were breaking new ground and pushed to keep things on track.

A newer, less popular theory at the hospital postulated that these trips were not being made into the memory, but actually through time using the subconscious of the mind as a conduit. The little voice inside your head that advises you in times of need—traditionally referred to as your conscience—was really a telepathic message from your future self. This SOS alternates in a continuous cycle of call and response. You always ask yourself for help at the same point and always receive the same answer, thus never really altering the flow of time. Each performance uses the same setlist and stage banter, and your past and future incarnations always chime in with the same requests and the same heckles.

Sending subjects back within their minds was accomplished by stowing away on these brainwave transmissions. Riding the waves allowed one to visualize this common cranial action. Actually changing events came when the stowaway was able to break on through and take over as the conscience by sending a similar brainwave pattern at a stronger frequency, overpowering the incumbent message. A personal radio transmitter of sorts, knocking out the real 89.9 and instead playing its own signal from a pirate radio station.

The most thought-provoking facet of this theory was in how it made sense of a lot of the unexplainable, extending from conscience to include paranormal phenomena such as psychic ability and déjà vu. You sensed that something was about to happen since it already had. But it was still just a theory, and thus needed additional testing to find results that were both concrete and repeatable. Intrigued, older me signed on for another round.

This process of altering little pieces of his (or actually, my) life went on for years. In search of substantiation, the experiment was expanded and now had a dozen subjects being sent back in pairs to keep track of each other. Even with all of the extra help, older me was still the prized pupil. Some travelers could transmit minor persuasions to themselves, giving the scientists enough anecdotal evidence to continue. But old me was the only one with the unique (and dangerous) ability to make calculated changes to events of the past. He was also the healthiest of the group, with no known side effects to his travels. Other subjects often ended up comatose or worse, but the only thing I knew how to do was to keep on keepin' on.

He made sure to use this to his advantage. The doctors kept sending him on trips as they sought confirmation that what appeared to be happening was real, making sure to closely monitor his bodily functions and brainwave patterns at all times. Older me would make his trips and do what they wanted him to do, but he would also make secret side trips on his own after discovering as I had that he could transport himself into any memory without having to return to the present between trips. So he'd go back and persuade himself to graffiti a wall or bury a silver dollar under the corner of a building to be retrieved in the future, then blink off the grid for a more altruistic mission.

Although it would have been easier to manipulate his own life, the other me didn't know how long he could keep up these side travels without tipping his hand. He decided that his first mission would be to help improve the life of his sister. This would be more of a challenge for him, a chess game to maneuver our past self in subtle enough ways to enable change without making it obvious.

His sister had lived a fine enough life without his adjustments. Principal of a prestigious private high school, she cared deeply for the children who were under her charge and served as an inspiration to thousands. It was the best thirty years of her life. But something was missing. She never found that special someone to share it all with. Never got to fall in love. That's what he wanted to change. To make her life that much better. To give her that idealized missing puzzle piece behind the couch to make her sky complete.

He didn't really have strict criteria to go by, simply wanting a nice guy who would take care of her. Oddly enough, his working theory at the time was the complete opposite of my manifesto against "settling down." He felt that any person could fall in love with any other person given the right circumstances. His job was to enable those circumstances. Correct to a degree, but for a lot of the wrong reasons as I've indicated previously.

For months he used his side trips to observe potential candidates. He didn't want to set her up with one of his friends, so he focused on acquaintances and others separated by a few degrees. The rotating cast of characters that would play cards at my sister's apartment rotated for a reason, as older me would find himself in my head encouraging me to invite new players on a whim. The more my circle expanded, the more likely he was to find the connection that would lead to a suitable match. Eventually he settled on Nelson, a fairly successful guy who seemed nice enough, didn't date a lot, and was very polite to everyone he met. On the surface he appeared to be a man my sister could thrive with, making both of them so much better just for knowing each other.

The next part of the plan was to save our sister some pain by steering her away from beaus who would break her heart. After that, he slowly allowed her to hang out with some of his friends here and there, filling her free time and keeping her on their radar. Finally came the Hearts tournament where he was able to forge her first meeting with Nelson innocently enough, although he had to forego my fling with the roommate to facilitate this. He figured it was a small price to pay. All that was left was to maneuver me into making a few cryptic mentions to friends later on to help kindle the courtship along.

He discovered the wedding announcement on a later memory trip and was proud of himself for a job well done, completely oblivious to the horror that had followed since it wasn't actually a part of his own memory. He saw no need to follow up further, as this was all new to him and he didn't fully understand the dangers of futzing around in time. Instead he basked in the afterglow of his good deed and decided that next he would do the same for himself.

My anxiety caused me to interrupt again around this point.

"So you're saying that I caused all of this?"

"Not so much you. I caused this," he said with a frown. "We'll get to you. Let me finish."

On his next set of trips he worked to clean up his own love life. The redheaded girl was his first wife, but it ended in an ugly divorce that left him penniless and indirectly forced him to sell his body to this experiment. But since she was a sexual dynamo, he saw no point in losing her memory completely. He wanted to keep the fling alive, but accelerate it into a series of booty calls rather than a full on relationship. So he went back to that day at the bar and turned it on strong. Too strong, and she was gone.

I wondered why eliminating their relationship wouldn't eliminate his joining the time travel experiment, but decided it was a stupid question and held my tongue. Instead I hurried him along.

"I know this part. I was there. I saw you."

"You saw me?" he asked in confusion. "You couldn't have been there. We can't go to the same time twice."

"Well, we did. I didn't realize it was you at the time, but now I'm sure it was. In the bathroom and then outside. You wouldn't cooperate because you thought I was one of them. We hadn't met yet. Or at least you hadn't met me."

Thinking back, his babbling from outside the bar made more sense now. *"I refuse to undo what I've already done."*

This revelation was of great interest to him.

"I guess that means," he started, "that travel in the head and in full body must be different enough to allow some overlap to occur."

"You really don't remember meeting me?"

"I wouldn't, since you weren't there when I was there. But now there should be another version of us out there that will remember his meeting with you. I'd go back and check, but your being there…"

"Blocks you from being there. I know."

He smiled. "You're learning. Now, let me finish."

Comfortable with the lack of obvious side effects, the head doctor had become a subject in the experiment and now fully believed in what was happening. The new goal of the project was to allow an individual to take complete control over their past body. Not just timely persuasions as they had come to be called, but full conscious control of all functions and surroundings. Essentially the same idea as Project Quantum Leap, which always intended for Sam to occupy the body of his younger self until the experiment went "a little ca-ca."

"This real version went a little ca-ca as well," said older me. "They never could find a way to get full control of the body, at least not how they intended."

"But when I saw you, you were in full control of the body. It wasn't just persuasion. You were piss drunk and fully aware of your actions. You kept babbling on about refusing to undo what you had already done."

He pondered this a moment. "Must have been the alcohol. Body goes on autopilot, not expecting to have a designated driver ready to take over. I never thought of it before, but most of my successful persuasions always involved a slightly altered mind in some form or another. So theoretically a full fledged bender could allow for full control." He smiled a wide, thoughtful grin. "Never thought our misspent youth would pay off so well, eh?"

After the incident at the dive bar he tried to revisit other past relationships, but never found the harmonious balance needed to get it right. He'd either move too fast or too slow, ending each one in disaster. Some old relationships he couldn't get back to at all. At first this seemed odd, but he theorized that losing some girls from his life had a domino effect that eliminated others. To make matters worse, since whatever was learned in each relationship was now erased, each subsequent girlfriend was essentially the first. Since we all know it's one in a million that your first real girlfriend is your last, my love life was left in shambles and older me was none the wiser. He actually thought he was helping me.

"At least now I know why my love life has always sucked. It actually hasn't, just my version of it."

He ignored my outburst, turning to a more somber memory.

"I slipped away during some family vacation memory the doctors had sent me to, trying instead to head off a particularly messy date where I didn't realize it was the girl's birthday. I tried to blink into an end of summer family barbecue as my starting point, but instead of the goofy fun I remembered I found myself in the middle of a more serious gathering. It was a wake. Her wake."

He didn't need to clarify his pronoun.

"At first I didn't realize what the problem was. I knew my changes had to have played a part, but had no idea which change could end like this. Then I noticed the way everyone was avoiding eye contact with Nelson, and it suddenly hit me how grave of a mistake I had made."

A heavy silence filled the room. I had nothing to contribute, so I gave him time to let the moment pass before resuming his tale.

Shortly thereafter, the experiment had an accidental breakthrough that took time travel to the next level. A mixture of drugs, electricity, and self-replicating nanotechnology allowed for a microscopic time machine to be injected directly into the bloodstream of a subject. With the machine in the man rather than the man attached to the machine they were able to internally amplify the right brainwaves and theoretically take control of the body in the past.

This time, the theory was almost right.

Instead, they had stumbled upon the type of time travel that I had been experiencing all along. Invisible to any person, place or thing except for myself, yet able to fully interact with only a past image of me. They had control of the body, but only through brute force.

The sponsoring doctor became the first guinea pig for this new method, and it worked marvelously. He was only sent back a few days, but his reports as to what he saw and how he met with his past self astounded those involved. Initially he was met with the same doubt that older me had, but when he started recounting conversations he was never present for after eavesdropping on them in the past as a ghostly observer he quickly won over his critics.

Self-interaction both intrigued and terrified the doctor. Upon discovering this side effect of time travel he became obsessed with it, seeking in vain to understand and ultimately suppress that ability. The Catch-22 was that studying self-interaction required self-interaction, and the only person who could track the results was the person being studied. Concerned that others would want to expand this interaction trait to work universally, he adopted this subset of the experiment for himself, while the other scientists continued to fine-tune the injection serum to see how far they could push it.

The process was tweaked and enhanced on other subjects until eventually they had another breakthrough. Instead of being limited to their own experiences, a time traveler could now go to any time where humans had memories, riding on a huge subconscious peer to peer neural network of brainwaves carrying messages from the future to the past. The more people with memories, the easier it would be to get to that time. And more people with the same memory gave more pathways to more times. The overlap was the key. This left the window of opportunity at roughly the age of the oldest living person in the traveler's true present time.

Although the traveler was still only able to interact with their own past selves, they could go anywhere as an observer. The plan was to use this discovery to study history, creating more accurate accounts of events by having multiple firsthand witnesses on site to record what went on in an unbiased manner. But first they needed to test it, and for this they needed older me.

The needle pierced his skin, and a new age began. Having lost the ability to travel in his own head, the new and improved time travel injection method gave older me less flexibility to put right what once went wrong. The stowaway style trips were much better suited to his agenda. He had to find a way around this, as well as a way out of the hospital to have more freedom to set things right. The old, IV based machine had been retired, so that was out. Realizing that he no longer needed (or at this point, wanted) to be on site to blink, he hatched his theory on using a cause and effect pair to give his younger self the ability to time travel, thus springing himself from the hospital.

Knowing the doctor would try to find him, he realized that his younger self would be better equipped to save his sister from Nelson than he was, especially if he could get in touch with a self who was still reeling from her death and open to the possibility of revenge. That was what led him to me. He stole a syringe, blinked, and never looked back.

"You've been traveling in time non-stop since then?"

"I wouldn't say non-stop, but I've only been back to the present once if that's what you mean. What's there to go back to? This place? I'll take my chances as a man out of time."

In a lot of ways I agreed with his plight. I had been afraid to go back to the present after ending up in that hospital, and my fear turned out to be correct. But something confused me. "I moved away after my sister died. Shouldn't that have been enough to get you away from the study?"

He shook his head. "I thought of that. You didn't leave the first time; I talked you into going west for that exact reason. But I came back and I was still here. I've been afraid to try again since."

"What does that mean?"

"I guess it means they would have found you one way or another. And since you're here now, that appears to be true."

I returned to my earlier question.

"I still can't believe we caused all of this."

Older me put a hand on my shoulder to console me. "It's not your fault. My sister lived, but I inadvertently killed your sister. You can't save her, but you can set it right so the next versions of ourselves and our families can avoid the same pain."

"You're just fiddling with the words to make me feel better. Is there really a difference?"

"On a broader level there is, but you can view it however you'd like."

"In that case, won't everything just undo itself when I don't go into my younger head to set her up with Nelson?"

"Unfortunately it doesn't work that way," he said straight faced while I cried, killing my last ray of hope. "Once a head trip is made it becomes a brain pattern. You're essentially becoming your conscience, and with or without you the same message and actions will live on. It's only full body time travel that needs to be redone each time to ensure proper flow. Or at least it seems to be, it's all..."

"I know. Theory."

Regardless of his attempts to sugarcoat it with semantics, the simple truth was there. All the times I felt like I was to blame for my sister's death, I was technically correct. Me, myself and I: partners in crime. And I could have fixed it all, but instead I made it worse. She was still alive, but she was he, and he was with him. It was all a big mess that would continue to repeat for generation upon generation of other mes. The revelation had already left me dejected, and as the pronouns kept on circling I started to feel sick.

There had to be a way to fix this thing.

22 Days

Fixing this thing would require a minimum of three events, all easier said than done.

- I needed to get out of the hospital.
- I needed to time travel again.
- I needed to change my sister and myself back to my sister and myself.

In my mind, the best way to accomplish all of the above would be for older me to go back and stop me from getting to Dad. Three birds with one stone as they say.

"You're not thinking fourth dimensionally," he said after I outlined my plan. "I can't go back to stop you because you've already been there. I thought you understood this part. Only one trip, remember? You were there for so long the window is essentially closed for me."

"You could go back to before I even got there and warn Dad not to believe me when I show up," I argued back.

"Think about it. Even if I could convince him to ignore you, you'd just jump back even further to make it work. And if you landed on a date I had already been to, you'd negate my trip."

"Won't I be blocked from going anywhere you've already been?"

He glared at me with a look that evoked a professor who catches a student not paying attention in class. "If you make a trip at a younger age than I was when I made it, then I never made it because you just prevented yourself from making it when you grow up to become me. It's not the actual order we make the trips in, but the order relative to our ages."

"But if this version of me never made the trip, then I never did visit Dad. But if he didn't visit Dad, I'd still be me. One event causes the other. We're in a paradox, aren't we?"

Older me looked uneasy as he answered. "I don't know. Theoretically we should be, but also theoretically if this were a paradox we should cease to exist."

"You say correlation is not causation?"

"Perhaps," he said, still lost in his thoughts. "Unless it means that we still will visit your father. Or at least that we still can."

"If I can't do it since I'm trapped here, and you can't do it since I already have, where does that leave us? It should already be over. There's something happening here."

He shook his head. "You're right. But what it is ain't exactly clear. As soon as you returned to your present that should have been the end of everything, but I'm protected from paradox since I haven't been back to my present. And since I'm you, maybe we're both safe."

At least that was a relief. Changing gears, I had another idea. "What if you gave me a booster shot? Then I'd be able to blink back to Dad and prevent this place from happening."

The look from older me was now solemn. "I don't have the syringe with me," he said with neither smile nor nod.

"What happened to it?"

"I used it on you."

"But you showed it to me after…"

Again he was becoming impatient. "Afterwards for you, but before for me. It's gone."

This new theory of relativity was getting complicated, not to mention confusing.

"So why don't you go back and get another one, and then meet me here tomorrow for my shot?"

Professor look again. "If I go back to my present, I'll become future you, meaning future you who can't travel in time. Not to mention the fact that I'd likely unlock the paradox you've already caused with your father."

"But you said you haven't been back, so you don't have to go all the way. Can't you think of a time when you still had it, then meet me here?"

He would have hit me with a ruler if he had one.

"It doesn't work that way. It's gone. Accept it and move on."

Although the time travel rules and theories still confused me, I was able to stop grasping at straws and understand his plan. And I didn't like it one bit.

"You want me to just wait it out, hoping I have a chance to steal a syringe like you did? They don't even have that kind of syringe yet."

Nod, but no smile.

"Are you even serious?"

The door suddenly opened. It was the head doctor.

"Who are you talking to?"

Older me shook his head in warning. I didn't know what he was so worried about, as I could answer truthfully without attracting suspicion. "I'm just talking to myself again."

He didn't buy it. "I know what's going on, and I know that this experiment is going to be successful with or without your help. With your help will be better for both of us. Are you going to cooperate or not?"

My first instinct was to assume he was bluffing.

"Tell me what's going on and I'll tell you if I'll help."

The doctor took a long look at me with pursed lips. It seemed he couldn't quite get a read on me, but eventually decided there was nothing left to lose since I was his captive.

"I believe you when you say you were talking to yourself. My primary interest is in which self you were talking to, and how that came to pass."

Older me gave a confused shrug while the doctor waited for a response from me. Getting none, he continued.

"A thoughtful man may have an internal debate with himself inside his own head. An angry man may speak to himself aloud out of frustration. A crazy man may speak to himself aloud for attention. But you were talking differently. You were having a normal, logical discussion. Don't try to hide it, I could tell. Why do you think I let the conversation go on for so long?"

I supposed he was smarter than he looked. But he still hadn't explained what he wanted.

"I'm not quite understanding how I can be helpful," I said, trying not to look at my other self. A plan had come to me that he wouldn't approve of, and I couldn't risk his presence being uncovered or his altruism knocking me off track. With one hand in my pocket, I groped to verify the contents. Wallet, keys, phone. Good thing this wasn't airport security.

"What were you talking about? How can we make it happen?"

"I'll confess," I said, trying to sound as remorseful as possible.

"Excellent. I'm listening."

"You caught me trying to plan my escape. I called my brother-in-law on my cellphone. His name is Nelson, and he is going to try to break me out tomorrow."

Nelson wasn't actually my brother-in-law anymore, but that wasn't really important now. The doctor was taken off guard by both my answer and the incompetence of his staff. "They let you keep your phone?"

Luckily enough they had. Nobody bothered to search me. That was remedied quickly, as the doctor snapped his fingers to summon his henchmen. They confiscated everything I had, giving me a rather rough pat down for good measure. Convinced I didn't have anything else on me, each one grabbed an arm and awaited further orders.

"Take him back to the room, and send someone to pick up this Nelson character. Between the two of them we'll get our answers."

—⁂—

Confined again, I pondered what had just happened. This newest strategy had fallen into my lap, as the overheard conversation probably couldn't have gone better if I had planned it. I wasn't sure if I could get Nelson to take the full blame, but I was sure he'd get his fair share when they tried to force information out of him.

The next question on my mind involved the doctor's description of how I was talking to myself. It certainly sounded like somebody who was wise to what was going on and not just starting to uncover the secrets of time travel. Was I overthinking this since I really wanted to believe that he could get me out of here? Older me had said this was the place that made him a slave to their studies, but he also said it wasn't supposed to have started yet. Did I do something to start it early? And if I had, was it evolving fast enough for the result I so urgently needed?

After a couple of hours the door opened and the two thugs pushed Nelson into the room. It was the moment I'd been both waiting for and dreading for much of my adult life. I had often wondered what I would do if I were ever alone in a room with him. The guy who killed my sister. Who tore my family apart. Who ended lifelong friendships. Who figuratively smothered my sister to death, and was now doing the same to my brother. Who didn't even have a clue as to the pain he had already caused, and was so oblivious he owed no allegiance to the facts of the situation.

"Why don't you like me?" he had asked me once upon a time.

Interesting question. Let me count the ways.

Hate is a strange emotion. The polar opposite of love. Or is it the same emotion with a different weight? Equally difficult to define, yet far more widespread. It's probably the only emotion that everyone experiences. Not everyone finds true love, but we all find an archrival to despise. Why? Maybe because it's so often one way and without reason. Unlike love, you never really hear of someone having unrequited hate for another. Just the act of letting someone know you hate them makes them hate you back. That's quite different than love, where the act of professing love or even like for someone more often than not leaves you feeling shunned and falsified if the feeling isn't mutual. The pain of rejection may even turn the emotional tides from end to end, causing love to morph into hate, confusion, or suffering.

Love is a mystery, sometimes better off as a secret. Hatred is the other way around. You'll tell anyone who will listen about your enemies, but it's only your closest confidants who know the identity of your current crush.

People love to hate, and sometimes get so caught up in hatred that they can't even pinpoint the cause of it. Not so much hate at first sight, but certainly hate at first conversation. A person who just rubs you the wrong way. Who spews negativity all the livelong day. Who picks fights just for the sake of it, thinking they're a Mr. Knowitall but not really knowing enough to formulate an intelligent argument.

We all know the type of person we hate. The schoolyard bully. The strict teacher. The mid-level manager with a top-level ego. The clueless CEO who can't take constructive criticism. The next lover taken by your ex. The guy who drives your sister to suicide by putting a metaphorical full nelson on her.

I always felt a certain sense of pride in myself for giving people second chances and not heavily weighing first impressions, but it was tough with Nelson. As I said before he's not necessarily a bad guy, but he certainly wasn't a good guy. He was just sort of there, taking up space in a world full of heroes and villains. Try as I might, I could not remember one redeeming thing Nelson had ever done for anyone, nor could I recall anything particularly terrible aside from the one event that his personality helped to fuel. That was bad enough for me. Hate can be just as irrational as love in some cases. It's always contrived and delusional to a degree. But when the moment of opportunity presented itself in the here and now, I couldn't do much more than have those thoughts and glare at him red-faced.

"What are *you* doing here?" spat Nelson upon entering the room.

I knew we were being watched, so I tried my very best to keep my emotions in check as I turned to my nemesis and set my vengeance into motion.

"Me? You know damn well what I'm doing here. You sent me undercover to steal a syringe for you."

"Syringe? What are you talking about?" He looked scared, and I loved it.

"They heard me on the phone with you planning my escape. I confessed and told them where to find you. If you don't tell them what they want to know they'll kill you. They might kill us both."

Nelson started to cry. "I don't know anything. I don't want to die. I don't deserve this."

"Neither did she!" I roared back.

The doctor had heard enough. His thugs returned to collect Nelson, who continued to rant and rave and scream and cry as they dragged him away. A success of sorts for me I suppose, but did it really matter? This wasn't the same Nelson I hated. Well, it was, but many of the reasons were now moot. The victory would be pyrrhic at best, and essentially (not to mention hopefully) undone presuming we could get this situation resolved. Part of me felt almost guilty for helping to inflict whatever was about to be inflicted on him. Then again, the other part of me was overjoyed. Revenge is sweet, and so are you.

Before I could finish analyzing my feelings the doctor entered to talk to me.

"I took care of your problem. Now will you help me with mine?" he asked.

"I still have no idea what you are talking about."

"Look, you wanted us to pick up that guy, and we did. You never called him though. Cellular phones don't work in this building."

Damn. He definitely wasn't as dumb as he looked.

The doctor continued. "As I told you before, you don't act like a crazy man. Based on observing you in that room and your scores on our tests, I have reason to believe that you are the one we've been looking for. The one *I've* been looking for."

Gracious as I was for his help with Nelson, I still refused to give in. "Once again, I have no idea…"

A chair screeched as the doctor dragged it across the room in aggravation. He paused for a moment, then regained his composure and thoughtfully sat down. "I know you will be a time traveler in the future. I know this because I share the same fate."

He went on to describe the origins of the time travel project to me as best he could. His older self had come back to him much in the same way I had visited my younger selves. After a similarly awkward start, he convinced himself to rent space at this hospital and start a study. He told him what ads to run, what tests to administer, and what to generally look for in subjects. Everything except for what made time travel possible.

"Is he here now? Can I meet him?" I asked quietly.

"He hasn't been around for a while. But even if he was, you wouldn't know. Only I could see him. But you already know that, don't you?"

"Why wouldn't he tell you everything?" I asked, ignoring the question. "I mean, why start early if you're not going to *start* early?"

The older doctor was very worried about paradox, especially cause and effect. He wasn't willing to take the same risks that my older self did in creating new cause and effect pairs. He knew that telling himself outright how to create time travel would run the possibility of a paradoxical loop where time travel is created because time travel is created. That defied his logic, and thus was an unacceptable risk.

Instead he encouraged himself to get an earlier start, making an appearance to use his past self as an insurance policy against future travelers in the study manipulating the past for their own benefit. He gave himself a list of names to monitor the activities of, plus general quirks to look for in personalities. The key indicators included a certain knowledge of future events and constant conversation with ones self. Seems the best defense against self-interaction was self-interaction.

He taught himself to look for the signs, and if anyone matched the profile he should detain them and study them. Studying them would ensure the future discovery of time travel, while detaining them would ensure that any changes they may later invoke could be corrected or avoided in the future.

"Theoretically," I chimed in.

"Yes, of course it's theoretical. But adhering strictly to the theory is the only way to ensure survival."

"What do you want from me?"

"He needs to know what your other self had you change so we can make sure to fix it when fixing becomes possible. I need you to use your future self's knowledge to make the machine work for me."

Naïve, but still fascinating. I had to admit that their system did impress me to a degree. They had thought about almost everything, and in their shoes I likely would have done the same. You need a system of checks and balances to ensure success, especially when dealing with something as complicated and dangerous as time travel.

But thinking of "almost" everything wasn't good enough. I was pretty sure the doctor was missing two crucial pieces. He suspected that I would become a time traveler, but he had no idea that I had already been one. I mean, how could he? If I still had the power he might have been able to figure it out from some history and maybe some blood work, but that was a different me altogether. The signs wouldn't be here.

Second, I was fairly certain his older self had no idea about the father clause. If he did he would have set up shop another full generation in advance just to check in on all the possible changes. The entire system was based on the assumption that you could only interact with yourself, thus greatly narrowing down the margin of error. I didn't know for sure, but it wouldn't be too far outside the realm of possibility that I would be able to interact with my grandfather, great grandfather, and so on down the line of my fragile family tree.

Although he hadn't expected the study to have started yet, older me must have had some knowledge of the preventative measures. That's why he needed to inject me. He needed me to do the dirty work since I wouldn't really be a suspect. They would be looking at my actions, but my time traveling wouldn't be what they were looking for since the ability wasn't supposed to be discovered yet.

Or maybe not. If I could only interact with myself they would still monitor younger me. They'd expect oldest me to contact him, but having real, middle me contact him would still raise an alarm. That could explain my first trip back to this hospital. Younger me had been discovered much like I had been now. The flyer on my car was the bait, and I fell right into the trap. I was more goldfish than guinea pig.

I decided my best bet was to continue to play dumb until I could earn another chance at blinking back. But before I could do that, I had to make sure to keep the new Nelson from repeating history.

—∞—

After giving things a day to cool down, the experimentation started up again. They wouldn't hook me up to the prototype time machine, but I did have a few more heart to hearts with the doctor. He'd alternate between being my best friend and my worst nightmare. Neither approach got him what he wanted, as I stuck to my strategy of ignorance. I'm not even sure he really knew what it was he was after. He just wanted to get there faster.

From my perspective he wanted two things. The first was exactly as he had explained it to me. He was being a good past self, respecting his elders and following orders from his older and wiser counterpart. But his other agenda was to figure out how time travel worked. He knew he would create it, but wanted it done immediately so he could become that other self. To be the one with the power to delegate the grunt work on the maintenance side of things to his younger self while he basked in the glory of creation, praise, and notoriety. Like any aspiring middle manager, he always did his job while simultaneously looking for a way to show up his boss. A little more complicated than that since the mentor and the trainee were the same, and the apprentice already knew he'd become the boss one day. Meet the new boss, same as the old boss. Regardless, I was pretty sure that could be used against him. My only fear was that it was all an act, and that the doctor's future self would see right through it if he returned at an inopportune time. I wanted to talk through this plan with my own older counterpart, but he had been keeping a low profile since Nelson arrived.

One sleepless night I thought of the cute little redheaded girl. Something told me she had a larger role in this than older me was revealing. He said she would be my first wife. That implied that I would have a second wife also, if not more. How'd this come to have to pass? The relationship with her that I remembered was essentially just sex. The one I witnessed ended immediately due to interference from my older self. The version I lived (albeit briefly) in this new life seemed more related to my relationship with my mother. Or more accurately her relationship with my mother. Which is probably why I nearly lost her. (Ok, I really lost her. But I couldn't resist the lyrical allusion.) Of course, my continued deceit was also a contributing factor. If you happen to get another chance, balance is necessary.

Back to the question, how did we end up married? And would we still end up married if I could take the same path again, or is who you end up with just a game of random chance? Does foreknowledge prevent events from occurring? Will knowing that the marriage once failed make me try harder, or not try at all? Knowing I'm supposed to have two wives may prevent me from having any at all. Just like the doctor, who by knowing he'll invent time travel may never fulfill his dream. That was what drove him to succeed, and it was also what had driven him to the brink of madness as I had witnessed here.

I wished that we could start all over, or that the time machine nano-technology potion had an antidote. Something that could put it all back how it once was. A reset button to invoke when events escape your control. Don't like the results? Just give it another whirl. That would be the true scientific breakthrough: an extra life like in a video game. Revelity: the reincarnation drug that works wonders.

The next morning I awoke to my body being violently shaken. This was new. Normally they used the buzzers and sirens from the sleep deprivation portion of the program. I sat up and rubbed my eyes to discover that I was actually trying to wake myself. Older me had returned.

"Where you been?"

He shushed me, motioning towards the two-way mirror. I rolled away from the window, pretending I had been woken by a bad dream and was going back to sleep. Then, very softly, I spoke.

"They're onto us even more than you know."

My aged doppelganger knelt at the opposite side of the examination table while I feigned sleep and continued speaking in a quiet whisper.

"The head of the project is a time traveler. I mean he will be. That's why it's starting earlier. He's been visited by his older counterpart, probably the one you told me about. He has a machine, but he doesn't think it works."

He nodded. "I figured there was something like that going on. How much does he know?"

"He said his older self is too cautious and doesn't want him to know how everything works, but his basic job is to look for signs of time travelers and bring them here before they can do too much damage. And he thinks he hit the jackpot with me."

Older me was confused. "It doesn't make sense that his older self wouldn't tell him everything. Unless he did originally and has since undone it."

"Undone what?"

"Nevermind, it's just theoretical," he smiled at the use of his favorite word. "It makes sense though. That's probably how you blinked out of the hospital the first time. If I only knew about Dad before."

He realized that I wasn't understanding at all, and allowed the thought to sink before abruptly changing gears. "Anyways, he's here."

"He who?" I asked.

"Our father, who art in the car out front. I recruited him for a jailbreak."

Confused, I repeated what he told me at our last meeting. "I thought you said our best bet was staying here and waiting things out?"

"I know. But I blinked ahead a bit to check it out. You're stuck here for a while, with no sign of a way out. Getting you and Nelson out of here may alter time enough to light a fire under the doc so he takes a chance on something new."

"Nelson stays," was my petty response based on instinctual hatred more than anything else.

"I know how you feel, but Dad says it has to be both of you. Besides, this Nelson doesn't have blood on his hands. He's not our man."

"You mean not yet."

At least my reasoning was right. He didn't have a suicide hanging over him, but he never really did originally either. It's almost as if we had framed him. Accomplices at the very least. I figured I could reason with Dad later, as it was definitely time to tell him more than he knew.

23:59 End Of The World

THE PLAN ITSELF WAS ACTUALLY QUITE GOOD. Dad entered the reception area at the front of the building and flirtatiously asked the woman stationed there if he could be allowed to visit his sons. He gave our names, at which point older me looked over the receptionist's shoulder to find which sector of the facility we were listed under. He already knew where we were physically located, but needed the sector code to give to Dad for later use.

The receptionist denied our existence at first, but Dad said he had a message from me regarding the experiment and had followed the van that brought Nelson here just for peace of mind. The woman at the desk said she was just following orders, but as Dad laid on the charm she conceded to finding her superior.

As soon as she was gone, Dad marched right in using my older self as his scout. Older me had previously obtained the seven digit entry code to the corridors leading to our holding area by wandering the building and watching authorized personnel come and go. Employees were instructed to be discreet with the combination at all times, but most of the staff didn't really know the full extent of the experiment. When they were alone they were easy targets. The head doctor knew there was a possibility of time travelers wandering about, but as far as everyone else was concerned how much discretion did you really have to use when you were by yourself in an empty corridor?

They stopped at a supply closet to get my father into some hospital scrubs so as not to be so conspicuous. After other me saw that the coast was clear, he showed Dad how to access the wing we were located in and where it was in relation to the main electrical room.

My role in the plan was to make sure Nelson and I were in the more easily accessible main room of our wing rather than isolated in separate cells. The timing would have to be perfect to ensure that both of us would be rescued. What a shame it would be to leave one far behind…

Putting my petty and self-serving feelings on ice, I lived up to my side of the bargain. Or at least I intended to. After getting out of bed and having the usual basic breakfast provided by my captors each morning, I requested a meeting with the head doctor. The man I spoke to said he was away, but I insisted that it was urgent. He still resisted and wanted me to wait until I told him that I was ready to cooperate. Those were the magic words.

Thirty minutes later the doctor arrived. I told him that this involved Nelson as well, and I wouldn't talk unless all three of us met together. He happily complied, being more accommodating then he had been over my entire stay here. He even offered me a cup of coffee. What a host he could be when he wanted something.

I accepted the offer, stalling for time as I waited for my older self to peek in and check for my signal. He still hadn't shown up after Nelson was brought in and I had finished the coffee.

"Why do you keep staring into your cup?" the doctor asked.

"I had a dream there were clouds in my coffee."

"I think you're wasting my time." He stood and turned towards the door. "Are you ready to cooperate or not?"

His impatience was forcing me to wing it.

Winging it isn't really the right word. I actually did have a partial plan in my head. It had nothing to do with what older me had arranged with my father and was more of a rogue solo plan. Although Dad wouldn't approve, after we explained everything to him I felt I wouldn't need to justify my actions.

"I'm ready." Here goes nothing. "I confess. I have been in contact with an older version of myself, and we did have the intention of altering the flow of time."

The doctor returned to his seat, utterly delighted by this turn of events. "Please, continue."

"Our mission is more complicated than you may imagine. It involves my stepbrother Nelson, and a murder."

"Murder?" asked the doctor, even more curious.

"Murder!" Nelson echoed in unison, confused and angry. "He's crazy! I didn't murder anyone. He's just a homophobe who doesn't want me fucking his brother."

"Homophobia has nothing to do with this," I countered. "My brother can make his own choices and I'll gladly support him. But they are his choices to make, not yours. Nelson is going to murder my brother."

"He's lying! He's a lying alcoholic!" Nelson continued to whine.

I hadn't actually lied up to this point, but I was about to. "Nelson is going to be a time traveler in this study. And when he meets up with himself, they'll orchestrate my brother's demise to fix their own future. My older self tracked down your facility here, traveled back, and enlisted me to prevent this tragedy."

"Lies! Lies! Lies!"

Nelson was still fuming, but his monosyllabic tirade didn't really do much to convey innocence.

"That is a most noble cause," answered the doctor, ignoring Nelson and keeping his focus on me. "But he's not on my watch list. How can I know if this is true?"

"Obviously we can't prove anything, but I propose a test run. What if we were to show you how to send Nelson back into his own memories to pinpoint the exact moment that he became capable of committing murder? It could be the breakthrough you need."

The doctor pondered this. Throwing the blood onto his hands seemed to rattle him, and dangling the instructional carrot iced it. "I do suppose that as long as we have both of you boys here it wouldn't hurt to experiment a little bit. The results could be beneficial."

Nelson continued to protest, but his cursing devolved into sobs and tears.

The doctor snapped his fingers. "Prepare the machine."

While they were hooking Nelson up for his trip, I saw older me poke his head through the wall. I smiled and nodded back at him, holding up five fingers to signal I was in position but I needed more time. He returned the smile and nod combination and disappeared into the wall.

Nelson was wired up and ready to go. His blood was steady gushing through the device. The green light started blinking. Eyes wide, his body tensed as he entered the trance. Without warning his heart monitor flat-lined. This was the first time I'd ever witnessed the backend of a blink. It's hard to explain exactly, really just the glassy eyes of someone transfixed in a passing sad daydream.

The machine continued to hum. I was starting to worry that things wouldn't go as I had intended. I wanted to strand Nelson in his own head, essentially getting him out of the way for the time being. The doctor wouldn't know how to revive him, and I'd have more leverage to get what I needed from him after the escape. At least that's what I was counting on.

Remembering my own trips to the past, I always returned to the exact moment I had left from. I hadn't really thought about what was happening to the body that I left behind. Did it stay exactly where it was enraptured in a trance for all to see, only to have memories of that trance erased as soon as I returned? Did I flatline as Nelson seemingly had, or could they revive me? What if someone shot, strangled, or otherwise killed my sleeping body while I was in the past? Would I die, or instantly return? Were there versions of the timeline where I had fallen into a coma for an unknown reason, but had no memory of this because I always returned to the place I had left from? Worlds such as this one where time travel was deemed impossible and every would-be traveler lived in a vegetative coma? Maybe that was why travel to the future wasn't possible, as in that version of life you would have to be a vegetable for the duration of your trip. Or maybe it was possible, and that explained how on rare occasions patients awaken from an extended comatose state with minimal ill effects.

That was about as far as my thoughts had gone when the power went down.

The machine stopped whirring, the low room lights went dark and the green strobe stopped blinking, engulfing us in blackness. A white beam of light emerged from the doorway and erratically scanned the room. I worried that it was the doctor's goons back to spoil our escape, but was relieved when the beam turned upwards to illuminate the face of my father.

"Let's win one!" he shouted as his flashlight panned the room. On our way out, the glowing shaft abruptly stopped on Nelson's limp body lying on the machine.

"Don't worry about it. He's safe, just not here." I explained as I pulled Dad towards the exit.

"Not so fast," screamed the doctor. As he said this, the auxiliary power kicked in. A security crew surrounded us.

So much for the jailbreak.

—⁂—

The doctors tried to revive Nelson, but he remained in his time travel induced coma. They were able to find a minor heartbeat and had him on a respirator, but all felt it was just a major shock to his system from which he might never recover. Although a few may have believed he had moved on to another place, not a single person suspected that this other place was not a where but a when.

My father and I were placed in separate rooms for obvious reasons, but we still were able to keep in contact using my older self as our messenger. Dad was trying to figure out what he'd tell Nelson's Mom regarding her son's mysterious disappearance, while I was being lectured by myself regarding the stupidity of my plan.

"He's not gone you know. He's back there, and he has foreknowledge. I assure you no one won."

"What good is foreknowledge if you can't act on it?"

"As I've told you, we still don't really know much about time travel. What we do know is that intense emotional suggestions allow you to act as your own conscience. Whenever he may be, there's a chance that Nelson will find a way to gain control. And when he does, he'll be out to get you."

I had a point. It brought me back to thinking of the concept of hatred again. Maybe those times when you hate someone for no good reason had to do with time travel. They burned you once in the future, your subconscious picks up on this, and mortal enemies are preborn. Because you hate each other earlier you will screw each other over later in life. It's a self-fulfilling prophecy.

As I saw it, Nelson met the same fate as John Cusack at the end of *Being John Malkovich* when he's trapped in his daughter's head, always able to view the world around her but never able to do anything about it. Simply along for the ride, good or bad, with no cognizant choice or free will.

I remembered one of the rules I had tried to teach myself but still didn't fully comprehend. "If Nelson doesn't find his way here again, won't he undo putting himself in his head?"

Older me thought for a moment before responding. "It really depends on some of the unproven aspects of time traveling. I see two possibilities. My theory always assumed there was only one timeline, and you had to retain cause and effect pairs to prevent paradox. If that theory is true, and Nelson finds a way to persuade himself to steer clear of here, it could cause a paradox so damning that I'm frightened to even consider it right now."

"And the other possibility?"

"If our meddling hasn't caused a paradox yet, it opens the possibility that we're really dealing in alternate dimensions. Paradox is impossible since both options are real."

"But you said we undid the paradox because you haven't been all the way back yet."

"No. I said we *prevented* the paradox, but that was…"

He didn't have to finish. "I know. Theoretical."

Older me didn't smile this time. "Maybe it doesn't matter anyway. Since mind travel is different and he's just a passenger he will most likely keep reliving his fate, helpless to avoid it. He may become an uber-Nelson of sorts, repeatedly nested inside himself like a matryoshka doll. But he'll retain the memory each time, so after a few rounds of built up frustration he'll be so angry he might just harness enough emotion to lash out."

"That makes it all the more important for us to set things right again. If Nelson is looking to get revenge via his retired musician stepfather and two stepbrothers, he won't know to go looking for a random man with a son and a daughter." I took comfort in the fact that at least uber-Nelson would have no knowledge of my sister.

"I suppose you have another plan," older me observed. "But they'll never listen to you this time."

"Maybe not, but they'll listen to someone if we really play ball. I think it's time for you to tell Dad everything."

"Everything? But I haven't even told you everything yet." With that he disappeared through the wall en route to Dad's room, leaving the smile and nod to my imagination. We grew up to be quite a mysterious son of a gun, hadn't we?

After a few hours my elder returned and gave me the rundown of his conversation with our father. Dad was blown away by how terrible Nelson had been and wondered why he hadn't tried to stop it. He was glad that we had made all of the attempts to set things right, and felt guilty that he was to blame for the mess we were in by doubting the prophecy and getting back together with Nelson's mother, albeit briefly.

He also wanted more of an explanation regarding his former life, the one where he never fulfilled his musical dreams and was a loving father to a son and daughter and stopped womanizing after a message from that special girl. Older me was selective in what additional info he provided, since if we were to succeed Dad would have to relive that life again even though for him it would be just like starting over.

Despite his curiosity and shock, my father did understand what we had to do to fix things. He had to find a way to get hooked up to the machine and take control of his younger self. His mission would be simple: Just say no.

The doctor had learned his lessons from my earlier (and future) stunts and kept both my father and myself under a much stricter watch. During our waking hours it was too risky to use older me as our go between. We were never left alone and prohibited from speaking unless spoken to. At night we were able to pass messages using the false sleep and whisper technique I had used before, but after formulating our plan for if and when we got back on the machine there wasn't much else to talk about. We just had to bide our time and be model patient/prisoners.

—m—

For the next few weeks I was tasked with pinpointing the timeframes of the memory trips taken by other patients due to my knack for using pop culture and music as a means of estimation. From this I was supposed to be able to show the doctor how to target the trips. He didn't know that the research wasn't necessary, but my keeping busy seemed to be a good idea for now. Music was universal and omnipresent. As long as the trip was to a reasonably populated area I could usually get enough info to take an educated guess. Oldies stations threw me for a loop at first, but having the subjects focus in on the DJs often helped. Getting the name and call letters was best, but context clues between songs also helped me to do a fair job. Offhanded mentions of an artist's death, upcoming birthday, first tour in X years or the Nth anniversary of blah blah blah on this date in rock and roll history were all good clues to follow.

Dad charmed his way into being dubbed guinea pig in Nelson's absence to ensure I wouldn't try anything funny. They ran him through the same barrage of tests that I was given upon my arrival here, and also a job interview style oral version of the program questionnaire. He rated well enough to qualify and began prepping for his first trip into the machine.

I was never very clear on what criteria the test was looking to establish. Back when I took it, I wanted to believe it was looking for time travelers, but since the doctor already had that information from his past self it could have just been looking for a specific psychological profile of some sort. Probably a little bit of both. After hearing the doctor explain his purpose as monitoring time travelers who may be trying to effect the past and then essentially "recruiting" them, I was worried that they would uncover Dad's meetings with me in 1969. I wasn't sure what would happen if the true level of my involvement were known.

That night I told myself that Dad would be put on the machine the following day, potentially giving us our shot at setting things right once and for all. I was ecstatic.

"But we can't go through with it yet," said older me, immediately dashing my hopes.

"Yet? Why not yet?"

He explained by elaborating on his earlier theory of being protected from paradox while time traveling. Phase one of our plan was to have Dad convince himself to ignore my blink to set him up with Nelson's Mom. This would get me back into my normal body and turn my brother back into my sister. But there would be trouble if Dad made the change while I was still in this version of the present.

"Remember, we're not changing your past, just a version of it. If you make a change that causes a change in yourself, you will return to a present where you then live in the results of that change. That's how this happened," he said, pointing at me. "But if another traveler were to make the change, you wouldn't even notice if you stayed in real time. Life would just go on. Ob-la-di, ob-la-da."

"So what are you saying?"

"If your father can trick himself into avoiding you, we have no idea of knowing what becomes of you. Maybe you become yourself again. Maybe you cease to exist. Or maybe you start your quest over again. Regardless of the outcome, you won't remember any of it if you're here when it happens. We need both of you to be back there concurrently. If he makes his change and you immediately make yours, everything will be bypassed and you'll retain your memories. At least that's the theory. I have no way of knowing for sure."

He had to add that theoretical, didn't he? Couldn't give a straight answer.

"But I don't want to wait. And what happens to you in that scenario?"

"Nothing. Things will change around me, but I'm not in my present so I'll recall both sides of it. You'll remember both sides too since you'll be out of time as well."

"I understand that. But when you go back to your future, what happens to me?"

"Don't be concerned with that. I'll be the one in control then since it's my time. But we're the same person. We'll live on."

That bastard. As we had already learned, returning to an altered future causes the time traveler to replace his real time alter ego. Maybe they merge to a degree, but for the most part control is relinquished. So I would do all of the dirty work, and old me would then just pop in and take over the best life I could come up with for us.

"It's not fair!" I cried.

"Life isn't fair," said old me, his tone turning a little curmudgeonly. "What's more important, you living out all of your life yourself, or saving your sister and reuniting your family? You get the best end of it anyways. Forty or so great years to do anything, and I'll just pop in for the swan song. The only thing you'll really miss is dying. I think you're far in the lead on this one."

Of course he was right. I was the selfish one, not him. Or he was, but when the same self is involved in both equations, does it really matter in the end? Perhaps that's what no one wants to see.

So we continued to wait it out. Dad made a handful of trips without altering anything. His favorite was being inside himself for one of his concerts. Normally he concentrated so hard on remembering the songs that he didn't really have a chance to enjoy the moment, but now he had the best seat in the house. He could see the mastery of his fingertips dancing over the strings. He could study crowd reactions when his body gave the required directional glances. He could really ponder the meanings of the lyrics, and like me analyzed what they meant and why I chose those songs to be his.

One night while recapping my father's travels with myself, I tried to concoct a new plan without success. What if we threw the doctor a bone and pointed him towards the injectable time machine as one of the keys? Or asked to sit in on one of his meetings with his future self, hoping the older and wiser version may be more lenient with us since he could vouch for the years of good behavior we had only just begun?

Older me shot each of these down as being too risky. The plan we had in place was our best option provided we could ever get the timing right. But if our timing ain't just right what purpose would that serve?

—⁂—

I was becoming increasingly impatient waiting around for the proper moment. My older self was spending more and more time with Dad as of late. I hadn't asked him why, but I assumed he hadn't been able to spend much quality time with his version of our father in quite some time. Old me was … well, old. Actually not that old, probably less than ten years older than Dad if you compared them side by side. Old enough to know better I guess. Dad wasn't immortal, so it was only logical. I didn't ask questions about their relationship, as I didn't want to deal with the hows and whens of the eventual passing of my own father, nor did I want to force my other self to relive the memory either.

Instead I was spending more and more time with the head doctor. He would pick my brain, and I would give elliptical answers that seemed to point him in the right direction. I even went against my own good advice to suggest that an additional machine wouldn't hurt things and may help him find the results he was looking for faster. He agreed and constructed another model to bring the total number in his arsenal to three. He also agreed to send Dad and I back in tandem if I could find a way to prove the effectiveness of such a trip. I proposed a method of starting us off in separate rooms and having a password that we'd share in the past, proving to the doctor that we were both there. I didn't want him to know that Dad and I could interact with each other, so the "plan" was to have the word be transmitted from me to past me to past Dad to current Dad. Since this was inspired by the way the older doctor would prove his time travel abilities in the future, it wasn't difficult to talk his current counterpart into it.

Older me was able to check the schedule to see which day Dad and I would be sent back simultaneously. It was four days away, giving him three chances to teach Dad how to break out of their subliminal suggestions enough to guide himself to the specific double jump we needed.

On the day of the first trial I had gone back to relive a debaucherous Halloween party from college. Much to my surprise, I wasn't in attendance this time around. Instead, the new me was holding a clipboard and making rounds in a dormitory. Rather ironic that I spent my college daze avoiding the resident assistants, and now I had become one of them.

After returning to the present and completing my debrief, I was lying on my cot and pondering how much of a lifestyle is determined by environment and how much is genetic. All of a sudden my older self barreled through the wall in a panic.

"Something's gone wrong, and I don't understand it."

"How bad could it be?" I asked, throwing discretion to the wind.

"Your father."

"What? Did he change something? Is he trapped back there like Nelson?"

"You don't remember?"

"Remember what?"

Older me paused, took a deep breath, and then just spoke.

"He died."

24 Hour Party People

THE SHOCK OF THE NEWS HIT ME HARD. It was my fault. Again. Now I had two deaths on my hands, albeit in different timelines. And any chance of setting things right seemed to have gone out the window as well. As this realization set in, the teardrops came.

"Don't worry, he's fine," older me clarified upon recognizing my horror.

"He's fine? How can he be fine? You just told me he was dead!"

"No, I told you he died. But now he's fine. As if it never happened, but I don't fully understand."

My shock turned to relief, but that didn't stop the tears. "They revived him? Or you did? Did you save him?"

"I didn't do anything, and neither did they. I'll have to think it through, but I'm starting to have a theory…"

He had entered the room with our father and witnessed him being strapped into the machine. Dad had been through this a number of times already, so he was very calm and collected. The doctors gave him instructions, and older me gave one last reminder on how to break the spell while in the past. The machine started up. Blood started flowing out of his left arm, through the tubing, and back into his right as always, but almost instantly Dad flatlined just like Nelson had.

Something had gone wrong. They tried to revive him, but it was already too late. Another doctor came into the room in a panic. The same thing had happened to another subject. The head doctor was livid, screaming at everyone in his path and throwing things. Older me had come and given me the news. He said I reacted much as I've already detailed, although there was no comfort in the end. I asked my older self if he could go to the body and pluck me a lock of hair to remember him by. He agreed.

But when he got there, everything was fine. Dad had just finished his post trip interview with the doctor. He was sent on to the wrap up stage where he would write a report summarizing what he had witnessed. Upon seeing my older self he winked and said it worked like a charm.

The other subject was also fine. Items the doctor had tossed aside were still lined up in perfect order on the exam room table. It was as if none of it had happened.

"So what's your theory?" I asked.

"I'd never observed a full experiment before. I'll need to watch some more to confirm, but I think this happens every time."

That couldn't be right. "You think the patient always dies?"

"Exactly. He dies, and his mind goes back in time. He does his thing back there, and when he returns he's inserted back into the body of the version of himself that lived out the timeline he has changed. You and your new body are a most extreme example of that."

"But I've made close to a dozen trips by now, and I don't always change something. Neither have any of the other subjects as far as we know."

"You always change something just by being there. All of you do. I think you died each time. When you return to the spot you left from, it's the same spot because you never left. That version of your body never made the trip. It's all mental. Upon returning your mind takes the place of the youngest host."

I was discouraged. "It's brand new. We'll have to start planning all over again."

"None of this is new. Don't you see? The death part is the last missing piece!"

I didn't understand. "That doesn't make sense. Why haven't we noticed it before? And why don't I remember it happening?"

"You have noticed. You said your memories changed while you were watching yourself at the bar with my wife. That's because I was there too, and my change rippled around you since you were displaced. It's the paradox protection principle. You didn't see yourself pass out at the bar when I was in control. You saw yourself die, and then the death was undone in time for you to drag yourself home."

It was coming together. "And you said you noticed things changing around you when I was back with Dad, but you couldn't figure out what it was since you didn't trace it back that far."

"Exactly. This is the same basic idea." Older me was talking a mile a minute. "Since I'm displaced I think I'm seeing things undo themselves around me, but instead I'm just being bumped into the most forward timeline. You, on the other hand, stay put. You don't remember your father dying because he didn't die here. You aren't the same you I've been talking with all this time, you're just the most recent version. The 'youngest' as we said before."

I started to answer, but older me still had an excited look and rambled on.

"It would also explain why things didn't end when you didn't visit your father and teach him songs in this body. Paradox isn't possible under this type of theory. Each timeline operates independently of the others. There are multiple realities."

A smirk appeared on my face. "So what about your rule that each time trip needs to be repeated?"

Smile, nod. "I was wrong. And I could be wrong again. Although … I suppose if your conscience can transcend worlds, then repeating trips to narrow events down to a single cause and effect pair would ensure that positive changes are allowed to repeat universally rather than risking they'll come undone accidentally."

"Huh?"

"Don't worry. It's only a theory."

But the theory still had a flaw.

"What about Nelson? Why did he stay a vegetable?"

"I guess he hasn't tried to come back yet. The changes only happen upon a time traveler's return. He might really be trapped."

"But they found a faint heartbeat."

"The old time machine is based on a heart-lung bypass apparatus. That could have kicked in to cause the universal heartbeat they are tracking."

His theory still had some holes and required a few leaps of faith, but the pieces were starting to form something with reasonable plausibility. Amazingly, the only thing that had been holding this entire plan together was the fact that my older self never returned to his own present after giving me my powers. Without that, we'd all be on our own. But that would mean…

"Does that mean that there are other versions of the world out there where I died?"

"Of course. Theoretically, there would also be worlds where time travel experiments resulted in a slew of dead bodies and nothing more, and an exponential number of worlds where just one time traveler survived, or two, or three, or four, and so on."

Which would further mean that there are now quite a few worlds where my parents lost both of their children to early deaths. What was saving my sister really going to accomplish if it was leaving so much pain for others? Nothing was really being erased or pinched off completely; it was only being eliminated from our limited perspective.

Older me saw my spirits drop and asked what the problem was. I explained my realization, but he saw things differently.

"There may be an infinite number of variations out there. Before humans started harnessing time travel, corrections were always accomplished automatically via your subconscious. Each new version of you would have more information available from an alternate future you in order to live a better life. Allowed to play out, it would eventually lead to perfection. Once perfection was reached, it would theoretically repeat through all versions for the rest of eternity. We're just helping that process along. Even though we might not be around to appreciate setting things right for our sister, the generations of us that come next certainly will. She'll survive in every new world that comes along! Taken collectively, the dozen worlds that you died in are just a drop in the bucket of infinite perfection."

Once again, other me proved to be older and wiser. Timely persuasion as a means to infinite perfection was just a law of nature. It was almost beautiful in its simplicity, and I was now feeling oddly at ease with what had to be done next.

—⁓—

Older me further confirmed the dying aspect of his theory by witnessing the demise and resurrection of both my father and myself on our next experimental trips. He deduced there was some sort of lag before the new timeline caught up to his displaced self. This was what allowed him to briefly see things both ways. There wasn't much time to celebrate his discovery, as it put even more pressure on our simultaneous mission. Now if our timing wasn't right, we'd run the additional risk that one of us would be dead from the other's point of view.

Complicating matters further, since being reintroduced to time travel my aim wasn't as true as it used to be. Historic red letter days were still as easy to hit as they had become for me previously, but the methodology the doctor was using relied on more personal situations. Memories of past lives did me no good, and outside of recent experiences I didn't have much else to grasp hold of. At least I was able to land on Halloween for the college trip, but what I'd be doing when I showed up was always a mystery to me. I was popping in all over the place since the memories I was riding back on weren't my own. If the doctor knew how unlikely it was for me to meet up with Dad on a simul-blink, the little bit of trust I'd built with him would be shattered and all bets would be off.

The day of reckoning was upon us. The subliminal persuasion given by the doctor for my father's memory trip involved a time when he felt his greatest sense of disappointment. As the procedure went, he'd write a short essay on when he felt that disappointment, after which they would try to send him back to the same point in his memories. With my help, they thought the process had evolved well enough since we had been here that they were quite adept at getting the target right. Little did they know that my help had nothing to do with it.

I was able to read my father's essay before he went back. To the best of my recollection, it went a little something like this:

The greatest disappointment in my life was the birth of my second son. You see, I was expecting a daughter. Expecting one so much that it was a foregone conclusion that the child would be a girl. When my wife went into labor and I saw my child for the first time I insisted there had to be some mistake. But there was not and I now had two sons. This event really made me question my life, question its purpose, and question the direction I was taking with it. As such, I decided to leave my family. I had grown to love my wife and my son over the years, and in the years since have found love for my second son and now have legal custody of him. We all still keep in touch and I am very much a part of their lives. But with the birth of the wrong child in my mind I had to see if there was something better out there. Something different. Something that if I didn't do I'd end up regretting forever. So I left them for a former girlfriend. In hindsight, the decision was hasty. In the end I knew that I was wrong and should have stayed with my real family. They were my destiny, and I had missed out. I hope one day they can forgive me for my lack of patience.

If that wasn't a farewell note, I didn't know what was. Almost like suicide, as Dad knew that if all went wrong this was goodbye more or less, and if all went well he still wasn't coming back from this trip. At least not this version of him. This could be the last time.

He was strapped into the bloodflow machine as he and me and so many others had been before. One moment green pulses of light, the next his kitchen. Our kitchen.

Back at the home of my childhood. Where he once built his family, and also where he once left it. He was in the past of the latter, and the first sight he saw from inside his head was his right hand applying a signature to that Dear John letter to Mom with a blue ballpoint pen. His hand put the pen down emphatically, then held up the letter to give it a final read before leaving it on the table to be found. It had to be just right, as it would be serving as his legacy here. The final memory that turns love to hate. The thought that would always overpower the good times, seeping in at the most inopportune moment to cheapen the treasures of the past.

Seemingly satisfied, Dad witnessed his own hands putting the letter in an envelope, sealing it with his tongue, and printing my Mom's name in large block letters. Each action was performed just as deliberately as he had nearly twenty years earlier. In his own head he just kept thinking of how sorry he was, hoping he could have that old life he never knew back if our plan worked.

It was then that something changed. His hand turned over the envelope and added a postscript. A new line of text that he was certain he hadn't appended before. Although his thought was the spark, he had no conscious control over the rain of thoughts going into this brainstorm. He watched in anticipation as they played before him like the alternate version of a dumb film's final scene. The last words read:

Something tells me I'm sorry and shouldn't be doing this. I guess it's just my guilty conscience. But it also tells me we'll all be together again. And I believe that part and hope it is true. I'm not telling you a secret, I'm not telling you goodbye.

His eyes turned to the clock, then back to the envelope that held the last thoughts that would (hopefully) not ever need to be read or remembered. Inside, Dad realized that he had better get blinking if he wanted to begin the process of erasing those words.

He thought of the hospital clothes.

He thought of the lawnmower.

And he thought of me.

Not me his son, but me his friend. The strange friend who provided the songs that led him to become Local Boy. He thought of their first meeting, and then he was there.

His bare feet shuffled along the grass, inches behind the motor of the mower. He recalled how his father had always told him not to mow the lawn without shoes unless he wanted to lose a toe, but the feeling of the fresh mowed grass on his skin always excited him for some reason. Too bad he couldn't relive that feeling again here. When living like a refugee in your own head, all you have are your own thoughts and your own senses of sight and sound. No smell, taste, or touch. He wondered if he should report that to the doctors, or if anyone ever had before. If only he could feel and smell that grass again. Even though he was doing the right thing, he was almost sorry that it would have to end like this.

A car horn honked. His body didn't stop mowing and his head didn't turn, but in the peripheral vision of his host he could make out a carload of girls doing a drive-by as they often did. The whistles and catcalls always made him smile.

Another car drove by the yard. This time his body did stop the mower. An inverted bottle of beer entered his vision and the Dad inside wanted to smile again. He used to call this one the beer commercial: Glug, glug, glug, ahhhh followed by an exaggerated motion to wipe the sweat from his brow. Drove the ladies wild.

His eyes stole another sideways glance to assess the audience, but an approaching figure obstructed his view. *Something tells me he's been here before.* This was it, the single moment he needed to change to fulfill his part of the masterplan.

He heard himself speaking.

"My parents aren't home, but if you come back later they may want to make a donation."

"Donation?" asked the confused visitor in the orderly uniform. Dad felt his eyes drift to the hypnotic circular logo on the man's chest.

"Yeah. I figured you were from the hospital when I saw that outfit on you. Never heard of LBDG though."

Yes I have. But where?

He felt a confused sense of déjà vu as thoughts from the past mingled with thoughts of his present. Why did he think this guy was from a hospital? Something about him was familiar, but at the same time it wasn't quite the same. *You would see if only…*

The visitor snapped out of his daze. "Oh, yes. I just…got off of work. I wanted to talk to you. Ask a favor, actually."

Inside his own head Dad started thinking intensely just as the man who stood before him would one day teach him.

Fucking jerk interrupted my show. Now I'm not getting laid tonight. Probably escaped from the mental institution. Fucking jerk. Fucking jerk.

They were thoughts he hadn't had in quite a long time, but he knew he had to revisit them if he wanted to convince himself to blow his top.

"Who do you think you are, interrupting me when I'm entertaining the ladies?" he heard himself say.

Throw down the bottle.

On cue, he threw the beer bottle down at the visitor's feet.

"You've got me wrong. It's more of a challenge. There's this girl…"

"I don't need any help getting dates from the likes of you. Now get outta here."

"If you'd just let me explain…"

No explaining was to be done by me on this trip, as Dad watched in disbelief as he sent his future son to the ground with one punch.

"Are you gonna get, or do I need to knock you into next week?"

It was hard to tell from his reaction, but the visitor seemed almost amused by this comment even though he held his tongue. Regardless, the threat didn't need to be repeated. The guy in the hospital gear ran off with more spring in his step than one might expect considering the beating he had just received. Dad wasn't sure, but he thought he saw him disappear into thin air rather than run off into the sunset. He left the lawn half mowed and marched into the house to find his cousin.

At least that's the way part of my brain remembers the story now. Seems accurate enough, though I'm not completely sure of my trustworthiness as a narrator given the circumstances.

This version I am sure of. While Dad was being prepped for his memory trip, I was with the doctor awaiting the mystery word I'd supposedly have to pass on to Dad in the past.

"I'm of the opinion that I'm a lot closer than I think I am," he started. "But I need proof. Your father needs to bring back proof."

"We will. What's the good word?"

Cupping my ear, I leaned closer in anticipation.

"Nelsonification."

"Nelsonification?" I repeated.

"Nelsonification. I couldn't use a real word, so I made up something you're not likely to come up with on your own."

So Nelsonification it was. Not the 'Rosebud' I was expecting, but it would do. Nelsuicide would have been more appropriate, but there wasn't any need to argue since it wasn't going to happen anyways. All I had to do was humor him.

"All right. One Nelsonification, coming up."

I actually had a better word for him.

Sucker.

25 Minutes To Go

WHEN THE GREEN LIGHT SUBSIDED, my surroundings left me startled and disoriented. On a plate in front of me were the remnants of a porterhouse steak from a big old steer, the best meal I'd seen in ages. Sitting across from me was the cute redheaded girl. It was obviously before our breakup, but from the scene here you would never have known it was coming.

A sea of red liquid careening below a translucent archway briefly obstructs my view of her. My hand lowers the wine glass, but never lets go of it. I notice an empty bottle on the table, as well as two empty rocks glasses. She asks a question, but my response is lost in an unintelligible slur. I take another swig of wine to help clear my vocabulary, then tap my glass and nod my chin. She giggles and pours another for each of us, draining a second bottle.

We were sloshed.

The scene before me gently rocked back and forth as my host swayed in his chair. This must have been something that happened to the new me, as I had no memory of it. Would that mean it was happening to a new new me? At least we seemed to be having a good time. Despite the rocking and the alcohol, I still couldn't shake my focus from the beauty of her face.

Inside, I thought *I want to tell her that I love her, but does it really matter?*

And then I did tell her.

I thought to myself *reach out our hands, hold on to hers,* and just like that I clumsily reached across the table to entwine our fingers. Since I hadn't lived through this before I was unable to tell if I was really helping things or not, but suggesting actions from the inside was suddenly far easier than it had ever been previously. But it still wasn't flawless. Although I knew what I was telling my host body to do, he was still having some trouble actually doing it.

Tell her you'll be right back. Go to the bathroom.

The words continued to have trouble escaping from his mouth, but he stood up right on cue. I was a puppeteer, but a ventriloquist would be more appropriate. My dummy and I awkwardly managed to stagger into the bathroom. I looked at myself in the mirror—really looked at myself— for the first time since initially discovering that I wasn't really me anymore. Searching my eyes for a hidden answer, I remembered that I had to act now. Maybe I could tell her everything before Dad completed his half of the changes, and then we...

For an instant I saw my real self in the mirror, and then there was blackness. When the picture slowly came back into focus I was watching a television monitor. Twelve. Twenty-two. Twenty-four. Forty-seven. Sixty-nine. All five numbers shared the screen.

I was back at the beginning.

The vision in front of me panned down to the ticket, then back to the screen, then back to the ticket before crumpling it up and dropping it into the open bowling bag. I tried to stop myself from damaging the ticket, but I began to lose control and couldn't. Why?

"Play 'em," said a voice beside me. My eyes involuntarily gave a sideways glance, just as they had before. And there I was, an old man, taking a long sip of my beer. My young host pretended not to notice and did the same.

Beer! I thought. *That's it! Finish it!*

A familiar voice inside the head inside my head spoke the flashback: *"The body goes on autopilot, not expecting to have a designated driver ready to take over."*

Psychic ability, conscience, reflexes, love at first sight, impulse purchases, schizophrenia, instinct, and déjà vu were the building blocks of time travel. A future version of yourself giving advice and guidance when you needed it most by way of an excited utterance straight to the brain. A drunken night where you can't remember anything in the morning must work the same way. The thoughts are somehow more easily conducted due to the inebriated state and the lack of competing brainwaves, allowing a future mind to take over. This was how I survived so many alcohol-induced blackouts. Easy when somebody else was calling the shots, both literally and metaphorically. And if you eventually remember later, it's because you've become the version of yourself who actually lived those drunken minutes out of sequence. It wasn't death as older me had hypothesized, but it was close.

My host kept the glass pressed to his lips, opened his throat, and poured back the remaining four swallows.

"Your loss," said the old man.

"Excuse me?" was the reply I heard myself give.

The bartender looked towards the empty glass in my hand. My head looked at her and nodded, slamming the glass down on the bar with authority.

I chanted to myself internally. *Let's get hammered. Let's get wasted. Let's get let's get let's get let's get rocked.*

"And a shot of bourbon," I said as the bartender handed me my beer.

"Your numbers. This is your game," the old man continued. I could see some worry in his eyes, as he knew our tolerance for hard liquor just as well as I did.

"I think I'm about done. They're not coming up twice. I'd rather save the money for booze."

The shot arrived. My body downed it in one and quickly asked for another to satisfy the internal craving I was stimulating. Anything to quiet that voice.

The man took another long sip and smiled, continuing to follow the same script as before. "Twelve, twenty-two, twenty-four, forty-seven, sixty-nine. They all come up this time. When you're feeling greedy you think about adding two, four, and seven. Now would be a good time to follow through. This time you got it."

I threw back the second shot, gagging slightly as the whiskey burned the back of my throat. I took a few hearty swallows of the fresh beer as my vision clouded from the alcohol-aided tears in my eyes. An arm appeared and wiped them away with a wrinkled shirtsleeve.

"If it's such a sure thing, why don't you play it?" I slurred as my body stood up and stumbled slightly.

Old me continued to look concerned, but that didn't alter his speech. "It's not possible. And it's your lucky day, not mine. My lucky day has come and gone."

It's coming back around again.

"Whatever. I'll be right back," said my drunken host as he turned and stomped towards the bathroom, nearly falling as he took his second step but managing to recover. He looked back at the invisible obstacle that impeded his progress, then swung the bathroom door open via a heavy lean into it with his shoulder.

This time the mirror confirmed the good news I had glimpsed at the restaurant.

Me.

Real me.

The me that I knew and loved and thought I'd never see again. I willed my hands to splash cold water on my face, noticing my limbs were once again becoming easier to command. Staring hard into the mirror at my wide bloodshot eyes, I knew what I was thinking without actually reading my thoughts. Why the hell did you decide to do shots? Don't start me on the liquor. You know what happens.

Now I do.

And that's exactly what I was banking on. I needed a full-blown blackout so I could take control. And as a special bonus, this me from the past wouldn't remember what I was about to do.

A wave of warmth engulfed me from the inside, and from within that wave I could feel intelligent use of my faculties return. In full control of my drunken host body, I returned to the bar and slapped my older self on the back.

"I know who you are and why you're here. Meet me outside."

The look on his face was priceless. The element of surprise was mine this time. I slowed my walking pace so as not to seem so drunk and headed out for some fresh air.

When older me emerged from the bar I jumped him much as he had done to me the first time around. Or at least I tried to, but my coordination was still off from the booze. We struggled for a brief moment, ending as before with me pinned to the car.

"Don't inject me! I don't need it! We can save her!"

He released me from his grip and stared in disbelief.

"What do you know? How do you know?"

"We played this scene before," I replied. "And it didn't go particularly well."

He was still puzzled. "We couldn't have done this before. We can't both be here at once."

"Apparently we can. I'm just a stowaway, but I managed to pull off a mutiny. Yo ho ho and a bottle of rum. Or at least a couple shots of JD."

A glow of recognition came to his eyes. "Of course. We have done this before, haven't we? On the eve of the wedding."

We chatted for a bit, with me recapping select portions of our adventures, but not everything. Nobody should know too much about his or her own future, even if a lot of that future is in the past. This time it was he who asked the magic question.

"How can we still save our sister?"

"It's simple. You just have to strand me back there."

Older me gave a confused look, but it turned to a smile after I recounted Nelson's fate for him.

"Do you think it could work?" he asked.

"Theoretically," I answered with a nod, adding a wink for good measure.

Across 26 Winters

Darkness. I felt a sharp pain in my neck, and then the colors started. Green black green black green black green flashed before my eyes as the machine whirred. The whirring turned to silence, and the silence was interrupted by my voice. My older voice.

"Blink now, or you'll ruin everything!"

He squeezed my arms just above the spot where the IV tubes entered me, using enough pressure to stop circulation and start an electric feeling of pins and needles. Trying not to wince too noticeably, I took the semi-subliminal advice and forced my way back into a memory.

I woke up with a headache like my head against a board. When did I fall asleep? For some reason I was on the couch with headphones on. I had been dreaming about something, but couldn't for the life of me remember what it was. Neither deep sleep nor coherent thought were options the way my head was raging with pain. I hadn't had a headache this bad since…

I sat up suddenly, trying to catch my breath from my last thought. Was it all a dream? No. At least I hoped not.

Still pondering like a poi dog, my body rose from the couch against my will. I ended up in the bathroom brushing my teeth. The mirror told me I still looked like myself, but the uninterested passing glance given to the reflection indicated there was no reason for me to look like anyone else. I wanted a closer look to be sure, but I no longer had control over my actions. I remembered asking my older self to trap me, and I certainly felt like a stowaway.

Teeth cleaned, my host lumbered into the bedroom and buried himself among the covers. I tried to think my way out of bed, but it wasn't happening. The darkness had me feeling claustrophobic. The last thing I wanted to do right now was sleep. What if the doctor found a way to retrieve me? What if I couldn't ever take control? What if I had to replay all of these events as nothing more than an internal witness? And what if Dad never made it back? I still had a lot of work to do.

These were the thoughts that spun through my subconscious. Although I couldn't make my body act, the brainwave activity seemed to be having some effect on my real being. Occasional violent rotations and blurred red lines interrupting the opaqueness told a familiar tale of insomniatic clockwatching that I knew all too well. Thinking and tossing and turning and looking and listening continued for a couple more hours until my body had had enough. It got up, walked to the kitchen, and pulled a bottle out of a cabinet.

As the alcohol circulated my arteries en route to my brain, I felt the familiar warmth begin to take hold. *One more!* I screamed from backstage, smiling inside as the bottle went down and the glass went up. My eyes tensed shut, but I was able to force them open. Excited to be back in the driver's seat, I blinked.

—⁂—

Driver's seat. Driving.

I was driving somewhere. Or at least I was a passenger in my head while another me was driving. Maybe it was you. I wasn't sure where we were headed, and to be honest I didn't really care. The important part was that they couldn't revive me. Here in your head was where I needed to stay.

I thought about everything that had happened to us so far, or in your case hadn't happened anymore. You never went back in time, though sometimes you had a strange feeling that you had. Nothing specific, just a vague premonition of what might be (or what once was). Don't worry, that's just normal everyday persuasion. You may have it stronger than most now that I'm here to passively share memories with you, but it happens to everyone. How else could you explain Jeff Tweedy using all of that post-September 11th imagery when writing *Yankee Hotel Foxtrot* in a pre-September 11th world?

As far as this self was concerned, a strange old man wanted you to make a crazy Hot Spot bet on the same numbers for two consecutive drawings. You were in a bad mood so you blew him off and decided for some unknown reason to get blitzed. You knew that meant you wouldn't bowl worth a damn, but the voice inside your head just screamed for it and you caved. You don't remember much more after that. But I do.

You never lost your bowling ball during league night. You couldn't have since I can see it here in the car with us now, on the floor of the passenger side where you always kept it. You like being able to glance at it while driving, giving you comfort that you're still grounded in reality. Passengers get a bit annoyed when they have to straddle it, but you tell them Glitzy is too good for the trunk and to just deal with it.

You've never had a tattoo or a scar that wouldn't heal, especially not on your neck. We barely even remember the cute little redheaded girl, even though part of me still thinks we might have a shot if I ever see her again. And we certainly didn't steal hit songs from the future and then teach them to our father before they were written.

"These are all things I thought you knew. Oh things just don't seem like they used to," were the lines I found myself singing along to on the radio.

On the radio? Uh-oh.

The car screeched to a halt as I took control of our body in a rare moment of sober clarity. You fumbled with the dial to turn up the volume. Who was singing? It certainly sounded like Dad's version. At the end of the song the station went right into "Captain Jack" by Billy Joel. At least that was normal. After three minutes and thirty-four seconds that seemed to last forever, the DJ returned and recapped his set.

"That was piano man Billy Joel, and before that we had a great one by request from the archives, Local Boy with 'Won One.' Remember tomorrow is two for Tuesday, where we always play two songs from your favorite artists. You won't be hearing 'Won One' then, as it's the only song Local Boy ever released. Quite a shame to see his talent go to waste, but that's why we call them one hit wonders. We have The Beatles and America coming up next, so stay tuned."

I made you shut off the radio. Won One? I couldn't possibly have had anything to do with that. We didn't even have the power to do so just yet, and having Dad undo it was a big part of how I got to be here now. Did that mean that we would still go on to relive it all later in life? That since the possibility still existed it continued to be so?

I thought of Local Boy.

And Dad.

And a telephone call.

And then I blinked again.

—⁂—

We were at home. You poured a drink and picked up the phone to call Dad while I eavesdropped. He answered on the first ring. After the usual polite how are you small talk you asked my loaded question, thinking it was your own.

"I heard 'Won One' on the radio yesterday. Do you remember when you wrote it?"

I could feel the smile in his response.

"Son, have I got a little story for you. It was the strangest thing. I was mowing the lawn when some guy came up looking for donations. I was in a bad mood and he wouldn't leave, and I ended up having to forcefully persuade him. Right after that I stormed into the house, picked up my guitar, and played that song on the first take. Didn't even try, didn't write it down. It was already in my head and I just knew it by heart. Funny too in that it's such a pretty song, but just moments before my blood was boiling."

Now I was smiling. Dad must have taught it to himself as one of his last actions in that other life. Very sly.

Dad continued walking through the reminiscence. "It still amazes me how easily it came that day. I try all the time to write something else, but success it never comes. They say everyone has one book in their head. I guess I just had one song. Got by pretty well on it. You could say I really won one there. The royalties put you and your sister through college. God rest her soul."

My sister. It was good to hear someone else acknowledge that I had a sister again. But she was still gone. At least for now. We'll have to find a way to fix that.

If I can blink around within our own lifetime to subliminally guide you, infinite perfection could be just around the corner. I'll be there to protect you, making sure none of it ever happens. There will be no experiment. There will be no escaping and sending my younger self on a mission. There will be no need to contact Dad. There will be no setting sis up with Nelson. No wedding or bad relationship or bad marriage or bad life. Everything done would be undone. The road to infinite perfection doesn't necessarily intersect with the route of timely persuasion. It's a road best left untraveled, unless maybe you have a chauffeur who has seen it all as your guide…

—⁓—

Years went by as I bounced around our lifeline, and as far as I could tell I somehow managed to live a fairly normal life.

I didn't marry the cute little redheaded girl. As anticipated, the pressures of foreknowledge were all too much for me to take. If you can't let human nature take its course it just doesn't work out. They say you can't fight fate, but you can't force it either. Hence the fickle finger. She'll be with you if you want her to, unless she finds out that you do, then somehow she won't want to be. Look at it this way: What would you do if someone you weren't dating walked up to you and said with complete confidence that they were going to marry you, and there was nothing you could do about it since it was destiny? Not that I tried that line.

Actually I didn't really try much of anything. Had myself pseudo stalk her for a while, partly for the sport of it and partly just to see her smile now and again. I could never manage enough control to really turn up the charm, and even if I could charm was Dad's gift, not mine. We did have an occasional pleasant conversation after "randomly" bumping into each other on the street. But there wasn't any real spark, no inciting incident. Que sera sera.

On one blink I saw her out on a date with someone else. For a few seconds jealousy flared through me, but upon realizing her date was with Nelson the feeling dissipated. I wondered how much influence the internal Nelson had over the external Nelson in that scenario. Was this the

Nelsonification the doctor was referring to with his last word? Though I considered having a drink and doing something about it, I decided against it and stayed away. I needed to keep my eye on the long term endgame. Maybe it was just sour grapes, but it did make me decide that I didn't really want her anymore. The past was gone, but something might be found to take its place.

Enough about who I didn't marry. The girl I did end up with was about as good of a bullseye into my quote unquote type as you could probably get. A smart, short haired girl who sometimes wears it twice as long and likes music and cards and wants to save the world and who everyone is in love with but she either doesn't realize it or doesn't care, only wanting to live her life on her own terms and not be caught up in the ways and means of traditional society.

People often tell me my wife reminds them of my sister. I hadn't seen it previously, but after hearing it multiple times I could admit there was a resemblance of sorts. Subtle, but definitely there. Maybe I was picking up on it subconsciously. Or maybe my mind did it on purpose to remind me of what I had to do. Or maybe my older self had a hand in our set up and this was his Freudian idea of a joke.

I say my older self, as I honestly had nothing to do with it. At least not directly. Looking back, maybe admitting to both my internal and external selves that the redheaded girl wasn't the one lifted enough baggage to pave the way for this one. Or maybe having me inside as a confident confidant during similar scenarios gave the youngest me the self-assurance that cupid needed to do his thing. After all, I'd had my share of misses, and they say he only misses sometimes.

It didn't matter. We were both very happy with the relationship. My only curiosity was whether or not we were together in another version of our lives. Was she originally the unconfirmed second wife I had presumed myself to have? In a different time, were my romantic misses actually my missus? It was probably better that I didn't know, as I'd have more than likely found a way to screw that up as well.

But if she was a brand new girl, what did that say about destiny and soulmates and the concept of finding "the one" that's out there somewhere? Can anyone settle down with anyone else in the world as long as they play their cards right? Do the cards played matter as much as the cards that I'm dealt? Is there not really a specific "one," but instead many similar options that could be equally blissful depending on probability and other mathematical factors? Do I think about this far too much?

I thought back to Dad & Mom and Dad & Nelson's Mom and Nelson's Mom & Nelson's Dad and Nelson & my sister and Nelson & my brother and Nelson & the cute redheaded girl and me & the cute redheaded girl and me & tree house girl and me & the roommate and me & my newfound angel. So many permutations that I could hardly keep it straight. Might as well just enjoy what I have while it lasts.

—⁂—

Blink. I am somewhere in the city. I am climbing up a fire escape.

—⁂—

Blink. I am staring out the window, seeing the world fly left to right. Why do I end up in the car so much? I guess it's the only place where a mind wanders enough to accept an intruder. Where your guard is let down enough to let me in.

We're in the back seat this time. I'm young, sis is younger. I'm not sure if this is something I remember, as it could be one of any number of similar car rides. *Maybe Mom took a photo I can match it up with.* In sync with that thought, Mom turns from the front seat.

"Who else is going to the party, honey? Are you the only girl?"

Sis turned red. I suddenly remembered this drive. We were dropping her off at a birthday party for a boy in her class. Probably her first boy-girl party. Originally I chimed in with a "little sister got a boyfriend" chant right about now. *Don't be so immature,* I thought to myself. *Let her go and start over.*

That was enough to suppress the peanut gallery.

—⁂—

Blink.
Red lines.
The clock.
Insomnia again.
I wonder should I get up and fix myself a drink?
Glug, glug, glug, ahhhh.
Working my way back to the computer, I sat down and started writing about everything that had happened. I've been doing this for a while

now, ever since you upgraded to a new model you couldn't afford. A total impulse buy as far as you were concerned, though now that you've read this far I'm sure you realize my role as the voice inside your head had something to do with it.

I've been careful to keep the names to a minimum in case someone else found this manuscript and read it before you did. Character names aren't needed when you're telling a tale to somebody who knows you as well as you know yourself. You'll know who I'm talking about when I refer to me or my sister or Dad or the cute little redheaded girl. No need to give names just for the sake of it. Except for Nelson. Hate needs a name, especially a hate as strong as this one. If it wasn't for him, none of this would have ever happened. Maybe his name wasn't actually Nelson, but it's close enough. I'm sure you know who I mean. That is, if you even happen to find this file hidden on the depths of your hard drive. Some writers say they're driven to drink to help find their muse. You never realized how true that really was. Lou Reed called it the power of positive drinking.

Maybe our sister will still end up with Nelson. Maybe we'll keep my current wife. Maybe we'll still end up with the redheaded girl. Maybe you really will play the Hot Spot numbers and win that drawing. Maybe I'm amazed at the way you pulled me out of time. Maybe it doesn't really matter in the long run.

For now I feel a sense of relief. Whatever happens next will happen for the right reasons. I might not be around to remember it, but mentally I'll be with you all the while. Older us will be too. I am he as you are he as you are me and we are all together. I have a feeling that you and the other younger generations of us might like it better this way.

Prologue (Reprise)

"I CAN'T BELIEVE YOU'RE GETTING MARRIED!" That was the last thing I said to my sister. At least it was the last thing I said today before she hung up to relay the news to the rest of her friends. She wanted me to be the first to know, and I was very happy for her.

Her fiancé was practically an adopted member of our family already. Everyone adored him. Fun loving and easy to get along with, he integrated himself into all of our lives as if he was meant to be there all along. This was especially true of his relationship with my sister.

He brought out the best in her, melted away her worries and insecurities and just let her do her thing. They were one of those perfect couples that make you realize that maybe there really is such a thing as true love. In a world where everyone seems to settle for second best, they were unequivocally a match made in heaven.

I was so proud of her. There were times growing up where I would question her judge of character upon meeting some of the guys she dated, but I never spoke up. I never really had to. A little voice inside my head always seemed to say "Don't worry, she'll be fine." And the voice was always right.

Sis always managed to separate the good from the bad much faster than her friends did and never had a bad relationship. You could say she lead a semi-charmed kind of life, as if someone was looking out for her.

And maybe somebody was.

www.lb-dg.com
www.timelypersuasion.com

Acknowledgments

I promised too many people I'd mention them here, so please don't be offended if you're referred to by a group and not a name. In rough order of the sequence that led to this, I'd like to thank:

- The musicians who wrote the songs that inspired me.
- iNetNow (for folding at the right time for me to start) and Voce (for letting me leave at the right time to finish).
- Jon Mack, for talking me into trying this and letting me mooch on his couch, laptop, and Internet in Lux for two months. Also thanks to Jon's roommate Andreas for putting up with the whole idea, and to everyone in Luxembourg and at the Arizona bar who made me feel so welcome during my stay.
- All of the early readers and editors who provided valuable feedback, especially Lynne Vu, Adam Johnson, Nate Pepper, Kathy Legendre and the extended CarriageHaüs family.
- Chris Evjy, for letting me have "Won One."
- Dave Eggers, for teaching me that the copyright page is meant to be read. (Mom, your mention is there.)
- Jessica Francis, who put up with the constant rewriting, diligently read and reread, and may be the reason my future self wanted me to write this book in the first place.
- José Roberto for the perfect cover image.
- Jeff Winston, Pamela Phillips, Henry DeTamble, Jud Elliott, Billy Pilgrim, Sam Deed, James Cole, John Titor, Dan Vasser, Livia Beale, Tru Davies, Daniel Eakins, Sam Beckett, Al Calavicci, Marty McFly, Emmett Brown, Bill S. Preston, Ted "Theodore" Logan, Hiro Nakamura, Eckels, Aaron, Abe, Will, Sherman, Mr. Peabody, and anyone else who has walked in their shoes.
- And last but not least, thanks to Neil Janulewicz, whose very existence made this novel necessary.

—JL